ORION

SHANE COWDEN
ISBN: 978-1-7390100-0-3

Dedicated to the men and women who
continue to fight their war at home.

Prologue

Backwoods, Alaska
Present Day

"Stay down," a muffled voice whispered in the darkness. "Accept it ... it's OK."

His crusted eyes started to open. The harsh cold stung his nostrils as he labored to raise his eyelids in this unknown place. He let out a forceful wet cough and cleared his lungs of what felt like a flood of debris made of liquid iron and phlegm.

Bright red painted the white canvas as he regained focus. Blood on snow, fog from his breath, reflections of sunlight breaking through the tree branches. Everything started to take shape as his senses regained clarity. Raising his head, he realized he was lying face-first in the snow. Bruised and dirty, he adjusted his vision, endeavoring to recognize his surroundings. Beside his face, a spattering of blood tainted the snow like a galaxy of red stars.

"You don't need to do this," the voice whispered again. "Sleep. It will all end."

The voice was not normal, nothing like you would expect it to be. For years, it had haunted Jason, speaking to him in riddles and negativity. It was a voice that every person had within. Some were quiet and reserved. Others were boisterous and insurmountable. Recently this voice began to envelop his reality as it became inescapable and obsessed with him. Ever since coming back home, it had become all-consuming.

Painfully, the rays of the rising sun hit Jason's eyes as he rolled onto his back, his corneas stinging from the burst of brightness. He took a deep breath, stinging his lungs with the crisp Alaskan air. Jason's head rang with confusion, struggling to focus his mind to some semblance of understanding of his circumstances.

Where am I? Where is that voice coming from? Everything hurts.

He thought about these questions and used his arms to sit himself up. Spitting out a wad of thick red phlegm, he wiped the dried, crusted blood from his eyelids. "Fuck me," he moaned as he felt his rib cage, his hands shaking from the cold.

While looking down at his abdomen, he noticed a much larger patch of blood soaking his shirt. "Agh, shit," he groaned as he instinctively removed his hand from the wound. The pain shot through his side like a lightning bolt. Jason spotted another large, unusual-looking wound on his left calf. Something had ripped a chunk of flesh off him, leaving a painful gash.

The cliff must have been about thirty feet and almost straight up. How he survived the fall was beyond him. Nothing around him was familiar except for that voice. Rolling onto his hands and knees, he crawled toward a nearby tree. Fumbling his way toward the base of the trunk, his knees scraped against the protruding roots that hid underneath the snow. Jason's hand struck something in the snow that made him pause.

With his vision still adjusting, he desperately dug around the object, feeling it out until his fingers wrapped around it. The item began to feel familiar in its shape and weight. With a firm grasp, he ripped it out from underneath the snow.

Seating himself against the tree, he placed the object on his lap. Inspecting it, he tried to regain his memory. It was black and brown with a tan camouflage pattern dyed along its side. It also had a sling and optical scope affixed to it. *My rifle.*

The weapon's bolt was locked back, indicating it had recently been fired and was either empty or had encountered a jam. Anxiety set in as he glanced around in all directions. A looming sense of horror embodied his soul as he lifted his shirt to inspect himself. Seeing blood dripping from a three-quarter-inch hole, he placed his hand on his back to examine himself further.

Probing around in desperation, he detected an even larger hole in his back, opposite the hole in the front.

"I'm shot," Jason mouthed to himself in disbelief. *How did I get shot?*

Jason's pupils dilated as the cloud of confusion began to dissipate. He always hated that familiar feeling of oncoming clarity and how it came at him like a bullet train. It always felt like falling through ice and into cold water, having the ability to kill you in less than a minute—like being in one of those blissful dreams, then having wakefulness rip you back into the complex realities of life. He found that there was a lot less pain in the cloud.

With desperation, he started to feel around his pockets for something, anything. His muscles felt like they were acting faster than he could think, moving on their own, instinctually. Raising his hand from his pocket, he caught the glint of sunshine against the pale-yellow brass he now held in his hand.

In haste, without much thought, he threw the brass 7.62 caliber round into the rifle's chamber. Smacking his hand against the side of the rifle, he released the bolt catch loading the gun with a single bullet. The bolt slammed forward with a familiar metal clutching sound.

He raised his head and placed the rifle on his shoulder in an instinctual state of readiness. Jason stared out into the distance, now completely aware of his reality. The voice echoed throughout the wilderness with contempt and aggravation.

"You don't quit, Orion, do you …"

Chapter 1

A snake that cannot shed its skin perishes.
—Friedrich Nietzsche

Backwoods, Alaska
Present Day

Echoes of animosity shot through the wilderness with each swing of Jason's axe. Each downward strike carried more strength and aggressiveness than the last as he grunted through physical exertion. He was unsure how long he'd been chopping this fallen tree, but it felt endless. Bounded by the emotions swirling within him, he struck it unheedingly.

It wasn't an activity of sustenance. Jason had enough firewood in the cabin to keep him warm for weeks. This tree happened to be an unfortunate target of his aggression. Call it a workout or call it stress relief; whatever it was, Jason felt some alleviation doing it, as he had on most days.

"ARGH!" Jason roared as he swung the axe one final time, embedding it into the center of the giant fallen log. Chips of wood and bark sailed through the air in all directions. Panting and out of breath, he shuffled backward and sat down on a nearby tree stump. Exhausted, Jason rubbed the left side of his numb face. The numbness was always there, but he found it more discernible the stronger his heart beat. Slouching, with his elbows on his knees, Jason gazed toward the beaten-up log. Although his eyes were fixed on the lumber, that was not what he saw. It never was.

Jason sighed as he pulled his bandana, now soaked in sweat, off his forehead. His wavy black hair fell across his scarred face like a veil to the world in front of him. His misty breath dissipated into the cold air, moving his hair with each exhalation. He wore a white T-shirt and ripped blue jeans that were held up with a faded brown military-style belt. He never dressed warmly when he knew he would get a good sweat on—overheating often made him uncomfortable. Jason preferred the cold. This was one of the reasons he chose his solitude up north. Not many people liked the cold.

The rays of sunlight struck his eyes through the trees. The falling sun had begun to set on the horizon. *Another day is almost over.*

Standing up, Jason slung his rifle over his shoulder. His eyes were transfixed on the log as he thought back to his hometown, his friends, and his family. Sighing, Jason left the axe in its wooden bed as he pivoted to return to the cabin.

It was never a far journey from his workout site, but Jason always brought his rifle. He figured he'd rather be in a situation of having a gun and not needing one, compared to being in the dangerous position of not having a rifle and needing one. He'd encountered many predators in his life. All had different aspects in their danger: bears, cougars … *humans.* Having a weapon on him made him feel comfortable. *Old habits die hard.*

Jason stepped out of the tree line and into the clearing, where he spotted his wooden cabin. Situated on a slight hill fifty yards before him, it wasn't the best-looking place or the biggest, but it was home. The weather-beaten abode looked as if it had seen better days. The one-story dwelling with a dark wood exterior was the only shelter for miles in this rugged wilderness.

Opening the door with his boot, Jason set the rifle in the corner and began throwing dry logs into the cast-iron wood stove. Placing a cigarette between his lips, Jason struck a match, illuminating his scarred face in the dim cabin. Igniting it, he took a deep breath of pacifying nicotine and tobacco. *Old habits die hard,* Jason thought to himself. He threw the lit match into the prestocked wood stove, setting it ablaze. The heat rushed through the air toward him, ready to provide warmth for the cold night ahead.

Jason opened the fridge door and scanned the contents within. The light illuminated the contents within thanks to a small portable generator Jason had lugged with him on a previous outing. Fresh game meat filled the fridge, accompanied only by condiments, alcohol, and dried jerky. Slamming the door shut, he cracked open a beer can and took a large, refreshing gulp. The taste of a cold beer at the end of the day always calmed his nerves before bed. Other times it took more than one to do the trick. He stood in the kitchen and examined the wall above the wood stove.

"What are you looking at?" Jason asked. "Not much to say, eh?"

It never had much to say. Besides, what could you expect when you talked to the head of a black bear mounted on the wall? A beast, one of many that he had struck down during his hunts. The heads of bears, moose, wolves, and bucks were a collection of trophies that filled his cabin. All taxidermied memoirs of his adventures and achievements. In these woods, at least, he was the apex predator.

"Yeah, stop badgering me. Here's an idea, how about you go fuck yourself. You're not even alive. Why should I listen to you?"

Sometimes Jason wasn't sure if he spoke to the bear or himself. As time had passed, the lines had somewhat blurred. Isolation could have differing and unpredictable impacts on the mind.

Sighing, he made his way through a door to the small bed in the corner room. Kicking off his boots, he lay on the mattress and gazed up at the ceiling. His weathered body settled into the soft sheets. Closing his eyes, Jason began to take long, deep, purposeful breaths. He had learned to use this tactic if he was in a stressful situation. Most recently, he used it as a measure to prevent his mind from running away from itself. Nothing disturbed his sleep like overactive thoughts; of those, he had many. *One … two … three …*

"Jason." A deep voice whispered in the dark. His eyes snapped open, alerted by the unknown. *Did I hear something? Did I imagine that?* The strange voice paralyzed him.

"Come to me …"

* * *

Although born with the name Jason, a nickname was bestowed upon him many years ago, one that he was referred by often out of respect and admiration. Orion. It was a nickname given to him during his time overseas. Knowing how much of an avid hunter Jason was, he was called Orion once by one of his teammates, and the nickname stuck. He further earned it after suppressing the enemy in a firefight shooting accurate volleys from his M203 grenade launcher. He ended up expending all the rounds from his belt with deadly accuracy, ending the firefight. He often carried those rounds in a belt wrapped around his waist. Orion's belt.

In Greek mythology, Orion was a huntsman and venerated hero that Zeus placed among the stars as the constellation of the same name. Many stories of this ancient mythological figure have been passed on since ancient times, with different plots and outcomes. These ranged from his appearance in Homer's *Odyssey* to his mentions in *Astronomia*, a lost work by Hesiod.

One of the more common versions of the story had Orion becoming such an indomitable hunter, the pinnacle of human excellence, that the gods sent a creature to Earth to teach him a lesson. To show him that no matter how good he might be, he was no god like them, just a mortal. That creature also earned its own constellation next to Orion's. Its name was Scorpio.

On that day in Afghanistan, the heat was like a scorching oven, made worse by the sand infiltrating every part of his body. The desert was miserable and compassionless. It was a land that had been baptized in blood from the lives of countless souls throughout the decades. The land was no stranger to death and no friend to foreigners. Nobody left this desert without it taking a part of them.

"Fucking Orion's belt, bud!" Brad Redman, one of Jason's fire team partners, shouted joyously as the enemy was no longer engaging them, having been neutralized during the battle. The lull in the ear-splitting gunfire was a welcome relief to all.

"One section! We'll push past that tree line and clear out those fighting positions! Move!" The section commander hollered out his orders, and his soldiers immediately obeyed.

Jason climbed out of the wadi, a dry riverbed typical in Afghanistan, and moved with his section. His platoon was ready to meet any resistance with a blanket of deadly firepower. They pushed across the arid ground toward the tree line they had recently taken fire from. Most were confident that the enemy threat was neutralized or had retreated. The return fire they had provided during the ambush was all-encompassing. No one could have survived. Yet, it was still good practice to check the spots the enemy was fighting from to assess the damage and search for any valuable intel that might be recoverable.

The soldiers made their way across the open plain. Their eyes were fixed on the position they had just bombarded, prepared for any counterattack. Moving forward, the sandy rocks shuffled under Jason's feet as he kept his teammates beside him within his peripheral vision. Reaching the sparsely wooded tree line, he could feel his heart pounding as he peered into the ditch before him.

"Well, fucking look at that!" Brad yelled. "You fucking nailed them with that 203, Jason! Attaboy! I told you, it's Orion's belt, bud!" Jason wasn't as excited as Brad as they stood at the top of the ditch. Below them, past the tree line, was a bloody mess of mangled bodies.

Inside the ditch lay three dead enemy fighters. Their faces were twisted and flattened. Unrecognizable as humans. They were all killed by the explosive grenades shot by Jason. Many thoughts ran through him at that moment, yet he didn't feel bad. After all, they were trying to kill him and his teammates. Jason didn't feel anything. After six months in Kandahar, Afghanistan, he had become indifferent to the human suffering that the war had forced men to commit upon each other.

Sergeant Bass, his section commander, smacked Jason on his shoulder, snapping him out of his daze. "Let's go. Orion, we're moving." Jason was rarely called by his real name after that day. Some nicknames had a habit of sticking.

* * *

"Come to me," the voice whispered again.

Jason snapped his head to the side as he glimpsed something out of the corner of his eye, a thin white leg stepping out of the doorway.

His heart pounded as he got out of bed and took slow, cautious steps toward the main room. The light from the woodstove fire flickered across the cabin as the logs crackled in the heat. The place was now a warm, comfortable room temperature as it blazed while Jason had been napping. He scanned the area with his senses on overload but saw nothing of concern. Taking a few more steps into the room, he analyzed the interior further.

Doors closed, jackets on the hook, and unwashed dishes on the sink. Wouldn't that be nice to have someone break in to do your dirty dishes? Everything seems normal.

Jason moved to return to his bed until an ominous feeling grew within him. He froze in place. Slowly, Jason shifted, his eyes to the right, where the head of the black bear hung. It looked the same, but something about it was different.

Cautiously he walked toward the mounted head of the bear. *There's something off about it.* Closer and closer, he moved his face to the bear as he stared deep into its empty marble eyes.

Abruptly, the bear bellowed a deafening roar, snapping at his face with ferocity. Startled, Jason fell onto his back in absolute horror. The bear swung its head back and forth, bursting at the air as if trying to escape its eternal mount.

The cabin grew louder with the sound of wild animals. The barking of a moose and the howling of wolves all raged in the heated cabin. Overwhelmed and frightened, Jason placed his hands on his ears to soften the wall of pain caused by the chaotic noise. Desperately he staggered to his feet.

His hunting trophies were now alive and seething. With animalistic instinct, they thrashed and bit, trying to escape their positions on the wall. Horrified, Jason began to hyperventilate.

What is happening? My gun, where's my gun?!

Jason spotted the gun where he had left it, near the corner of the back wall. Unfortunately, that also happened to be beside the bear's head, which was now snarling and drooling out of its large black face, foam dripping from its gums. Stepping toward the gun, he was stopped by a different noise that brought him even more concern. This time it was the sound of wood cracking and breaking apart.

The black bear smashed through the cabin wall, and timber exploded throughout the room. Falling into the floor, the bear stood up, shaking off the splintered wood remnants covering its body. It was now whole and free, snarling toward Jason.

In horror, Jason screamed in fear as he abandoned the thought of grabbing his rifle, instead running toward the cabin door to escape his homestead. The cabin was now filled with the sounds of feral rage from all his hunting trophies. Approaching the door, Jason tripped over the leg of a chair, causing him to stumble toward the nearest wall.

Catching himself by placing his hands against the wall, Jason's eyes widened in horror as he looked at the face affixed to the wall in front of him.

What should have been another one of his hunting trophies now took on a different shape. A deep, bloodcurdling scream shrieked from the deformed human head facing Jason.

"ORION!" its gurgled voice screeched. The bloodied face was disturbingly familiar. Its head was flattened as if its skull was crushed. Mangled and deformed, shrapnel wounds covered its face. Where the eyes had once been were now two deep empty holes. Its head was somehow mounted on one of his trophy placards in a gruesome display of horror.

Jason screamed in fear as he pushed himself off the wall and crashed out the cabin door into the frigid snow. Desperate to escape, he crawled through the cold snow as fast as he could. Moonlight reflected off the white ground creating a ghostly glow in the wilderness around him. His breath rapidly dissipated into the frosty night.

Jason hysterically persisted in crawling through the white powder. Gasping and hyperventilating, he saw something familiar emerge before him.

Standing before him were two tiny legs barefoot in the snow. The skin was nearly as pale and white as the snow it currently stood in. Raising his head, Jason drew his gaze to the ankle and up along the leg. He stared up at the corpse-like figure above him. The child spoke in a soft feminine tone.

"Come to me, Orion."

Chapter 2

They sent forth men to battle, but no such men return; And home, to claim their welcome, come ashes in an urn.
—Aeschylus

Kandahar Province, Afghanistan
Fall 2010

A scorpion scampered over the sand-encrusted rocks, its oil-black skin baking in the desert heat. *Is it looking for shade? Does this heat even bother it?* Its body seems hardened like a suit of ebony armor. Sinister and deadly, it emitted an aura of caution, warning anyone who crossed it that they would suffer the consequences.

The platoon was hunkered down in a large wadi. Jason had been watching his arcs during the listening halt from an ideal firing position, peeking up over the edge of the wadi. He was scanning for enemy fighters when the scorpion scurried a few feet in front of his face—confronting him with a threat just as deadly as his enemy. The scorpion appeared to stop before him as if it was assessing a threat.

Jason and the creature eyed each other. Its portentous gaze judged Jason's soul. He felt, in some way, that this creature was reading him, assessing him. It was a predatory arachnid from a different part of the world, yet Jason felt as if it seemed to know him intimately. *Snap out of it.*

"Don't let that thing sting you," Sergeant Bass warned. "There are many ways to die out here. I would be pretty disappointed in you if you went out at the hands of an insect." The scorpion scurried away from Jason, off to find whatever it must have been looking for. "Prepare to move," Sergeant Bass ordered, slapping Jason on the shoulder.

"Brad, come on, let's move," Jason called out, cautiously shifting his eyes from the black creature. "This heat is getting to me."

Jason shuffled his gear around his body into a more comfortable position. You could only get so comfortable wearing eighty pounds of gear and armor in hundred-degree heat. Adjusting your equipment to suit your needs was the best you could do.

"Brad, let's fucking move," Jason repeated to his fire team partner. Although a solid soldier, Brad Redman seemed to be struggling at this point in the patrol.

"I'm fucking moving, man, chill," he responded, adjusting his radio to a more desirable position.

"If you need some water, get it in you now. We've got about three clicks to go before we're back at the FOB." Sergeant Bass, a well respectable section commander, always had his soldier's welfare at the front of his mind.

The forward operating base was situated ten miles southeast of Kandahar City. It had been their home for the better part of five months now and would be for another four. They had gotten to know their surroundings quite well over the months, well enough to know when things seemed to be amiss or odd. Such as a bustling village going quiet or a busy road often taken by locals becoming deserted. For these men, everything, down to the smallest detail, was a possible threat indicator.

Frequently, these presence patrols would end at the base uneventfully, with nothing notable except the dirt and sweat covering their bodies. Other times, returning to the FOB would be a sweet relief after an intense confrontation with the enemy. The members of Jason's platoon were eager to get this patrol over with.

"When we return to the FOB, I'm having a nap. I don't give a fuck what the Sergeant tells me to do." Brad Redman was often outspoken, yet obeyed every command he was given. It had become a running comedic theme, his threats to disobey an order.

"Sure thing, Brad." Jason rolled his eyes. It was yet another empty complaint from his friend.

"I'm serious. Sergeant Bass can get somebody else to prep the vehicle radios for the night. I ain't doing it. I always do it." Brad moved, inspecting his surroundings.

"You always do it because you're the secondary signaler, Brad. You could always be the primary latrine cleaner if you don't like it. I'm sure you'd be great at that." Jason smirked.

"Yeah, whatever."

The platoon moved over the uneven ground, ripe for ankle sprains and awkward falls. During these patrols, Jason's body was often tired and ached in the blistering heat. Yet he always kept his mind sharp and attentive. Sometimes it reminded him of his time hunting back home in the backwoods of Nebraska. He would frequently brave the elements, which brought challenges and rewards. Even while soaking wet during a rainstorm or swarmed by insects and mosquitoes, he would always remain sharp to his surroundings, focused on the objective of fetching his prey.

"We're moving off this path and onto the road. Ack Ack formation," a voice squawked over the radio, directing them to split up on either side of the roadway in pairs. Jason lunged to get up onto the road, an elevated hardened route covered in dirt and dust. This was one of the few main roads in the area that was paved.

They began walking down the road, placing themselves on either side in a staggered line. The team of soldiers straddled each side on command. This created distance among them and ensured they did not bunch up. Their FOB was visible in the distance, the closest thing they could call home. The large guard towers on all four corners of the base loomed over the Hesco barrier walls, daring anyone to attempt an attack.

After the hours-long dismounted patrol, a hot meal, fresh water, and showers awaited them all. "Orion, what's the first animal you want to hunt when you get home?" asked Brad, turning around to face Jason.

"Not sure, a bear maybe? It won't be moose season, so it all depends. But whatever I decide, they'll be stocking my freezer and making a nice conversation piece on my wall." Jason lowered his head, his mind drifting to when he shot his first bear with his father.

A warm feeling of nostalgia washed over Jason as he walked down the desert road. Just ten years of age at the time of his first kill, he couldn't stop vibrating with adrenaline as he stood over the animal. His proud father stood behind him, his hand on his shoulder, beaming with joy for his son.

"Always confident, huh? Does anything ever get away from you?" Brad's comment brought him back to his precarious reality.

"Well, of course. Never for long, though. I like the chase." Jason looked down at his tanned boots as he kicked a rock out of his path.

"Well, I hope poor Winnie the Pooh gets away. What the fuck did he ever do to you?" Brad spoke as he walked backward, facing Jason.

The sound of a motor began getting louder in cohesion with his platoon mates' rising voices. "CONTACT!" Jason heard the panicked shout from one of the men up front. Snapping his head up, Jason raised his rifle into his shoulder, pointing down the roadway beyond Brad.

Seeing this, Brad spun around with his weapon and pointed it toward the threat at the front of the formation. An orchestra of alarm and desperation erupted as the five soldiers to the front screamed commands at the approaching vehicle.

Shots rang out toward the car as it barreled down the road to the front of the platoon. The Toyota Corolla charged forward, white and rusty, its chassis weighted down with something heavy in its trunk. Powder and dust kicked up all around the vehicle as it was showered in a hail of bullets. The dull sound of lead on metal filled the air as if a thousand hammers were hitting the car. Yet the car was not slowing. It continued to charge with incredible speed.

Flipping the safety to full auto, Jason held down the trigger for a prolonged burst of his rifle. The recoil punched into his shoulder like a jackhammer as he attempted to hit the driver through the windshield. *Come on … Come on … Come on!* His heart sank as the vehicle approached.

FLASH.

A deafening explosion ripped through the air and turned the world into a haze of dust and rock. The sky was no longer visible; no sounds echoed, no voices spoke, and no gunshots were fired.

The world became silent.

Chapter 3

*There are seeds of self-destruction in all of us that will bear only
unhappiness if allowed to grow.*
—Dorothea Brande

Backwoods, Alaska
Present Day

Jason gasped for air as he struggled to take the bedsheets off.
Covered in sweat and breathless, he looked around the room at his
surroundings.

"Fuck," Jason wailed as he pushed the palm of his hands into his
eyes. Sleep never came easy. After a vivid nightmare, he often wondered if
his dream was a reality or not. It all seemed entwined together in a hazy fog,
memories and emotions mixing with subconscious narratives. Sitting on the
mattress, he took deep breaths to collect his thoughts.

"One ... two ... three ..." With his eyes closed, Jason slowly
counted his breaths to control his racing heart. "Ten." The pounding drum
of his pulse subsided, and he began to regain composure. Opening his eyes,
he drifted his gaze to the doorway.

Come to me.

He remembered the voice. The pale white legs. The familiar
deformed faces on his wall and the terrifying roars of animals from his
dream. *Was it a dream?* He was unsure what to do for a moment, still
somewhat scared and in shock; he felt frozen in apprehension, yet too
hesitant to step out from the doorway. *What if it wasn't a dream? Are the
animals alive? What about that bear? That girl? Those faces?*

Jason's face wrinkled with unease. His eyes weighed heavily as he moved to sit at the side of the bed. His facial expression remained weathered and gloomy as it usually did. Standing up and favoring the side of his stiff hip, he began to limp his way to the doorway.

Although he was only in his midthirties, his body sometimes felt like it was in his eighties. Mornings were the hardest. It was as if he needed to take an hour to chisel his body from a concrete casing before he felt completely awake. He laid eyes on the bear head hanging on his wall as he stood in the doorway.

"Hmph," he grunted, noticing nothing different about the trophy mount. Jason let out a sigh. A sigh born out of shame? Relief? Embarrassment? He found it hard to analyze his emotions, but he knew he was glad this ordeal was just a dream.

Jason strode to the bathroom and poured water over his face. Another tactic he utilized to manage his anxiety. Turning off the tap, he scrutinized his face in the mirror. His bright gray-blue eyes told a story of pain and loss. Scars blanketed the left side of his weathered face. Jason felt as if he was staring eye-to-eye with a stranger. The more the days passed, the more he questioned who he was and why he had bothered to come here.

Returning to the main room, Jason grabbed the paper filters from the top cupboard and began to brew his morning coffee. He always stood in front of the pot while it brewed, an act of patience he found worthwhile to complete. The machine's humming and bubbling sound brought a soothing feeling to him. Patiently waiting on his morning kick-starter had turned into a type of ritual.

Jason, with his hands on the counter, peered to his left. Outside the cabin door window, snow covered the fields and forests. Smooth and white, it was a serene, untouched canvas of the northern sky blending with the earth in an overcast gray.

"Agh!" Jason screamed as his forearm touched the now-burning pot of coffee.

"Fucking, God dammit!" Jason hollered. Seizing the pot of coffee, he hurled it against the back wall. The glass pot shattered and spread across the floor, causing dark coffee stains to drip down the wall and pool all over the floor. Panting, with rage on his face, Jason clenched his eyes shut and lowered his head. His jaw tightened as hard as his fists.

It happened so quickly. It was an instantaneous transformation from calmness to rage. Something Jason had a hard time controlling. It came with an almost out-of-body experience. During these episodes, Jason could recall floating over his body and watching himself act in a way he had no control over. It was hard to contain his anger, and it would frequently be replaced with shame and guilt when it dissipated. Just as it was doing right now.

Rubbing his elbow, he contemplated the rash decision he had just made. "God, you're an idiot." *Stupid idiot.*

His inner thoughts were never kind to him. It was an overwhelming bombardment of negativity—extreme self-criticism, overreactions to minor failures, and pessimistic voices toward himself and others. Over time they grew louder and more discernible.

With a sigh, Jason peered into the corner where he had left his rifle. The weapon leaned into the corner with a steadfast ambiance. It was the one object he could count on and trust. He cherished it as a child would cherish a security blanket.

"Let's do it." Jason looked for anything to shake him from his mood, and hunting would be just the thing.

He walked to the front door and began getting dressed. A spontaneous hunt would hopefully help Jason escape his current mood. Lacing up his black military-style boots, he knotted them tightly and tucked them into the side of his boot. He grabbed his thick brown corduroy jacket from the closet and threw it on. Another ritualistic hunting item he had was his ball cap. He wrapped a bandana over his head and ears and placed his tattered brown baseball cap on top of it.

Sunglasses, backpack, rifle … good to go.

Jason often filled his bag with items he might need if he was out in the bush for more than twenty-four hours. He packed it with water, a first aid kit, rope, hunting knives, ammunition, a thermal blanket, a tarp, lighters, and other related supplies.

The door slammed behind him as he exited the cabin with the rifle slung on his shoulder. Jason didn't even bother cleaning up the mess he'd made inside. He just needed out. *I'll deal with it later.* Snow crunched beneath his feet as he began hiking north, taking the foot trail that carved through the enormous boreal forest.

It was decent weather for a hunt. Overcast, chilly with a light breeze, not comfortable but not unbearable. Hunting in the winter had its benefits and challenges. On the one hand, tracking animals by their prints in the snow was more manageable. But the lack of vegetation limited concealment, a double-edged sword for predator and prey. As the air was thinner in winter, sound also carried farther, so Jason would stop walking to conduct a listening halt every so often.

He assessed his surroundings as he crouched down, closed his eyes, and tried to hear for signs of wildlife. The only noticeable sound was the crisp wind blowing through the branches above him and his foggy breath.

Hours passed by with Jason roaming the forest. Now a few miles from his cabin, he was deep in the woods with no man-made trails nearby. On a few occasions, Jason came close to finding prey—footprints of a bear, deer droppings, the messy, chaotic footprints of a pack of wolves. Unfortunately, none of them were fresh, and he had yet to see any animals.

Jason stopped and threw his backpack on the ground next to a tree. *Time to go back, not getting anything today*, he thought as he slid down the tree trunk for a respite.

Drinking from his canteen of water, he wiped the moisture off his face. Jason leaned his head back and closed his eyes. Taking deep, slow breaths, he inhaled the cool winter air. Crisp and refreshing, it was a sensation he cherished. It brought him a sense of calmness and flooded his mind with childhood memories of hunting with his father.

* * *

"Dad, I'm tired. Can we go home now?"

"It's been a long day, hasn't it, Jason? Let's make our trek back after a little break. How about a snack?"

"Yeah! Do you have those protein bars?"

"Sure do, bud. Let's sit here."

Jason and his father brushed the snow off a fallen log and made it their bench. Chewing on a chocolate protein bar, eleven-year-old Jason took in the springtime wilderness of Nebraska. It was the third time he had been hunting with his father, and he was still getting used to the whole thing. Jason remembered how the adrenaline shot through his veins when his dad let him take the shot on his very first hunt. It was a feeling like no other.

This time, however, there had been no such luck. No wildlife. Just the father and son wandering around in the woods.

"Dad, it really sucks when you don't catch anything. It makes it so boring. All we did was walk around the forest wasting time." Jason kicked some sticks from his feet.

"Son, if you consider an unsuccessful hunt a waste of time, then the true meaning of the chase has eluded you altogether." His father looked down at him with a look of amusement.

"What do you mean?"

"Jason, some people in the world have forgotten where we came from. We came from the woods. There are fifty-thousand-year-old cave paintings depicting ancient people going on a hunt. This sport used to be a necessity of living and a cultural ritual. It's how humans bonded within their tribes. They worked together for their common survival. The hard work involved in hunting makes it all the more rewarding when you're successful. Some hunts can be miserable with rain, cold, and rough terrain. But misery can make good company and help lighten everything else in your life," his father continued.

"In Alaska, there are Native Americans of the Athabascan tribes. They were hunter-gatherers and moved throughout their land, keeping in touch with the animals. They respected animals greatly and believed that some had mystical powers and represented spirits. It's an exciting way of life."

"Dad, that was a long time ago. We can just grab something from the grocery store if we don't catch anything. We don't need to be out in bad weather if we don't want." Jason finished his protein bar.

"That's exactly what I mean. Somewhere down the line, we became too domesticated, too spoiled. Everything is easy now. Do you want a certain type of food? Go to the store. It'll be there. Do you want to speak to a relative or friend that lives far away? There is no need to send them a letter or take a long trip to see them, just pick up your phone. Curious about something? Just look it up. Things have become too easy. We forgot what made us human in the first place and, in the process, have lost some of the experiences life has provided us. I don't want you to forget that either, son."

"I won't. I enjoy spending time with you, Dad." Jason looked into his father's loving eyes.

"Me too, Jason. It's not always about the end result ... But you should know one more thing, and this is important." His father placed his arm around young Jason.

"What's that?"

"When a hunter returns holding only a handful of mushrooms … don't ask him how his hunt went."

* * *

Jason opened his eyes toward the sky. Branches swayed back and forth above him, a rhythmic dance made possible by the northern wind. He decided he had rested long enough, and it was time to head back to the cabin.

"Fuck." Hanging his head, Jason mumbled a curse as he remembered the mess waiting for him back home. A mess of broken glass and coffee stains made by his own short temper and impaired judgment.

Alright, whatever, let's go, Jason thought, but something made him pause before standing up.

He sensed that he was not alone. Something else was in the woods, watching him. Frozen and looking around with piercing eyes, Jason scanned the forest in front of him. *There!* A brown shape appeared between the tree branches in the distance. A doe stood gracefully in the snow.

The deer had a long dark snout, and her chest extended forward in front of her legs. Mature and good for the kill, the doe was still, staring off into the distance and oblivious to Jason's presence.

With great care, Jason slowly grabbed his rifle and placed it into the crutch of his shoulder. Aiming at the deer's heart, he exhaled a slow, steady breath and gently squeezed the trigger with the pad of his index finger.

The shot rang throughout the wilderness as the birds in the trees overhead flew away. The doe made an initial twitch and sprinted away in a desperate act of pure instinct.

"Got it!" Jason lowered his rifle and scanned the target area.

Adrenaline surged through Jason's body as he grabbed his equipment. Sprinting through the woods, he arrived at where his doe was last standing. A trail of blood and footprints were all that remained on the spot. His deer made a trail that led through the woods and down a snowy embankment a few dozen yards to the north.

Standing at the embankment's edge, Jason spotted the deer down below at the edges of a softly flowing river. *It's a pretty steep hill—the deer must have fallen down it in a panic. It's going to be a bitch carrying her back up.*

Carefully, Jason began to make his way down the hill. Hanging onto some branches and sliding his way from tree to tree, he lost his footing several times but was able to stop himself from falling. Ice that had formed underneath the snow made it harder to traverse than he thought it would be.

Reaching the bottom, he ambled toward his trophy. The doe lay at the foot of the slow-moving river that was partially covered in ice. The deer's gorgeous shape looked pristine, lying on the white canvas and appearing as if it was sleeping in a tranquil dream.

"Two hundred pounds? Maybe?" Jason spoke to himself.

He estimated the size and weight of the doe as he crouched down and placed his hand on her chest. *A clean kill, she didn't suffer long.* A smile came to his face, and excitement coursed through him. The work, however, had only just begun. He had to gut it, quarter it, and bring it back to the cabin. A process that would take a lot of time and effort.

Excitedly Jason took his pack off and placed it between his legs for support. Rummaging through it, he brought out his custom-made bowie hunting knife. The knife, made from Damascus steel with a stabilized wood handle, was his favorite knife for skinning.

"There we go."

Jason held the knife and began cutting at the animal's ankles until something made him pause. *I'm being watched.* He looked across the river. A fawn was standing on the other side, staring at him. The baby deer watched in silence and confusion as its mother lay dead on the ground with this strange man kneeling over her.

Jason sensed his blood cool. Staring at the fawn, he felt sadness, regret, and guilt. He had killed its mother. Jason had done this a hundred times, but seeing the fawn across the river resurrected something deep within him that he could no longer suppress. A deep pain arose from within him as his heart rate accelerated. Breathing heavily, he felt as if he was being transported into the past.

His eyes glazed over as he stared off into another world. He was looking at the baby deer, but he also wasn't. He was staring a thousand miles beyond it. A massive migraine began to form at the sides of his temples, making him light-headed and confused.

Jason looked down at the mother and moaned in agony. With one hand on the deer and another on his head, he felt like something in him was trying to rip his skin off and escape his body. Overwhelmed, Jason felt like he was being pulled in a million different directions, his soul squirming to

escape his own skin. Yet his body lingered, kneeling over his kill. Jason's heart began beating faster as his throat started closing up. *What's happening?*
Jason collapsed into the snow.

Chapter 4

No guilt is forgotten so long as the conscience still knows of it.
—Stefan Zweig

Kandahar City, Afghanistan
Summer 2010

"Orion!" The voice was muffled, unrecognizable over the ringing in his ears.

Dust particles clouded the air creating a haze of sand in the back of the vehicle. In the chaos of the moment, the sand calmly hovered in the air like thousands of stars. It was all Jason could focus on. Confused and disoriented, he tried to grasp what was going on but could only hear the breathing of his tightening lungs.

"Orion! IED!"

He was staring at a face in front of him, but it wasn't registering. *Brad?* It was Brad, shouting at him in urgency. He was sitting across from him with a rifle between his legs and it seemed like he'd been trying to get his attention for a while. They were in the back of their light armored vehicle. *On patrol?*

"IED! Out! Out! Out!"

Jason snapped out of it, and his training kicked in after realizing an improvised explosive device had struck them. Luckily their vehicle still stood upright. Although shaken up, the explosion wasn't powerful enough to flip it, and by the looks of it, everyone was still alive.

With as much strength as possible, Jason pushed the back hatch open as hard as possible. The explosion had caused the door to warp and made it considerably more difficult than expected. *Get out, get out, get out!* It was the only thing that was going through his mind. Nothing was more perilous than being sitting ducks in an ambush zone. Your best chance of survival was getting out and bringing the fight to the enemy.

"Hngh!" Jason let out a labored grunt as the hatch finally gave way. He tumbled outside onto the ground with a thud. Jason had clear vision from underneath their vehicle on the dirty sand-crusted road. He could see many legs running around the vehicles to his front, attempting to organize themselves in the chaos that surrounded them. Shouting commands, his fellow soldiers were taking up firing positions around their vehicles. Underneath Jason's armored vehicle was an astonishing-sized hole, some overturned dirt, and … *a scorpion?* The black scorpion stood underneath one of the tires, its eyes fixated on Jason with its tail raised toward him.

"Here!" Brad lifted Jason to his feet and shoved a rifle into his chest. "You dropped this!" Jason grabbed it and quickly checked to ensure it was functional.

"Rooftops!" Panicked voices shouted out all around him.

Their patrol was on its way back to camp after a three-hour presence patrol in Kandahar City when it was ambushed by a roadside bomb. Gunshots echoed in all directions like an orchestra of chaos and violence. The bomb had turned the world on its head in an instant. Bullets rained down upon their armored vehicles from the rooftops. The platoon returned fire up at them. A storm of lead enveloped the street.

Snap! Crack! Ting! The rounds were snapping over their heads and striking their vehicle. The gunfire coming from the three-story building was kicking up dust near their feet. Brad took a kneeling position with his SAW 42 machine gun and let out a suppressing burst above. *Tunk, tunk, tunk!* The cannon on the light armored vehicle fired at the opposite rooftop across the street. With the enemy keeping their heads down, Jason and three others sprinted to the base of the building.

Reaching the concrete structure, they flattened themselves against the wall for protection. Aiming their rifles in different directions, they tried to cover all potential threats in their location. Sergeant Bass and Brad were the last to leave the kill zone and arrive at the wall.

"Orion! We're taking this building! Our section is to clear this out and hold it until reinforcements arrive. Our vehicle is fucked, it can't drive, but it can still fire. The patrol is to stay put."

"Yes, Sergeant!" Jason responded. His heart pounded, and his legs felt weak. Knowing what awaited them inside the building brought an adrenaline rush that could not be matched in any other way. Jason began to harness his predator instinct with discipline and controlled aggression.

"You and Brad take point. We're moving in with all six of us," Sergeant Bass shouted with authority.

"Got it! Stack up!" Jason cried, issuing the command that they were about to take the door. Each soldier huddled in close behind one another. When they were set, they squeezed each other on the shoulder, starting from the man at the back. The squeeze was passed down one by one until it reached Jason at the front, signaling his section was ready to enter on his move.

Crash! Jason burst through the door with his teammates following close behind him. Moving immediately to the corner of the room, he scanned the area. Somewhat empty, with a couch, a small table, and a few prayer mats on the ground. It looked as if no one had lived there in a while.

"Clear!" Jason hollered.

"Clear! We've got an open door to the front leading to another room!" Brad announced, pointing his weapon at the doorway.

"Flow through!" Jason issued the command that instructed his section to forcefully take another room.

Once Jason issued the command, Brad and another soldier entered the room in unison. The moment they stepped into the doorway, gunfire erupted immediately, and concrete chips blew off the wall above them. Jason saw Brad plunge to the ground.

NO!

Returning fire from the ground with a prolonged burst in the direction of the enemy, Brad was alive and still fighting. The deafening echo of his machine gun spraying from the floor was overwhelming. Brad lay there in desperation, spraying a tsunami of shots in one direction. Diaz, the other soldier who had followed him, happened to trip over Brad's body. Diaz, vulnerable and in distress, was straining to crawl for cover when the gunfire stopped.

"Jesus Christ!" Brad screamed as he stood back up. With his eyes wide open, he had his weapon still aimed at the area of contestation. Jason entered the doorway. Immediately upon entering the room, he saw two enemy fighters dead in the corner of the room, lying motionless on top of each other. The wall behind them was littered with dozens of holes— evidence of the deadly response from Brad's weapon.

"You guys OK?" Jason examined Brad and Diaz.

"Yeah … yeah … I think?" Brad was stunned. Being so close to death, he was shocked he was still alive, let alone uninjured.

"What about you, Diaz?"

"I'm good, man. Fuck!" Diaz yelled, trying to collect himself.

"Lucky bastards!" Jason cried while helping Diaz to his feet. Sergeant Bass entered the room behind them with the other two soldiers and began to take command.

"Alright, shake it off, boys. I'll take the lead this time. There's a stairwell leading to the upper floors. We need to clear two more floors to reach the rooftop. We saw at least two fighters on the roof while we were on the road, so chances are they are still there. Let's move!"

Sergeant Bass took point, followed by Jason and two others. Having the same individuals enter the room first was something that they tried to avoid. Being the first to enter a room was always the most dangerous position. Spreading out the danger among the men kept them all on their toes.

The team flowed through the stairwell with Brad and Diaz at the rear. They saw a short hallway on the second floor with two rooms on either side. Placed in a covering position, Sergeant Bass signaled to the others that they were to move past him.

Jason motioned with a hand signal to the men behind him, informing them of the plan. Jason and one soldier, Rodriguez, would take the room on the left. Diaz and the others would take the room on the right. Brad would position himself covering down the stairs to their rear in case someone came from behind.

Jason made a chopping motion to his front, holding his hand in the air. That was the signal for the team to move forward with their plan. Simultaneously, both teams took their designated room by force. With aggression, Jason poured through the doorway and turned to take the corner of the room.

Faster than Jason could comprehend, he was on his back. A Taliban fighter had waited for him behind the door and jumped on him, forcing Jason to tumble to the ground.

"Allah!" The fighter screamed as he mounted Jason and tried to rip the rifle from his hands. Elbows smashed down onto Jason's face. He began losing his grip on his weapon. *You lose this weapon, and you die! You lose this weapon, and you die!* That was all he could think to himself.

The fighter was dressed in light brown linen with a white turban. The Taliban fighter had a long black and gray beard, and his face was weathered, aged from what must have been years of fighting. Jason was surprised as the fighter released his grip on the rifle and began choking him, two hands around Jason's neck.

Jason instinctively grabbed onto the fighter's wrists to try and loosen the deadly grasp he had on him. *I can't breathe! I can't breathe!* In a panic, Jason began looking around for something to help him out of his predicament. The yellow eyes of the fighter were locked onto him with pure rage and hatred. He drooled through his clenched crooked teeth and continued crushing Jason's throat, attempting to snuff out his life.

I'm going to fucking die. I'm going to fucking die. Jason's thoughts ran wild as he stared back at the fighter. Holding onto his wrists, he continued trying to pry them off his throat. Desperately and with all his strength, he fought for his life. Jason began throwing punches at the fighter, each seeming less powerful than the other. His vision began to fade. As his world turned black, he looked at the fighter's forearm. There was a tattoo—a giant black scorpion.

BANG! The head exploded above him. The Taliban fighter's body collapsed on top of him, covering Jason with blood and brain matter. Jason pushed the dead weight off and began a fit of coughing while on his hands and knees.

"You good, Orion?" Rodriguez, the soldier who entered the room with him, shot the fighter.

"Fuck me, thanks." Jason continued to cough as he stood up with his weapon, aided by Rodriguez. His vision slowly came back. Nursing his throat, clarity began to rise within him. He recognized the room they had entered was a child's bedroom. The space was partially empty except for a child's bed pushed against the wall and a crib next to it. Lying on the ground near the bed were some traditional colorful dresses. Toys were also scattered about, along with one dead enemy fighter.

"Room clear!" Jason heard Diaz's voice cry out from the other room.

"Room clear!" Responding, Jason and Rodriguez moved back into the hallway, linking back up with Sergeant Bass and Brad.

Tink, tink, tink! The distinctive sound of bouncing metal coming from the stairwell caught everyone's attention. The metal ball bounced down from above, hitting each step until it landed on their floor.

"GRENADE!" Sergeant Bass screamed at the top of his lungs and jumped on top of Brad. Both of them fell down the stairs back to the first floor. The four soldiers in the hallway desperately tried to enter back into the rooms they had just taken.

BOOM! The building vibrated, and Jason's chest felt the dull echo of the detonation. A cloud of dust spread throughout the hallway and into the rooms. Their hearing became muffled as the dust stung their eyes and caused them to cough. Jason and his teammate were unscathed, as were Diaz and his partner in the room across the hall. The fate of Sergeant Bass and Brad was unknown.

Positioning himself inside the doorway and facing the stairwell, Jason cried out, fearful for his two comrades. "Bass! Brad! Are you good?!"

"Yeah, we're good! Goddammit!" Sergeant Bass responded from down below.

"Good! I've got the stairwell covered. You two move up to us!"

"Roger!" After acknowledging Jason's direction, Bass and Brad sprinted up the stairwell. Reaching the rest of his team, Sergeant Bass attempted to regain his composure.

"OK, listen, those dickheads are still up there! I could see only one room on the third floor, and the stairwell led up to the roof. We'll get this shit over and take it by storm." Bass grabbed Jason by the shoulder.

"Orion! You and Brad will take the room on the third floor first. Frag that fucking room before entering. Once you do that, the four of us will flow past you and take the roof immediately. Understood?"

"Got it, Sergeant! Brad, let's fucking do this." Jason's eyes hardened with steely determination.

Jason and Brad began proceeding up the stairs until they had eyes on the room that Sergeant Bass was referring to. The door was ajar, cracked and pushed open from the force of the explosion that had just occurred. Brad had his weapon trained on the stairwell above as Jason focused on the door.

Nodding at Brad, Jason grabbed a grenade from his tactical vest and pulled the pin. In one fell swoop, he rolled the grenade into the room and used his hand to shut the door, ensuring the explosion was contained within the room, amplifying its effects.

BOOM! The walls convulsed, and Sergeant Bass and his team immediately pushed past them to the rooftop. Thunderous gunfire erupted above them as Jason and Brad kicked in the door and entered the room.

What lay before them was something they were not prepared for. Lying in the room was a woman twisted on the floor. White concrete dust covered her legs, and her clothes had been partially blown off. She was dead. Her body lay in a puddle of blood and debris at the back of the room.

The gunfire from the rooftop had stopped, and Jason vaguely heard the commands of "Clear." He stood there fixated on the destruction he had just caused. Frozen within his own body, he was in a state of shock. A hand grabbed Jason's shoulder and his eyes filled with the devastation before him.

"Jason … you didn't know, man … Jason?" Barely hearing Brad's words, Jason's attention was captivated by a separate voice.

"Moor! Moor!" The voice of a child sobbed while screaming out for her mother. A young girl not older than five stood crying in the corner of the room, hidden behind a table. Tattered clothes and messy hair, she stood there holding a stuffed bear. Tears dripped down her dust-covered face as she called out to her mother, lying dead on the floor.

"Moor! Moor!"

Jason's chest felt tight and heavy. A terrible shadow drifted over him with the world's weight behind it. He caused this. This was his doing. There was no erasing it. No turning back time. No fixing mistakes. No ignoring the present. Jason stood in the doorway, incapable of moving, digesting what had just transpired.

The human suffering he had just caused was being tattooed onto his soul.

Chapter 5

Of all the things you choose in life, you don't get to choose what your nightmares are. You don't pick them; they pick you.
—John Irving

Backwoods, Alaska
Present Day

The wind whistled through the dark, barren branches above him. Hanging over him like hands reaching down to seize him, they gave Jason an ominous sensation of being unwelcome. The gray, overcast clouds blanketed the sky through the treetops. His eyes adjusted as he began to take in his surroundings. *I'm cold.* Lying in the snow, he heard nothing but the sound of the moaning branches as they swayed in the wind. Water flowed softly through the icy stream beside him. *How long have I been out?*

Turning his head, he came face-to-face with the lifeless deer carcass. Its empty eyes stared right through him. *Fuck.* Chilled to the bone, he rolled onto his knees and inspected his kill. The blood on its body had dried. Its crusted hair was a dark crimson red. Jason's rifle and backpack lay in the snow beside him. *My head …* He closed his eyes and massaged his temples as he tried to regain clarity. *Did I pass out?* He gazed at the dead deer, which jolted his memory as he recalled the fawn standing across the river.

Snapping his head to look across the river, he could no longer see the baby deer. *Must have run away, poor thing.* Jason moaned as he looked at the water, taking in the sounds of nature around him. Seeing the fawn watching its deceased mother had brought back memories that Jason harbored within. Memories that he long tried to suppress. His chest felt hollow as he closed his eyes, rubbing the left side of his face.

The silence broke with a chorus of low, dismal, far-reaching howls that came from the forest-covered embankment across the river. The thickness of the bush obscured it with darkness; he could not see through the trees, but he sensed what was behind it.

Carefully, Jason closed up his backpack, threw it over his shoulders, and tightened the straps. *Something's not right.* Twigs snapped, and bushes rustled. The howling grew nearer, close enough that he could distinguish that there were more than one. The grunts and barks began to spread across the tree line.

The wolves broke through the forest in unison, slowly lurking forward. Four of them, gray and grungy, looked wild and unhinged. They stopped their movement at the shore of the icy water. All four wolves stood beside each other, staring at Jason and his kill. With their jaws clenched, they licked their lips in hunger. Steel gray claws protruded from their large paws. It was a stare-down that didn't seem to end. On one side of the river was Jason, crouching by his deer. Four ferocious wolves were on the other. Nothing stood between them except for the frigid water coursing downstream.

What do I do? Jason debated shooting at one or firing a shot to scare them off. *They want the deer. They don't want you.* Jason took a deep breath as the stare-down continued. He had never seen wolves be so still. Like statues. The only movement they made was caused by their rapid breathing. Mist rose from their breath.

Jason remained on his knees and placed his rifle in his lap. Taking a deep breath, he contemplated what to do, hoping they would decide to go away. His only comfort was knowing a body of water stood between them. *They're still staring at me.*

The wind grew more assertive, filling the air with the sound of blowing leaves and branches. Jason began to notice that the overcast sky was darker than it had been minutes earlier. As if on cue, the wolves turned to walk along the shore. In pairs, they split in both directions, strolling purposefully to their destination. Their eyes never left Jason.

The wolves disappeared into the woods down the shoreline, but no comfort came to Jason. The encounter with these animals was disturbing and confusing. It was strange and foreign compared to what he had ever before experienced with wolves. *I've never seen something like that before. The way they looked at me. The way they moved ...* While scanning the shoreline, an unnerving feeling overcame him. *I'm still being watched ...*

Chills ran down his spine as his stomach tightened into knots. He began scanning in all directions and turned to see the forest behind him. A strong wind blew through his sweaty black hair, and he froze. He could feel his fight-or-flight instinct setting in, but he wasn't sure why; he could sense danger. Something dreadful was here.

Gradually, Jason focused his attention back across the water. Looking up, he saw a dark figure standing at the top of the embankment. A human figure stood in silence, watching him from above. Jason couldn't quite identify the features from where he was, but alarm bells began ringing inside of him that something was not right.

"Who's there?!" Trying to get a response from the figure, Jason began calling out.

"I see you! Who are you?" Still, the shadow gave no response. Stoic and unmoving, the dark figure remained in place.

"Listen, motherfucker. I don't play games, so stop fucking around and answer me! Who are you, and what are you doing out here?" *I haven't seen a human in months. What the hell is this guy doing here?*

No response, no reaction. The dark figure stood among the trees, its gaze fixed on Jason below. The wind picked up its swiftness, and the gusts tore through the trees. The breeze grew louder as the leaves blew and branches swung.

Jason's eyes remained transfixed on the shadow, trying to determine who it was. *Why isn't he answering? What does he want?* Disturbed by the situation, Jason turned his head and spat on the ground beside him. Wiping his lips with his sleeve, he turned his attention back to the top of the embankment.

The shadowy figure stepped forward from behind the branches. Its features were now clear as day. The man stood about six feet tall with olive skin and dark, sunken eyes. He wore a traditional brown linen dress with a white rope tied around his waist. A white turban sat atop his head as he stood in the snow, wearing nothing but sandals on his feet.

"What the … this can't be." Jason's eyes opened wide in shock at the familiar image above him. The Taliban fighter unslung his AK-47 rifle from his shoulders and aimed it toward Jason. Awestruck, Jason had trouble comprehending what he was seeing. *Is this some kind of joke?*

BANG! A shot rang out through the forest. Snow and dirt kicked up in front of Jason's knees as the bullet penetrated the ground. Falling backward, confusion and horror overcame him. *My rifle!*

In desperation, Jason grabbed his rifle and lay prone on his belly. Using the carcass of the deer as cover, he tried to get as close to the ground as possible. *BANG!* Another shot rang out, and he felt his backpack nudge rearward as if someone had kicked it. The Taliban fighter continued to take single shots at Jason. Each deadly round came closer to hitting him. Snow and dirt kicked up around him with each shot. He felt his backpack nudge rearward again as the bullets struck it. Rounds hit the deer carcass with a dull thud. It was reminiscent of the sandbags he had filled many times in his military career.

"Fuck, fuck fuck!" Jason pulled the rifle from underneath his belly and mounted it on the deer. He fired in the direction of the fighter. As his first shot missed, bark and wood blasted away from the tree beside the Taliban. The fighter didn't even flinch. *Five round magazines, one shot on the deer, one shot at him, I only have three rounds left ...*

CRACK! The sound of the bullet whipping past his ear was deafening. The fighter stood at the top of the embankment with his rifle still on his shoulder. Jason aimed his rifle at the chest of the shadowy fighter and pulled the trigger. *Hit.* With no reaction to the shot, the fighter lowered his rifle and stood still. *Did I miss him?* Jason again fired directly at the fighter's chest. No reaction came from it. The man stood still, holding his rifle in his right hand, arms by his side. *What the hell is going on?*

Confused, Jason's fighting instinct turned into flight, unable to grasp what was occurring. *Go!* Jason pushed himself out of the snow, causing a cloud of white powder to fly up from the ground. Desperately he turned to run back up the embankment that he came down from earlier. *Bang! Bang!* Shots continued to snap past him, hitting the dirt in front of him.

Goddammit! What the fuck! Jason quickly slung his rifle and ran behind a tree, attempting to climb the hill with his hands and feet. He felt his foothold slip while grasping onto protruding roots to help him climb up. *CRACK!* Another round smacked in front, just above his hands. The proximity caused Jason to lose his grip in the icy snow, forcing him to slide down.

Using his feet, he pushed up against a tree and stopped himself from falling further down the embankment. Panting heavily, Jason had a little cover from the tree he fell into. *Breathe, breathe.* Jason tried to regain his composure by taking a deep breath through his nose, pushing back against the panic he felt rising within.

Peeking around the tree, he saw the fighter still standing in the same spot across the river. "What the fuck do you want!?" Jason screamed, his voice echoing throughout the forest. The Taliban fighter did not answer but stood in silence, motionless. The two stared at each other, with Jason feeling dazed, trying to piece together what was transpiring. Without warning, the fighter began to make his first movements. He thrust forward down the hill making enormous strides to reach the bottom.

"Shit." Jason turned on his belly and began to crawl up the embankment in haste yet again. "Come on, come on!" He urged himself forward to the top, grasping a branch to help propel himself to the top. Looking back, he saw the fighter already on his side of the river, standing at the bottom of the hill. The fighter's ominous yellow eyes stared up at Jason with a look of revulsion. *How'd he get there so fast?* Now at the top of the hill, Jason turned and started to run as quickly as possible through the forest. Looking back occasionally, he could see the fog of his breath with every rapid exhale. He pushed branches out of his way, and his feet rapidly crunched through the snow. He ran faster and faster, beginning to feel confident he could escape the stalking fighter the farther he got.

He zigged and zagged and jumped over fallen trees. He felt like a gazelle sprinting through the wilderness. Nothing could catch him at this pace. *Get back to the cabin, get back to the cabin!* Winding his way through the trees, he sensed a strong breeze blowing. The noise turned the forest into an orchestra of nature with a strange thumping sound. He could hear drums beating but was uncertain if it was his heart or something else.

Without warning, the Taliban fighter stepped out from behind a tree in front of him and swung his AK-47 rifle, smashing the butt against Jason's face. He collapsed into the snow.

His world turned dark.

Chapter 6

*There is no such thing as closure for soldiers who have survived a war.
They have an obligation, a sacred duty, to remember those who fell in
battle beside them all their days and to bear witness to the insanity that is
war.*
—*LTG Harold "Hal" Moore Jr.*

Ramstein Air Base, Germany
Fall 2010

The sound of electronic beeping pulsed throughout the room. The
rhythmic throbbing of the noise was the first thing Jason noticed. Opening
his eyes, he saw the white eggshell ceiling above him. A window was
positioned to the right, and Jason could feel the sunshine begin to peek in
through the glass. Staring down at his body, he saw that he was lying in a
bed, covered in blue linen sheets. Wires were affixed to his body, and a hose
pumped oxygen into his nostrils. *I'm in a hospital.* The heart rate monitor
continued to broadcast its findings with every beat of Jason's heart.

Jason's heart began to pump faster and faster, causing an increase in
the tempo at which the machine chirped out its findings. Confusion and
terror began to boil up within him. Feeling numb and dazed did not prevent
him from mustering up his strength to try and escape his bed.

"Nggh." Jason's body felt like it was made of lead. His body weighed
so heavily that removing the covers off himself took a tremendous amount
of effort. With the covers removed, he now examined his naked body.
Bandages, scabs, and stitches ran up and down his chest, abdomen, and legs.
With his body covered in wounds and wires, it became clear that something
terrible had happened.

A flash of sunlight shone through the window and reflected off the medical equipment in the corner of the room, striking Jason's eyes with a piercing ambiance. The effect of the light and heat immediately jogged his memory on why exactly he lay in this bed.

* * *

"CONTACT!" The panicked yells and sounds of gunfire awakened Jason into the world he had been in. The white Toyota Corolla sped down the road toward him and his teammates. Jason was firing into the engine block rapidly, hoping to stop it, but it came too quickly. Like some monstrous demon barreling toward him within a dream, everything happened so fast, yet felt like slow motion.

He didn't remember hearing much of a sound, just a low, dull rumble that perforated his eardrums. He recalled his body beginning to feel as if it were being stretched molecule by molecule in all different directions. An intense heat encompassed his body, but he felt no pain.

Jason's head began to pound. Gradually, a furious ache rose and bounced around his skull, creating circles of discomfort that flowed above his left eye. He felt as if someone had struck him across the head with a baseball bat. His torso felt damp, and his shins ached in fierce pain. A tan haze hovered over him as Jason lay helpless in the sand.

Coughing the foreign dust out of his lungs, he rolled over and saw blood from his face dripping into the sand like a leaky faucet. Blood flowed out his nose and down his dust-caked skin. His uniform was torn and twisted, with blood pouring down his chest and stomach. The realization of what had occurred came at him like a bullet train.

Frantically, he began to feel the ground for his rifle. "Where is it? Where is it?" His voice was muffled and indiscernible. As if it was programmed into his brain, finding his weapon was all he could concern himself with. Gradually he began to tire, the pain in his head began to subside, and his eyes weighed heavy. His muscles became weaker and soon gave out. He fell face-first into the dust. *Get up, get up* … His world went dark.

* * *

"My rifle!" Jason frantically began feeling the side of his hospital bed, and behind his pillow, for the object he was now obsessed with. He rolled over and yanked on the wires that attached him to the medical equipment, popping them out of the machinery and causing a blaring audible alarm. The medical equipment could no longer sense signs of life.

The smack echoed through the room as he fell off the bed and onto the tile floor. Aching and numb at the same time, Jason was in a state of distress as he crawled along the floor, searching for his rifle. Arms suddenly grabbed him out of his manic state from above. Accompanied by soothing vocal mumbles, he was lifted off the floor as the nurses tried to snap him back into reality. Slowly, Jason began to learn he was in a hospital room.

"Calm down, Jason, it's OK! You're safe! You're safe!" The nurse pleaded with Jason as he struggled to avoid being placed back on the bed.

"Brad! Sergeant! Rodriguez! Diaz!" Jason could not control his actions. Despair and anguish overtook his emotions. *This has to be a dream. This can't be real.* Jason attempted to push the nurse out of his way but found he didn't have the strength to do it.

"Stand down, Jason! You're OK! You're safe. You're safe …" A soft hand caressed his scabbed face, forcing Jason to look at the person speaking to him. Her eyes were a pale brown with a sense of care and kindness behind them. He stared deep into the stranger's eyes, searching for answers.

Jason's heart slowed down, and he felt a tingling in his chest. The adrenaline coursing through his veins was dissipating and beginning to dump the effects it was having on his body.

"Where are they?" Jason asked in a weakened voice. "Where are they? Are they OK? Please!"

"Jason, please. You need to get some rest." The nurse continued to caress his face, but Jason needed answers.

"Where are they!?" He grabbed the collar of her scrubs as firmly as he could, demanding an answer.

"Jason, you need to get rest. Please lay down and relax. We don't want you to injure yourself more." Her voice was soft and commanded attention as she slowly lowered his hands to his side.

Jason's tunnel vision on the nurse's face began to subside, allowing him to notice that additional people were also in the room. Two more nurses and a man in military fatigues stood behind the nurse speaking with him. The man in military fatigues stepped forward and placed his hand on Jason's shoulders.

"They didn't make it, Jason. I'm sorry. They didn't make it. It's a miracle that you're even alive."

Jason felt his world crumble. The faces of Brad, Sergeant Bass, and the rest of his section flashed across his mind. The hard reality that they were no longer on this earth hit him like a horrific punch in the chest.

"Please lay down, Corporal. You need to rest and recover." The man in fatigues began to assist Jason back onto his bed.

Jason felt his eyes swell up and his trachea tighten. As if imprisoned within his own body, he now understood that nothing would alter the reality he now lived in. The loss of his friends and companions was absolute. He would never again be able to speak with them. Never again be able to joke with them. Never again be able to fight alongside them.

Jason had survived the explosion with severe but nonfatal injuries. The four other soldiers of his section died on the road that day. Corporal Redman, Private Diaz, Sergeant Bass, and Private Rodriguez had all sacrificed their lives doing their duty. Jason was left to live the rest of his days with enduring physical and mental scars. Reminders of the loss of his friends would remain written over his body.

He closed his eyes as tears seeped out. Slowly he fell back asleep as the drugs the nurses had administered kicked in. Wishing he would wake up and find out this was all a bad dream, he fell asleep.

Chapter 7

I feel no emotional connection to these outwardly human gestures. I am not there because I never left Afghanistan.
—Jake Wood

Plattsmouth, Nebraska
Fall 2011

Plattsmouth, Nebraska, was a small town south of Omaha situated east of the Missouri River. Like a time capsule, the downtown part of the city seemed frozen since the 1900s. It was a prosperous town that represented its history through the clean vintage architecture seen throughout downtown. Its detailed history saw the storied Lewis and Clark travel through this place on their journey westward. The city seal had a befitting motto for all who resided there: "Honor the Past, Plan for the Future."

Plattsmouth was the town Jason grew up in, remaining in this one town throughout his childhood. In this close-knit community, Jason knew everyone's name, reputation, where they lived, and their histories. But as Jason grew, the town became too small for him, and at twenty-five years old he decided to venture out for something bigger. Tired of stacking boxes in one of the town's general stores, he yearned for adventure. Jason gave great thought to the prospect of joining the military.

He was an avid outdoorsman, thanks to his father. They would go hunting every other weekend in the backwoods of Nebraska, traveling to different locations and searching for wild game to fill their freezer. The cookout they would have after the hunt would be a core memory for Jason, as the smell of cooking meat over the barbecue always brought him back to those good times with his father.

Jason was an only child. He also never knew his mother, as she passed away when he was only a baby. Cancer stole her from him. His father was his sole caregiver. Raising and caring for him, he did his best to teach Jason how to be a man and survive in the world. It was not easy for his father. The loss of his wife and the stress and burden it brought him weighed heavy. With angry outbursts, at times, he turned to the bottle in his middle age.

He wouldn't be a rotten drunk or violent; instead, he would become quiet. His father would often stare out to the street, sitting by a window with a glass of Glenfiddich scotch, always seeming deep in thought. Jason wondered what was going on in his head, suspecting he was thinking of memories from his past or merely enjoying the view outside. When you went through such a significant loss, trying to escape the pain in whatever way you could was inevitable.

His father was proud of Jason when he enrolled in the army. Skilled with the rifle and the outdoors, he knew Jason would excel in his new career. He also knew he would be losing his son to the distance it would put between them. Jason remembered the tears welling up in his father's eyes at the airport. They said their goodbyes and good lucks as Jason left for basic training to start a new chapter in his life.

"I'm proud of you, son. Your mother would be proud of you too. Always remember that. If things get tough or you feel lonely, always remember that you're never alone. You have people who love you no matter where they are, be it in this life or the next."

Jason excelled immediately in his training. Falling in love with his tradecraft, he escaped into the life of an infantry soldier. He achieved the top candidate award in most of his courses, and his professionalism and demeanor in stressful situations made him somebody his fellow soldiers looked up to. Jason traveled across different states and countries for training and deployments. Although it was tough, demanding, and stressful, he loved the career he had chosen.

It wasn't until the day he got promoted to corporal that news from back home dealt a crushing blow. His father was in the hospital. Having not been seen for a few days, he was found in his home by one of his concerned neighbors. It appeared that he had collapsed and remained on the floor alone for days without anybody to help him. The doctors diagnosed him with liver failure brought on by years of alcohol abuse.

By the time word reached Jason, his father had already passed away at the hospital. The sorrow and despair that he felt from this unexpected loss were all-encompassing. The guilt of leaving his father alone, his only living kin, was something he didn't consider before he left. Jason was too concerned with his adventures and dreams of leaving his quiet town. Once he left, he was too worried about his career to think about how being unattended would affect his dad. Jason blamed himself for his father's death. He felt alone. He also believed he deserved to feel alone, as loneliness was what his father had felt on the floor.

Jason became quieter over the years. Less joking around and less partying with his fellow soldiers. There were fewer feelings of joy or happiness as numbness was all he was beginning to feel. What did bring him happiness and escape, however, was hunting. He would head out to the same hunting spots he and his father used to stalk. He often found himself speaking to his father while walking through the woods. Updating his dad on his life, he would talk about how it was going. His successes and failures, his new relationships and old ones, how he was feeling, and his worries about the future. He would also say a few words to the mother he never knew.

"I'm scared, Dad. I'm deploying next week, and all signs point to this being a tough tour. I'm scared, not for my own life. But that I'll let my teammates down. I'm scared that I'll make a mistake." Jason often put others' well-being ahead of his own.

"I hope I have the strength and wisdom to make the right decisions. I wish you were here with me. I miss you, Dad."

* * *

The news of his platoon's deployment to Kandahar, Afghanistan, brought excitement. Within the company line, Jason and his comrades were nervous and itching to jump into things when they first heard of their tasking.

"It's going to be a hell of a year, Jason. When we get back, we'll head back to Plattsmouth to DC's Waterhole Bar on Main Street and have a whole bunch of beer to celebrate," Brad Redman asserted.

Brad was also from Plattsmouth and always spoke about the town. He never failed to fill the air with nostalgia when he brought up memories of the old town where he and Jason grew up. Although they knew each other growing up, they were not friends until they happened to join the army at the same time.

"Good idea, Brad. I promise I'll buy the first round," Jason retorted, slapping his good friend on the back.

"First three!" Brad pushed him backward with a playful shove.

"OK, first three rounds. But then you get the next six!"

"Ha-ha, deal!"

Years later, after his tour of duty, the memory of that promise stuck with Jason as he sat on the embankment of the Missouri River that ran parallel to the highway. Taking a break from his walk, he sat admiring the slow-moving water of the river. Jason decided he would go to the Water Hole Bar that day and opted for walking there instead of driving. He found long walks suitable exercise for the injuries he sustained on his legs caused by the shrapnel that had torn through his limbs. He lost some muscle mass due to the blast, but all things considered, he was in good shape and recovering well.

It had only been a year since Jason left the military hospital and came home from deployment. And now, the first anniversary of the explosion that took Jason's friends was here. Jason could think of no better way to spend it than at the bar he promised Brad he would go to when they got home.

"Alright, Brad. Let's grab that beer." Jason spoke to himself as he stared at the sunlight reflecting off the river.

Rising out of his grass seat, he slung his pack over his shoulder. Rubbing the left side of his numbed face, he tried to pull himself out of the memories that seemed to have swallowed him up while staring at the water. Parts of his face still felt numb due to nerve damage. Flying pieces of rock and metal from the blast had scarred his face above his left eye and made pockmarks on his cheek. Rubbing the left side of his face seemed to be a force of habit now.

Cars flew down the highway as Jason walked along the guardrail. The sound of his feet crunching in the gravel brought him back to all the ruck marches he would go on with his platoon. *Even on a simple walk, I'm reminded of the past.*

A few hours passed, and Jason was nearing the bar on Main Street. Reaching the bar as the sun set was perfect timing to grab the beers he'd promised Brad he would drink. His dark shirt, covered in sweat from the walk, was hidden only by the black softshell jacket Jason had recently put on.

Wearing boots and dark blue jeans, he removed his hat and slicked back his long dark hair as he read the sign above him. *DC's Waterhole Bar.*

A multitude of voices filled the room with laughing, arguing, and loud conversations echoing throughout the bar. The constant clanging of glasses and cutlery rang everywhere. Jason made a beeline to an empty chair at the bar. The bar top was square-shaped so that all patrons sitting at it could observe each other from across the way. Only the bartender stood in the middle at their station, filling drinks and taking orders.

"What can I get you, hon?" The cute brunette barmaid asked while placing a drink coaster in front of him.

"I'll have two bottles of Bud, please." Jason removed his hat and rubbed his face.

"OK, are you expecting somebody?" She smiled at Jason, leaning forward, and exposing her cleavage. *Oh, Brad, would you like to be here now …*

"Yeah, something like that."

Receiving the drinks, Jason placed one to the side. *Here you go, Brad. This one is for you.* He would leave that drink in its place untouched, honoring his friend who was not able to be there that day. A consistent reminder of his loss and the things that would never be.

Drink after drink, Jason chugged back beer until he felt numbness in more than just his face. He spent most of his time staring at the bar top or the television. The television played some sports highlights, but Jason no longer felt interested in such things. Once a rabid sports fan, the adrenaline and excitement it brought had lost its luster since he returned from the war. Now it all seemed so pointless. The adrenaline of war had toned down everything in life.

BANG.

The table shook, and glasses rattled across the bar top. Startled, Jason flinched in a way that made his arm knock over the warm beer Jason had bought in memory of Brad. Raising his head, his heart was pounding a million miles an hour. With wide eyes, he scanned the entirety of the bar, trying to find the threat that had caused this explosion.

Across the bar, he spotted a group of men laughing boisterously. The "explosion" was the act of one of the individuals slamming his hand on the table. In a fit of laughter, he continued to show his approval of whatever joke he had just heard.

BANG. BANG. BANG. "That's fucking hilarious!" the man screamed, again slapping the bar in rapid succession. Nobody else seemed bothered by it, not even lifting an eye toward the noise. Jason, however, could not take his eyes off the four men across from him.

A feeling of red washed over him. He understood that what had occurred was a regular event at bars. However, his body was acting in a way his mind could not control. Taking deep breaths and grabbing his beer, he chugged back the rest of the drink. *I need to leave.*

"Oh, hon, don't worry about the mess. I'll take care of it. Was that beer for a friend?" the barmaid inquired. "It seems like he's not coming anyways. It's been a while."

"Yeah … he's not coming," Jason slurred. *Of course, he's not. He's dead. They're all dead because of me. Because I couldn't save them.* He watched as the barmaid cleaned up the remnants of the beer he had bought in honor of his friend.

Hours had passed since he entered DC's Waterhole and Jason was already ten beers deep. Standing up from his stool, he braced himself against the edge of the table as he tried to maintain his footing. Not realizing how much of an effect the beer had had on him until he stood up, Jason rubbed the side of his face.

"Sorry about the mess." Jason shamefully placed his hat back on.

"Oh, don't worry, hon, this is a bar. These things happen." She gave him a caring smile as she rubbed a cloth along the table.

"Hey, be careful! This lady works hard enough. She shouldn't have to clean up your spilled milk!" One of the men with a white hat shouted from across the bar. Jason watched the man as he turned to laugh once more with his friends.

The four of them seemed like close friends. They were all dressed similarly in polo shirts with gelled hair. Most likely the same age as Jason, it was evident they were from different lifestyles. *Frat boys stuck in their ways.* They most certainly had different life experiences when compared to the injured vet. Clean-shaven and athletic, they had an arrogant aura about them. Jason guessed they had probably never experienced what a hard time was. *The most challenging time these assholes have experienced was not getting access to their dad's sports car.*

Just go home, Jason. It's not good here.

Jason placed a handful of cash on the table to pay for the tab, leaving a large tip for the barmaid. He held little value for money anymore. Jason recently cared less about it, and more than likely had just paid double what he owed. Throwing his backpack over his shoulder, he headed toward the front door. The door, however, was across the bar behind the four belligerents.

Approaching the group, Jason walked with his head down. They stood in a crowd blocking the path to the exit and paid no heed to Jason as he tried to get past them. Annoyed, Jason made it past by bumping into the back of one of them, who was wearing a dark green polo shirt. The bump caused the man to spill some of his beer onto his friend's white polo shirt.

"Hey, watch where you're going, dickhead," the man in the green shirt shouted.

Jason stopped in his tracks. A feeling of rage boiled up inside him. The only thing preventing it from erupting was standing still and trying to ignore it. Shaking off the comment, Jason once again made for the exit.

"Get the fuck out of here, bitch. Go drink alone at home." The man in the green shirt laughed along with his friends.

Jason stood still, eyes fixed on the exit. He felt a beast rising up within him.

"What's up, pussy? Did that upset you?" The men continued laughing.

Red rage enveloped Jason's body. A surge of hate and aggression rose up from deep within his gut, desiring to break free from his body. The emotion was too much. It became unmanageable and consumed Jason's actions.

He dropped his backpack and swung at the man in the green shirt. Connecting with a tremendous right hook, he dropped the patron to the floor. Immediately, Jason turned his attention to the man in the white shirt. Hitting him with a left hook, the force caused the man to stumble backward. Noises roared throughout the room as glasses dropped to the floor by his feet and stools tipped over. Chaos filled the bar.

Grabbing the man with the baseball cap, he cocked back his fist to deliver another blow but was stopped before he could connect. Jason felt an impact to the side of his head, knocking him off balance. Stumbling, Jason fell against the bar. The two still-standing jocks began throwing punches against his face and ribs, overwhelming his awareness of the situation. Realizing he was losing the standing fight, Jason tackled one man to the bar floor and mounted him. While on the ground, kicks soon rained down upon Jason's head and ribs, causing him to abandon his prey on the floor before him.

Struggling to stand up against the blows, he jumped toward one of the men. Catching him in a bear hug, they fell into the bar top. Jason threw a headbutt causing the man's nose to erupt into an explosion of blood.

"Fuck!" The man dropped to his knees in front of Jason. Holding his nose, he raised his other hand in the air as if to yield to Jason's attack. Shifting his attention, Jason saw the first individual he had knocked to the ground was now back up and attempting to tackle him. Sprawling with his legs, Jason blocked the takedown and snuffed out the attack. Forcing him to the ground on his belly, he now had him in a chokehold. Seeing red, Jason had an out-of-body experience. He felt like his soul was floating above and saw himself acting and moving with no conscious control of his actions. His rational voice was trying to speak with him. *Enough, calm down. Just leave.* But his body paid no heed, entirely in control of this fight-or-flight situation.

Losing consciousness, the man went limp underneath Jason. With the signal that his prey was now neutralized, he could focus his attention elsewhere. Suddenly people from all around were grabbing onto Jason and his adversaries. Attempting to break up the fight, bystanders jumped in, separating the men from each other.

"Calm down, son! Enough with this!" one older man yelled in Jason's ear as he restrained him.

"What the fuck is your problem, you psycho?" The jock in the white hat cried, holding his broken nose as strangers helped him stand.

"OK, OK, I'm good. I'm leaving. I'm leaving," Jason slurred, holding his hands in the air in a surrendering fashion.

The older man slowly let go of his grasp as silence fell across the room. Jason felt like a million eyes were on him, analyzing him, judging him. A mixture of liquor and blood covered his arms. Jason slicked his hair back and picked up his hat that had fallen onto the floor during the struggle. With silence still flooding the air, he placed the cap back onto his head backward and heaved a large sigh.

"OK … I'm going."

Throwing caution to the wind, Jason threw another unexpected punch out of nowhere, hitting the man with the broken nose and knocking him to the ground yet again. Chaos returned to the barroom as Jason reignited the fight. Turning his attention toward the other jocks, he began blindly throwing punches. Some connected, some missed, and some accidentally hit people trying to step in. The silence that once filled the bar was now an echo chamber of yelling and cursing.

A look of rage painted Jason's face as he endeavored to unleash violence on anyone who opposed him. Before he could do more harm, Jason was abruptly stopped and tackled to the ground from behind in the middle of his rampage. The force caused the wind to get knocked out of him. Somebody large had entered the fight and was clearly bigger than him by the weight of his body on Jason's back. Jason felt his arms being forced behind his back by two people. Continuing to struggle in this life-and-death fight, Jason resisted with all his might. It wasn't until the man on his back shouted down at him that he stopped fighting.

"Stop resisting! You're under arrest!"

Chapter 8

Every Criminal has a Good Mind Conquered by the Devil.
—Munia Khan

Plattsmouth, Nebraska
Fall 2011

Jason awoke with a pounding headache. His orbital bones throbbed with heat, courtesy of the beating he took at DC's Waterhole. Confused, he wondered why his bed felt so uncomfortable. *Where the hell am I?*

He painstakingly forced himself to sit up, his muscles crying out in pain with each movement he made. "Ugh, man …" Jason groaned as he swung his legs over to sit at the side of his strange bed.

The cell was a small and claustrophobic enclosure, illuminated with a faint glow by the artificial lights above. There were no wall decorations or fancy flooring. Everything was encased in cement with a door made of iron bars. *Oh … shit.*

The vague recollection of the night before came flooding back to him as he realized he had spent the night in jail. Jason slicked his greasy hair back and hung his head in shame. Dark, crusted bloodstains decorated his shirt. "Fuck me." He sighed laboriously and leaned backward, resting his head against the wall in despair.

"You're awake." An authoritative voice came from the cell door. "How are you feeling?" A male officer stood at the entrance to the cell, leaning his arms against the bars. Jason eyed the uniformed man but refused to acknowledge him, turning his head in avoidance.

"You caused quite the scene last night, Jason. The owner of the bar isn't too happy with you. Neither are the men you beat up." Jason continued to gaze directly to his front at the barren cement wall.

"Listen, man. We ran you through our system, and I understand that you have previous service in the military with a tour of Kandahar, Afghanistan. Is that right?" Jason's swollen face throbbed as his heart beat faster in frustration. Numbness overtook the left side of his face.

"I can't begin to understand what you may have experienced over there, Jason. And I'm sure you're dealing with some things that most of us couldn't begin to imagine. But you're not over there anymore. You're back home." The officer tried to make eye contact with Jason by lowering his head between the bars but was ignored. He continued his sermon anyway.

"I'm going to give you a card with the contact information of a doctor you can call. It's connected with the VA, and they can help you get on your feet and sort yourself out. I don't want to see you throw your life away, son, because I've seen this sort of thing happen before." Jason closed his eyes, endeavoring to suppress the whirlwind of negative emotions inside him. *I'm stuck in this cell, my head is pounding, and now I have to listen to this guy preach with no way to ignore it. For fuck's sake ... It never ends.*

"Now, you can ignore me all you want, but I know you can hear me. So please, give it a chance. Contact this doctor. I don't want to see you back here."

Jason opened his eyes and heard a metallic clicking noise followed by a large piece of metal rolling against the floor. The officer was now standing at the open door of the cell with a key in his hand.

"You're free to go." The uniformed man moved to the side of the cell door, allowing Jason a clear path to leave his concrete prison.

"I am?" Jason uttered his first words in disbelief.

"Yes. Neither the men you assaulted nor the bar owner have decided to press charges. You're free to go." The officer motioned with his hand, directing Jason to leave.

Painstakingly Jason stood, his muscles aching and stiff, making it hard to move fluidly. He cracked his neck, moving it side to side, and rubbed the left side of his face as he exited the cell.

"Here." The officer held out a white business card with the name and number of the doctor he'd spoken of. "Please give this person a call. There's no shame in a veteran asking for help."

Jason hesitantly grabbed the business card and analyzed it. "Thanks." He mumbled a halfhearted response.

"You're good to go now. Head to the front desk, and they'll hand you your wallet and phone." Jason made his way to the lobby and collected his belongings before exiting the main doors of the police station. The bright morning sun stung his eyes, causing him to squint as he walked through the cobblestone entranceway.

I'm glad that's over with. Jason reached into his pocket and retrieved the card the officer handed him. *Yeah, right.* Making his way back into society, Jason tore the card in half and tossed it into a nearby garbage can. *You can keep it.*

Chapter 9

Human beings, we have dark sides; we have dark issues in our lives. To progress anywhere in life, you have to face your demons.
—John Noble

Backwoods, Alaska
Present Day

Jason's eyes struggled to open. His head was ringing, and pain echoed throughout his skull. His face, numb and aching, hurt with every twitch of his muscles. Widening his eyes, he attempted to focus on what was hovering above him. He could feel the cold snow on his back and down the neck of his shirt.

A barrel? It hovered, pointing down toward Jason's face, only a few inches above him. The rifle holder had his cheek resting against the butt of the gun. A look of rage pierced over the iron sights and stared down at Jason. The Taliban fighter twisted his mouth showing his crooked yellow teeth.

"Zamaa badi shi ta!" the fighter screamed down at him. *I hate you.*

"Za niat akhes-tal zama badala!" *I will take my revenge.*

Jason couldn't understand the hostile words the hate-filled fighter was screaming. The look on the fighter's face was a mural of anguish and rage. His eyes were so wide they seemed like they were about to pop out of his head. Whatever he was saying, Jason understood the hatred behind it.

Click.

The Taliban pulled the trigger, but no bullet fired. Stunned, he looked down at the chamber on the side of his weapon to inspect what went wrong. Jason took his chance and grabbed the barrel of the gun. Quickly he pulled it to the side and away from his face, proceeding to kick as hard as he could upward toward the fighter's groin. The force of the kick caused the Taliban to bend over and loosen his grasp on the weapon.

With one hand holding the weapon away from him, he made it back to his feet. Jason's fight-or-flight response was in high gear. He was in a battle for his life as he wrestled over the enemy's rifle. *What the fuck is going on?! Who is this!?* Jason shoved his shoulder into the fighter's chest in an attempt to make him loosen his grasp. Unsuccessful in removing the weapon, he hit him with a headbutt. A flash of a vision emerged in Jason's mind, and suddenly he was remembering the fight at DC's Waterhole Bar.

The fighter's head snapped back on the impact. Lowering his head, he now came face-to-face with Jason. Blood poured down his nose as he grinned wickedly and spat a mixture of blood and saliva at Jason. Enraged, Jason released a feral scream and propelled himself to take him down. With as much strength as he could muster, he weaved under the weapon and picked the Taliban up by the waist. Jason ran forward and screamed, holding the man off the ground. The momentum was stopped as he slammed the fighter back into a tree, causing them both to stumble to the earth.

Jason and the Taliban began rolling around in the snow to get the best position. The weapon had now fallen from both of their hands. Looks of madness overcame both of their faces. Hatred and bloodlust filled the air. Rolling through the snow, the fighter maneuvered his way over Jason. He straddled his legs over either side of him, getting the best position. Before Jason knew it, he was being strangled.

The fighter sat on top of Jason, choking him with both hands. He could see nothing but the bloodied face and rotten yellow teeth above him. *I can't breathe.* Struggling with all his might, Jason attempted to undo the lethal grasp, but he wasn't strong enough. The cold and the pain had weakened him. Punch after punch Jason threw up at the fighter, each weaker than the last.

Memories of Afghanistan flashed within his mind. This same fighter had tried to strangle him over there. The same face, teeth, and look of pure, unfiltered madness above him. Except there was nobody around to save him. He was miles away from the nearest town in the backwoods of Alaska. His teammates were dead. This was it.

I'm going to die. Unable to breathe, panic and desperation kicked in. *How is this happening?* Jason glimpsed the same black scorpion tattoo on the fighter's forearm. Sliding his hand along the snow in distress, Jason felt something hard. Using all his strength, he grabbed the object and swung his right arm wide. The Taliban's face made a hollow cracking sound as he was smashed across the side of the head with a rock. The fighter collapsed into the snow face-first.

Coughing and wheezing, Jason struggled to make it on his hands and knees. He crawled to the nearest tree, scraping his knees along the ground. Jason could see the blood from his face dripping down onto the snow, creating a bright red track on the pure white canvas. Red-faced and sweaty, he slumped against the tree to catch his breath. Nothing but the sound of wind blowing through the trees remained. Attempting to gain his composure, he took deep breaths while staring at the motionless body. During the struggle, Jason's hat had fallen. His black hair fell across his face, acting like crooked strands of black prison bars. It flowed back and forth with his frantic breathing.

How did this guy find me? How is he alive? What is happening? Jason had so many questions. A routine hunting trip had so far turned into a nightmare. *I should have never left the cabin.* Rubbing the side of his face, Jason used the tree as a crutch to make it to his feet.

"Wake the fuck up!" he began to shout at the motionless body in front of him. "Who are you?" Jason's eyes were wide with anticipation and uncertainty.

He stared at the body, expecting movement, but none came. He spotted his backpack and rifle a few yards past the fighter, having fallen from the blow that knocked him to the ground.

"I said, who are you, motherfucker!" Jason hollered as he propped himself up against the tree.

Being on his feet and seeing his enemy face down on the ground gave him newfound confidence and energy. He walked with determination toward the unconscious body. "Come here, you piece of shit!" Jason grabbed the Taliban by the arm and rolled him onto his back so he could see his face. *What the …*

Astonished by what he was looking at, Jason stepped backward, nearly falling in the process. The face that once hung above him, complete with tan skin and crooked yellow teeth, was no longer there. In its place was something more familiar, more recognizable. It was like looking into a mirror. The turban-wearing man had white skin and facial features like his own.

The fighter opened his eyes, revealing a bright blue like his own. He smiled at Jason, a smile with clean white teeth, not the crooked yellow ones he remembered. The unusual-looking Taliban fighter made it to his feet until he stood face-to-face with Jason. They stared at each other in silence with a few feet of distance between them.

This can't be …

The fighter reached up to his head and slowly unraveled his turban. With the headdress off, it revealed long black hair that fell across his face. It was as if Jason was staring in a mirror, seeing himself standing right there. Untying the rope around his waist, he removed his traditional Afghan clothing. Piece by piece, he threw it to the ground, revealing underneath the same clothes that Jason was wearing. It was as if Jason was staring at himself. Everything was the exact same. The only difference was that the fighter was barefoot. That was, if this man was still that same fighter.

"Hello, Jason." The fighter smiled at him.

"What is this? Who are you?" He was scared, hurt, and confused. The situation was too much for him to comprehend.

"Don't be stupid. You know exactly who I am." The man's face twisted with disdain.

"I don't get it. What's happening?"

"You fucked up, Jason. You fucked up everything." The man began walking to the left of Jason, stalking in the way he moved.

"You thought you could escape by running out into the wilderness? To be alone? To find peace? Is this what you call peace? You stupid bastard." The man berated Jason as he walked.

"Who the fuck are you!?" Jason's emotions were pulling him in all different directions. He was having a hard time understanding the situation.

"I'm you, Jason. I'm everything you hate and everything you love. I'm your successes and your failures. Your dreams and your nightmares."

"I don't understand …" Jason clenched his fists, still anticipating an attack. Jason began walking in the other direction. Like the start of a gladiatorial battle, the two slowly walked in a circle. Never taking their eyes off each other.

"Of course you don't understand. You never do. Listen, Jason, if it makes it easier for you, you can just call me Jack. Like Jack Daniels! Kind of like the bottle you're so fond of hitting." The man stood still, sizing Jason up.

"What is it you want from me?"

"Want from you?!" the man retorted, flabbergasted at Jason's question. "There is nothing you can give me that I don't already have. I've been with you your entire life, Jason. I've seen the things you have done, the people you let down, the failures that could have been prevented." The man's face scowled in irritation.

"I am you, Jason. I am you, and I'm sick of it. Why did you come all the way out here? What are you aiming to accomplish? Running away from your problems? How can you escape your problems when you ARE the problem?" The wind picked up speed throughout the forest, bringing a bitter cold that surrounded the two men.

"You're just delaying the inevitable, Jason. You should have ended your life when you had the chance. You don't deserve to keep living your life while all the others around you are lying six feet deep." The shadowy man who named himself Jack glared at Jason with fury.

The two men stood in the snow, staring at each other. A profound stillness encircled the woods, the atmosphere frigid and ominous. "I don't know what this is all about or what type of tricks you're pulling. But I'm done with this game. What do you want? How is this possible?"

"You've got a lot of questions. There is something you could do for me, though." Jack answered.

"And what's that?"

"Die."

Jason eyed his hunting rifle that lay alongside his backpack in the snow a couple of feet away. Hesitation struck him. He was unsure if it would be of any use. He had shot this man when he was a Taliban, with no effect. This man appeared out of nowhere in front of him during his escape, like a ghost. *That was impossible.* And he saw this man turn from that Taliban fighter into … *Me? How practical can that rifle be?* From what he remembered, he only had one round left in the chamber.

"I want you to die. You should have died a long time ago. There is no point in you being alive anymore. You're useless and pathetic. You let your friends DIE! You let your dad DIE! You killed that little girl's mother! Do you really think you deserve to live? Kill yourself, Jason."

"I didn't know they were in that room!" The past came back to Jason like a sledgehammer.

"Didn't know? Or didn't care?"

"NO! I thought the enemy was in there! If I knew, I would never have thrown that grenade!" Jason was now sucked into his memories and the conversation, trying to justify his actions from many years ago.

"But you did, and now a little girl is growing up somewhere without a mother. Just like you did."

"Bullshit! Don't you think I regret that day? I do! I didn't mean for it to happen! I can't turn back time and undo it! If I could, I would have done that already!" Jason felt a deep sense of anguish build up within him. He hadn't felt that specific feeling in a long time, having pushed those sensations down as often as he could.

"That's just one of your failures, Jason. Or should I call you *Orion*? What about your section? Too busy walking with your head in the sand to notice a vehicle speeding toward your patrol?" The man spat a wad of saliva into the ground before him.

"You let them all die. You prided yourself on your skills, yet you failed when it came time to use them." They continued to walk in a circle, keeping their distance from each other.

"Behold! The mighty Orion! The great hunter! The apex predator! He can shoot the wings off a fly at one hundred yards! Nobody is more professional! More dedicated! More trusted to conduct his duties than he!"

"Fuck you!" Jason felt his left eye twitching, and his face began to twist.

"No, fuck you, Orion! You let them die! You had the skill set and the ability to stop that vehicle, but your shot was too late and not good enough! That's reason number two why you should kill yourself!"

The sky above began to darken. The overcast sky above the treetops made the forest grow dim, causing shadows to paint the snow below. Jason noticed a strange shadow cast by the man walking barefoot. The shadowy black figure walked in step with the man as it faded in and out while traversing the trees. Jack's shadow was not human but that of a scorpion.

"I tried! I wasn't at the front! I didn't notice it coming! I tried to stop it! I shot it, but it kept coming! There's nothing more I could have done!"

"Wrong." The man stood still now. Facing Jason, he shook his head. His oddly shaped shadow had now disappeared.

"There is always something you can do."

Jason felt a lump grow in his throat. These feelings growing inside him felt like cancer eating away at his chest. He was reminded why he tried so hard to suppress these thoughts and feelings. He hated how they felt; he always wanted to hide them. But now, this ghost of a man was forcing it out of him, and he couldn't seem to stop him.

"That's the second reason why you should kill yourself, Orion. You have done your brothers in arms no honor by wasting your life as you have been doing. Drinking? Isolating? Fighting? Hell, you already act like you're dead, might as well be it!"

Jason once again eyed the rifle that now lay behind him. Wanting to grab it, he paused as he did not want to take his eyes off whoever this man, this demon, was.

"And reason number three ... your dad."

Howling began to echo throughout the wilderness. Wolves in the distance called out to each other, and an owl hooted somewhere overhead. The sounds of ravens cawing surrounded the forest. Jason spotted them sitting on a tree branch above, behind the man. Their eye-piercing gazes punched right through Jason. The forest seemed to come alive in its darkened state.

"Your father died alone on the floor. Alone because you weren't there. Because you were too busy caring about what really mattered to you. Yourself."

"I didn't know he was sick! If I did, I would have gone back!" The levy broke, and tears began pouring down Jason's face. His windpipe was tight, making it harder to breathe. His heart pounded faster and faster. He felt it difficult to concentrate past these raw emotions that were taking hold of him.

"But you didn't! You didn't go back, and you left him to die! Maybe if you had called him more than once a week, you could have found out something was wrong! Your dad did everything for you! Raised you, taught you, loved you, and that's how you repaid him? With abandonment? Leaving him to spend the final hours of his life helpless on the floor?"

The image of his dad lying on the living room floor flashed within Jason's mind. He clenched his teeth in torment. He loved his dad so much that the thought of how his death occurred ate away at Jason for years. He could never overcome his guilt with everything this ghost of a man mentioned. He always tried not to think about it, but there was no escaping it now. This demon's words brought it out of him.

"Look at you, Orion. You're weak. Pathetic. You have no more fight in you. It's about time you gave up. Do the world a favor and place that rifle underneath your chin."

Jason looked at the rifle behind him and then back to meet the man's eyes. Jason felt weak and defeated. The words this man was speaking hit like a spell being cast upon him. Out in the darkening wilderness, he had isolated himself from society. Jason wondered what the whole point of carrying on was. Suppose the world would be better off without him. He was alone, depressed, angry, and tired. What kind of life was this to keep on living?

"That's it. Just do it."

Jason bent over to pick up the rifle. His body and joints felt like they were made of stone. Holding the gun with two hands, he stared down at it, contemplating his movements, inspecting the chamber of the weapon—*one round left.* He felt like his soul was hovering above himself, watching his body take these actions.

"Go on." Jack encouraged Jason to shoot himself. "Do it, Orion. It will all be over. No more pain, no more misery, no more loneliness. Things will be so much better. End your suffering, Jason."

Jason began to focus on what he had lost. He thought of his dad and all the times they spent together. He thought of his teammates and the struggles they went through side by side. He thought of his mother, whom he had never met, and wondered what she would think. A familiar voice spoke within him.

"I'm proud of you, son. Your mother would be proud of you too. Always remember that. If things begin to get tough or you feel lonely, always remember that you're never alone. You have people who love you no matter where they are, be it in this life or the next."

Jason threw the rifle down into the snow.

"You stupid motherfucker," the man said, twisting his face in disgust.

"Well, if you're not gonna do it, I guess I'll have to!" The man sprinted so fast at Jason he could hardly register the attack. Jack's shoulder drove into Jason's chest, causing him to go flying backward. Jason's body slid, stopping a few dozen yards away. Winded and hurt, he tried to stand but could only reach his knees. The man stalked toward him.

"You don't want to give up? You think you still have fight left in you? Well then, let's see it! Fight!"

The man kicked Jason in the ribs, making him tumble sideways. Jason cradled his ribcage and gasped for air as he reached his hands and knees again.

"Come on, you coward! Fight!" Jack kicked him again.

"Fight! What are you waiting for? Get up!" Another kick in the ribs. Over and over, kicks rained down onto Jason's torso.

"Get up and fight! Fight you, coward! FIGHT!"

An intense heat raged within Jason's chest. *Get up.* His soul was being pulled back from a dark abyss and back into his body. *Get up.* The blood pumping through his veins felt like gasoline. The sweat dripping from his brow was like holy water. *GET UP!* Something was changing within him. His instinct to fight rose. His will to survive and live another day grew stronger throughout his body. *Fight!* Remembering his dad's words and his love for him provided a foundation for resistance. His love for himself and all other things in his life, past and present, became an internal shield that made him feel unstoppable. *FIGHT, ORION, FIGHT!*

Jason felt a strange aura around his body. He felt as if he had an army at his back, filled with everyone who had ever loved him. It mixed into a hurricane of fury and controlled aggression. He felt like he had wings. Like he was no longer prey but a predator. Like the Orion his friends always knew him as.

Jason pounced up and drove his shoulder into the man. The man lost his balance and stumbled backward. With a primal scream, he attacked the demon with all his strength. Raging against this ghost, he fought, throwing punch after punch. The man's head snapped back repeatedly as he made a fruitless attempt to raise his hands in defense. The flurry of strikes he was receiving was too overwhelming to defend against.

With a warrior's cry, Jason tackled the man to the ground. Powdered snow flew up into the air as their bodies smashed into the earth. Their struggle continued as they rolled together in the snow. Each man was trying to get into an advantageous position. Slipping his leg over the man's waist, Jason came out on top, now mounting him from above.

Jason held the man's throat with one hand and continuously rained punches down upon him with his right fist. Over and over, he connected to the demon's face, blood bursting from his nose with each strike.

The man never once broke eye contact with Jason or blinked. His lack of reaction painted an unwavering grin on his face, like this was a game. Undeterred, he aimed to destroy this demon. Jason ignored his cold, tired body and pushed through the pain to continue his assault. The dull thud of flesh impacting flesh echoed throughout the darkening forest. Dark red blood splattered in all directions across the snow with each blow. Jason wouldn't stop until this demon was dead and gone from his world.

"That's more like it!" the man screamed as he grabbed hold of Jason's shirt. "Hello, Orion!"

With inhuman strength, the man shoved Jason off him. Jason flew backward over ten feet in the air, smacking right into a tree trunk. Falling into the snow, he tried to regain his senses.

What the hell was that? Now doubtful about what this man, this thing, was capable of, Jason needed something more than his fists. He desperately scanned the dim-lit snow for anything he could use to aid him in this fight.

My rifle. A few feet to Jason's right, he spotted his hunting rifle lying in the snow close to his backpack. *One round left, though. I need more.* Pushing himself off the cold ground, he sprinted toward his equipment, sliding to a stop at his backpack.

From a distance, the man sat up in the snow. Blood covered his face so thoroughly that he barely looked human. He turned his head and smiled at Jason, looking more like a demon from someone's nightmares.

Jason dug through the side pocket of his backpack, where he kept loose rounds of ammunition, and shoved some into his pocket. Picking up the rifle, he pointed it at the barefoot man, now standing where he once lay. A murderous grin showed through his blood-covered face.

The sun was so far below the trees now that everything was almost too dark to see; only a few shadows were visible. Jason spotted the strange shadow he had seen earlier being cast by the man. The outline of a giant scorpion was where the man's shadow was supposed to be.

Jason raised his rifle to his shoulder and fired the last remaining round into the man's face. The demon's head snapped back, and his body dropped limp into the snow. The gunshot echo reverberated throughout the forest, causing the ravens to fly away. Silence. Jason was frozen at the moment. *Is it over?* He could hear nothing but the gusts of wind that increased its speed as it swept through the trees.

The howling of wolves cut through the darkness. Ravens cried out into the night sky as they fled the chaos. Terror began to grip Jason as he scanned the forest to sense where it was coming from. The howling grew louder as it came closer and closer. Then Jason spotted two abnormally large wolves appearing out of the darkness at the head of the man's body. The same ones he'd seen at the embankment. Growling, they stood atop him as if guarding one of their own. *Load the rifle!*

Jason moved his hand toward his pocket to retrieve the extra ammunition but stopped dead in his tracks. He felt something watching him out of his peripheral vision. He could hear panting.

Two more wolves walked out of the darkness beside him. Their backs were hunched, and their razor-sharp teeth were visible like jagged knives. The other two wolves stepped over the man's body and walked toward him, growling, fixating on Jason.

It was then that one of the wolves pounced at him. With a swift movement, he swung the butt of his rifle at the animal, striking it just before it could grab his neck. The wolf fell to the ground and struggled to get up as it slipped into the snow. Before Jason could process anything else, the other wolf jumped at him. The massive bark he let out before leaping alerted Jason, and he reacted quickly. He cross-checked the wolf with his rifle, causing it to deflect away from him and into a tree.

RUN.

Jason turned his back on the four deranged creatures and sprinted into the darkness, seeing his opportunity to escape. He ran through the forest, desperately trying to outrun the animals. He could hear their panting and barking behind him. It was close.

RUN.

Jason continued to sprint through the dark forest, barely able to see what was in front of him. He occasionally stumbled but never fell. Pushing his way through branches, he ran farther and farther. The snow crunched under his feet, and his legs felt like they were going numb. He was cold, wet, and tired. The adrenaline of fear masked his body's pain, aiding him in his escape.

Soon all Jason could hear were his footsteps and his rapid breathing. No more barking. No more growling. He slowed his pace and turned around to see. There was nothing there. Thinking they either gave up or he outran them, Jason bent over. With his hand on his knees, he panted rapidly, trying to catch his breath from his frantic escape.

It was hard to see where he was. The sun was down, and he was stuck in the middle of the woods. He had lost all sense of direction. He had nothing with him except his rifle, having left his backpack behind in his desperate attempt to escape the wolves. *Fuck me.* It contained his extra ammunition, food, clothes, and a few survival items. He always carried it with him in case he became lost in the woods. *I'm lost in the woods.*

"Moor! Moor!" The voice of a child split through the darkness. Chills raced down Jason's spine.

"Moor!" The voice came from all directions, crying out from the darkness. His heart sank into the pit of his stomach. Terrified, he began to back up. He recognized the voice. How could he forget? After all, it was tattooed into his soul.

"Moor! Moor!" The little girl stepped out of the darkness and stood in front of Jason, sobbing and holding on to a stuffed bear cradled in her arms.

Please, no.

She looked cold. Her skin was a lifeless shade of white. Her pale legs stood barefoot in the snow as she cried out for her mother. Whimpering, she desperately looked around, but it was as if she couldn't see Jason.

Jason continued to back up. He was mesmerized by what he was seeing in front of him. He felt frozen in fear as if he was looking at a ghost. *God.* Unable to fully process what he was observing, the only thing he could do was back away. "Moor! Moor!"

Just then, the little Afghan girl's head snapped in Jason's direction as she made eye contact. Her face contorted into a spiteful look of hatred toward him. Her stuffed bear fell to the snow as she dropped it and clenched her fists. Frowning and squeezing her fists, she appeared to be shaking in anger.

"Argh!" Jason screamed out as a sharp pain struck him in his left leg. Limping backward, he looked to see what the cause was. A giant black Scorpion stood in the snow. Abnormal in its size, it was as large as a cat, and its pincers had just taken a chunk out of Jason's calf.

"MOOR!" The girl's voice was as loud as a jet engine. The trees shook from the force of the scream. Snow blew up into Jason's face, partially blinding him. Panicked, he limped backward as the Scorpion advanced toward him, its tail ready to strike.

The gust of wind from the girl caused blizzard-like conditions. Struggling to see through the flurry of snow, he shielded his eyes, vaguely making out the figure of a man standing behind her. He was holding something. *A rifle!*

BANG!

"God!" he cried out in desperation as a sharp pain struck him in his abdomen. He lost his balance. When he stepped backward, his foot never touched the ground. There was nothing under his feet except air. He had failed to notice the cliff behind him while backing away from the girl and the Scorpion. He fell off the edge and into the blackness. The abyss swallowed him whole.

Chapter 10

Even the devil weeps when he remembers he once had wings.
—Unknown

Plattsmouth, Nebraska
Winter 2016

Plows had cleared the highway after the latest snowstorm. Mountains of its dirty white remnants lined either side of the salt-stained streets. Cold and gray, the atmosphere could dampen anyone's mood, let alone one as fragile as Jason's.

Driving back from the supermarket, he returned home after a day of running errands. Jason was unemployed; holding down a job was another struggle he dealt with throughout the years since returning from the war. The decline in his work ethic and timeliness had a detrimental impact on keeping steady employment. He often showed up late to work, forgot his tasks, and procrastinated on all other duties assigned to him. He was recently released from the local hardware store for his poor performance.

Jason didn't have many close friends. His friends who still served in the military were often gone or lived too far to keep in touch with. He no longer spoke to any of his school or former workplace friends either. The conversations became too alien for him, and Jason hadn't been able to relate to them in some time. He felt as if he had been to Mars and back, and nobody understood him, no matter how well he described it. When Jason would attempt to talk to them about his experiences, they would become uneasy and awkward. They often tried to change it to a more easygoing, meaningless topic that he couldn't care less about. He found they did not want to know the reality beyond their suburban utopia. *They'd rather live in ignorance.* Due to this, Jason hadn't spoken to them in years.

It had been a few years since the incident at DC's Waterhole, and he had not fared any better. His run-ins with police were becoming more frequent. His criminal rap sheet was getting longer with every uncontrollable emotional flare-up. Assault and destruction of property, driving under the influence, trespassing, resisting arrest. Many charges had been laid on him, and he fell deeper into a void in society. A hole that was so deep he would soon not be able to crawl out of it. He no longer felt like the disciplined, composed soldier he once was. That Jason had remained in the desert, never to come home.

Home for Jason was now a tiny one-bedroom apartment situated outside downtown Plattsmouth. Located inside a two-story building, it was a simple residence that only had one window for the room. He didn't have much, and it was often bare; a sofa and TV were the centerpieces of his place.

A car horn blared behind him, startling Jason and making him jump and cringe in the driver's seat. Zoning out in his thoughts, he had missed the light turning green at the intersection where he was stopped.

"Hey, fuck you!" Jason shouted as he gave the finger out the back window. *Fucking dickhead.*

Jason continued to drive, checking his rearview mirror at the car behind him. He owned an old Ford pickup truck with shoddy black paint. It wasn't the best vehicle, but it got him from place to place. *Pasta for dinner, then I'll clean my rifle. I'll look into new areas to go hunting. Or just hit the bottle again, like it fucking matters. Some Jack Daniels will do the trick, good ol' Jack.*

Hunting was still a passion of his. It made him feel close to his father. He lived alone, but he never felt lonely, or at least admitted it. He increasingly preferred to detach from the nonstop hustle that society had become around him. Going to grocery stores became more difficult for him as his senses would become heightened while in crowded places. He found himself becoming suspicious of everyone around him. Jason could hear all the noises in his environment, creating a sensory overload that prevented him from focusing on why he was there in the first place. The sounds of cash registers clanging and the squeaky wheels of grocery carts spinning, along with the conversations of people around him, felt amplified to a level that he could not ignore. He often left with a headache and in a foul mood.

Is this guy following me? The car that had honked at him was tailgating Jason's truck.

"Back the fuck off, dickhead." Jason's cynical pessimism did him no favors in assessing reality. Everyone was suspect, and he always believed the worst.

The sun was shining behind him, making it difficult to accurately see who was in the car behind him. *Eat this.* Annoyed by the driver's proximity, Jason slammed on his brakes, brake-checking the driver behind. The driver swerved off to the side and hit his horn once again. "I told you to back the fuck off!" Jason screamed, barely paying attention to the road in front of him. His heart rate had begun to rise, pumping adrenaline throughout his body.

Driving was another task Jason had difficulty with. Being stuck in traffic was infuriating as he felt trapped and vulnerable. Every driver on the road seemed like an obstacle. He never acknowledged the occupants as ordinary people going about their day. For all he knew, they could be a threat to him. This mindset made him no stranger to road rage.

Keep following me, and you'll regret it. I swear to God. Jason took a right at the upcoming intersection, heading south to return home. The car behind him followed. His vision focused more on the rearview mirror than the road in front of him. The evening was approaching, and the gray sky was darkening. The clouds were like lifeless gray waves on an ocean above. Jason was prepared for the elements, as usual. His black toque and North Face jacket were his go-to outerwear for this climate. His usual black tactical boots, which he had worn for so long, adorned his feet.

"OK, motherfucker." Jason decided to pull into an approaching grocery store parking lot. *We'll see if you follow me now.*

He pulled into the parking lot and chose to back up into the nearest parking spot. The car followed him in. Jason's eyes went wide, concentrating solely on this potential threat in front of him. His heart continued to race, and the adrenaline rushing through his body caused his legs to feel light and his chest heavy. *You picked the wrong guy.*

Jason sat in his vehicle, observing the other driver. He waited as the driver pulled into the parking spot across from Jason. Waiting with anticipation, Jason prepared himself for the worst. He reached over the passenger seat and grabbed his Glock pistol from the glove compartment. Placing it on his lap, he waited.

The male driver exited the car in front of him and stood staring at Jason. He was a tall man in his thirties. Dressed for the elements, he looked angry and scowled in Jason's direction. The man took a step forward and opened the rear door of his car.

He's grabbing a gun!

Perceiving this man as a threat, Jason's fight-or-flight response went into overdrive. "Let's do this, motherfucker!" Jason exited the vehicle with his pistol in hand as the man leaned into the back seat of his car.

Standing in the cold, he gripped his weapon with intent, preparing to raise it and strike the threat before it could strike him. *Do it, you piece of shit.* The tension made time slow down. Jason could feel the soft snowflakes falling on his skin and the wind brushing them across his face. He could hear the traffic driving on the road behind him and the sound of a grocery cart being put away. He could feel the salt crunch beneath his boots as he adjusted his footing. His senses were in overdrive.

The man leaning into his car exited and turned to look at Jason with his two-year-old daughter in his arms. Before anyone could notice, Jason quickly placed the weapon behind his back. The man, who seemingly did not see the gun, frowned at Jason and began walking toward the supermarket with his daughter.

Jesus Christ …

In shock, Jason returned to his car and sat with his pistol on his lap. He hung his head and attempted to control his breathing, which was now rapidly accelerating. Jason began to feel light-headed and scared. Panic attacks often followed intensive emotional outbursts, but he never saw them like that. Jason never really thought of it at all. He just lived with it, believing his reactions were normal according to whatever justification he made.

He could have had a weapon. I thought he was following me!

Jason placed his head on the steering wheel and closed his eyes. Ashamed and angry at himself and those around him, he smashed his fist against the wheel. *Stupid. You're so fucking stupid.* Over and over, Jason punched the top of his steering wheel as he unleashed a primal scream. "AHHH!!!" Like an animal, he shook the steering wheel with furious aggression, unleashing all of the shame, anger, and adrenaline stored in his body from this recent incident.

After exerting himself with the outburst, he rubbed the left side of his face and attempted to place the key back into the ignition. Shaking, he missed the first few times until he eventually inserted the key and turned on the truck's engine. Continuing his journey home, he drove in silence. Reviewing the events that had taken place, he berated himself for being so reckless.

Upon reaching his apartment, he parked at his designated street parking spot and walked to the entrance. It was an old building that hadn't been updated in years. Weak on entrance security, it had an old-school passcode of silver push buttons and a flimsy lock mechanism. All it took was for someone to pull on the door forcefully, and they could get in.

Climbing the stairs, he reached his apartment door. Jason entered, threw his coat on the rack, and tossed his boots in the corner. They fell with a thud and scattered at the entrance. His home was cluttered, with empty beer cans scattered throughout the household. Those ornaments of misery were on shelves, TV stands, and in the kitchen. The sink was piled with dirty dishes, and his garbage overflowed. It was akin to the state his life was in. It was disorganized, sloppy, and depressing.

Jason opened his fridge. It was bare except for some beer and condiments. The only thing he had to eat was old leftover Chinese food that had been sitting in his fridge for the past three days. Rice and chicken balls were all he could have for dinner that night.

Heating the food in his microwave, Jason stood stoically in his kitchen. He stared at the food warming up but did not see anything in front of him. His thoughts and feelings of shame, embarrassment, and worthlessness filled him whole. *What kind of life is this?*

There was no greater demon he had than his subconscious voice. Hateful and critical of himself, it was inescapable. He was hard on himself in every detail of his life. He was consistently calling himself names in his mind and putting himself down. His soul was degrading with every thought he had.

Jason sat alone at his table, facing the bare white wall. No pictures were hung, and no decorations were visible. It was an unhappy home, but it was his only one. Finishing his meal, Jason pushed his plate away and sat in silence, his eyes gazing at the wall. He sat in a hypnotic state, not thinking of anything, sinking in his feelings. Jason couldn't describe it; it felt too intimate to give it a simple name like depression or hopelessness. Those labels didn't show what he felt. They gave it no justice.

Jason moved from his concrete position, with his joints feeling like they were made of stone. Making his way to the sofa, he sat down in his self-made prison. Reaching for his waistline, Jason removed his pistol from his lower back and placed it on the coffee table. He turned on the TV.

"KOLN Nebraska Local News. Six more US soldiers were killed today in an IED strike south of Kandahar City. All six were members of the 134th infantry regiment located here in Nebraska. Their bodies will be repatriated in the coming days. Here at home, a spokesperson for the unit spoke with us to comment on these tragic developments."

"These soldiers made the ultimate sacrifice. Their country called on them in a time of need, and they answered. Knowing the danger they faced, they still chose to go and fight. All citizens are indebted to their service and sacrifice, and we send condolences to the families here at home."

Just as quickly as he'd turned it on, Jason shut off the TV. He lowered his head and stared at the coffee table with a deep apprehensive sigh.

* * *

"Are you nervous?" Brad asked, sitting next to Jason on the Hercules aircraft about to disembark from the mainland United States.

"A little bit. Not sure if it's excitement or nervousness. I just want to get on the ground to get this thing started," Jason responded, fiddling with his Zippo lighter. It had reached the deployment date to Kandahar, Afghanistan. They would spend the next year in a forward operating base, conducting mounted and dismounted patrols in their area of operations.

"Yeah, I mean. I'm not worried about dying myself. I'm more worried about stopping your ass from getting hurt." Brad laughed, giving Jason a smirk.

"The hell do you mean by that?" Jason retorted.

"I'm fucking with you. I wouldn't want to lose you guys, that's all. Same with you, Rodriguez!" Brad slapped Rodriguez, sitting in front of them, across the back of the head, causing him to turn and give Brad a look of disapproval.

"I mean, we're luckier than most other sections. We've got a good leader in Sergeant Bass. I think we'll make it out OK. Lord help any Talib that chooses to fuck with us," Jason replied, opening and closing his lighter.

The plane was filled with hundreds of soldiers in all their camouflaged desert gear. It had been common transportation to the war zone for the past decade. Many soldiers went to Afghanistan, but not all came back.

"One year is a long time to be away from home. I'm going to miss my brothers. We're going to have the biggest party when we get back, though. The beer will be flowing. We're stockpiling a bunch of fireworks and plan to set them off all at once! It's going to be awesome," Brad expressed. "Think about how great that will feel, finally being home after a year in the shit. Coming home to women and booze and whatever else waits for you!" Brad elbowed Jason.

"Yeah, I don't care how long I stay there. I don't have any family left. It's just me." Jason placed his lighter back into his pocket. Thinking about his father, he stared straight ahead toward the front of the plane. *I miss you, Dad.*

"You're wrong about that, Jason," Brad replied.

"We are your family."

* * *

In his apartment, despair struck Jason in his chest. No longer able to see any future for himself, he wondered why he even bothered continuing to live in such misery. He missed the days when he was in uniform, professional and disciplined. He had adventures ahead of him and friends by his side. He longed for what he used to be but knew it was all no longer possible. The scars on his body and mind made him ineligible to return to service. Even so, he didn't have any desire to do that anyway.

Jason eyed the pistol on his coffee table. Lying next to an empty Jack Daniels bottle, the firearm gave an appearance of power and finality. It had the ability to save and take a life. Not many objects could do such a thing. It could defend, entertain, appease, and make him feel powerful and protected. It could do all those things, and did for many people. As with many others in this world, it could also put an end to suffering.

Without putting any thought into his actions, Jason reached for his pistol. Closing his eyes, he placed the barrel underneath his chin, gripping the weapon in an ironclad grasp. His hands faintly trembled as his finger rested on the trigger. *Do it.*

A sinister voice spoke to Jason from deep within him. "Ending it all would be better than living this dull life." *Do it.* The sound of drums began to beat in pace with Jason's rapidly pounding heart.

"You can't stand society anymore; you're a nuisance to everyone you encounter. Nobody will miss you." *Do it.* Sweat dripped down the left side of Jason's scarred face as the audible voice berated Jason.

"Hell, you couldn't even drive to the supermarket and back without almost ruining somebody's life." *Just do it!* His hand quivered as he began to squeeze the trigger.

Abruptly Jason opened his eyes and lowered his weapon, only to double-check that the pistol was loaded correctly. He had messed up so many other things in his life, and he didn't want to mess up his own suicide. Jason placed the barrel back underneath his chin and again put his finger on the trigger.

Before closing his eyes, something caught his attention. One of the old hunting magazines that were left was lying on the table. It was the only thing left in his life that he still had a passion for. So it was no surprise that this would take him out of his moment of despair, even if for only a second.

Ignoring it, Jason closed his eyes once again. He took a slow, deep breath and sighed, preparing himself for what was about to come. He was stuck between thinking about it and doing it. He knew he wanted to, but his finger felt frozen. His knuckles were like immovable granite, unable to conduct the downward motion of pulling the trigger.

"You coward, you can't even kill yourself," the voice spoke within him. Frustrated, Jason tossed his pistol on the table.

Staring at the discarded weapon, he weighed the decision he had just made. *You coward, just do it!* He wanted so desperately an answer to his problems. He could no longer go on in the way he had been living but could think of no other escape than ending his life.

Jason mustered up some courage to retry his final solution to all of life's problems and reached for it again. *Don't think. Just point and pull.* "Yes, that's it. Come to me, Jason …" the deep voice whispered.

As he grasped the pistol, he once again looked at the magazine. Something kept drawing his attention to it. "Ignore it, Jason! It will do you no good. You know what you have to do. Come to me …"

Hunt Alaska Magazine was the title. It was an issue that he had read a few months ago, and he was intrigued by the descriptions of that state's environment. Its wild game, beautiful scenery, and peaceful isolation in the northern part of the world gave an ambiance of utopia compared to the small town of Plattsmouth. It seemed like paradise to Jason, far from the chaos and triggers of society.

Gazing at the magazine on the table, he was drawn back from the abyss. Abruptly, the drums stopped beating. Thinking of the snow-covered Alaskan wilderness being so secluded, peaceful, and serene, Jason tossed the pistol on the table and held his head in his hands. The gun made a thud and knocked the bottle of Jack Daniels off the table.

Jason cried for what felt like an eternity. His body vibrated as he wailed heavily into his hands. He rubbed the left side of his numb face and cradled his head into his lap as he rocked back and forth.

Dad! Mom! I'm so scared! I don't know what to do anymore!
I wish you were here so much. I need you, Dad! Please help me!
God, I don't know how long I can go on. Please ... I don't know what to do!
I'm hurting so bad. I just want peace ... I want peace ... I WANT PEACE!
HELP ME!

Jason became exhausted after the emotional outburst and fell into the sofa. Silence filled the room as he eyed the magazine on the table. *Even living in a snow cave would be better than this damn apartment.* Jason thought to himself. With reddened eyes and salt-stained cheeks, he observed his backpack in the corner of his room. Always prepped and ready to go, it was his go-bag in case of an emergency. An old habit he brought back from the military.

This was an emergency.

Do it. Just do it.

Chapter 11

O, full of scorpions is my mind!
—William Shakespeare

Backwoods, Alaska
Present Day

"Stay down," a faint voice whispered in the darkness. "Accept it … it's OK."

His crusted eyes began to open as he struggled to lift his eyelids. The sharp cold stung his nostrils. He let out a wet cough and cleared his lungs of what felt like a flood of debris made of liquid iron.

Bright red painted the white canvas as he regained focus. Blood on snow, fog from his breath, reflections of light. Everything began to take shape as his senses regained clarity. Raising his head, he realized he was lying face-first in the snow. Bruised and dirty, he adjusted his vision. Having been knocked unconscious, Jason attempted to recognize his environment. Blood spatter stained the snow beside his face like a galaxy of red stars.

"You don't need to do this." the voice whispered again. "Sleep. It will all end."

Painfully, the rising sun's rays hit Jason's eyes as he rolled onto his back. Filling his lungs with that crisp cold air, he realized he was still alive. His head rang with confusion as he struggled to focus his mind back to some semblance of awareness. *Is it morning?* "Fuck me," he moaned as he felt his rib cage. *Where am I? Where is that voice coming from? Everything hurts.*

A much larger patch of blood soaked his shirt. "Agh, shit," he grunted as he removed his hand from the wound on his abdomen. The pain shot through his side like a lightning bolt. He detected a large wound on his left ankle at the spot where the Scorpion had torn a chunk of flesh off him.

The cliff must have been about thirty feet and almost straight up. How he survived the fall was beyond him. Nothing around him was familiar except for that voice. He lay beside a rocky cliff face amid dense forest and vegetation.

Rolling onto his hands and knees, he crawled toward a nearby tree, his limbs shaking with fatigue. He fumbled toward the base of the trunk, knees scraping against the protruding roots until his hand hit something within the snow.

With his vision still adjusting, he dug around the object, feeling it out until his fingers wrapped around it. The item began to feel familiar in its shape and weight. With a firm grasp, he ripped it out from underneath the snow.

Sitting back against the tree, he placed the object on his lap. Inspecting it, he tried to regain his memory. It was black and brown with a tan camouflage pattern dyed along its side. A sling was attached to it, and an optical scope—a rifle, recently fired.

Anxiety set in as he glanced around in all directions. An imminent sense of horror embodied his soul as he lifted his shirt to inspect himself. Seeing blood dripping from a three-quarter-inch hole, he placed his hand on his back to inspect himself more.

Feeling around in distress, he noticed an even larger hole on his back, opposite the hole on the front. "I'm shot," he mouthed to himself in disbelief. Jason's pupils dilated as the cloud of confusion began to dissipate. *That girl. That Scorpion. Am I losing my mind?*

With desperation, he began probing around his pockets for anything. His muscles felt like they were working faster than he could think. Raising his hand from his pocket, he saw the glint of sunshine against the pale-yellow brass he now held in his hand.

In haste, without much thought, he threw the brass 7.62 caliber round into the rifle's chamber. Releasing the bolt catch, he loaded the gun with a single bullet. The bolt slammed forward with a familiar metal clutching sound. He raised his head and placed the rifle on his shoulder in an instinctual state of readiness.

Jason stared out into the distance, now completely aware of his reality.

"You don't quit, Orion, do you …"

"No. I don't! And that's something you're going to have to deal with!" Jason shouted to the voice, using the tree as a crutch. It was the same voice as the man he had fought with above. The man who called himself Jack.

Jack took on different shapes. First, he was a Taliban fighter who tried to kill him. Then the fighter turned into Jason himself, trying to convince him to commit suicide. *Was he that little girl too? What about that Scorpion? How is a scorpion all the way out here?* These unanswered questions only came with one all-knowing truth. Jack had tried to kill Jason, and he wasn't finished yet.

Jack's voice came from everywhere, echoing within Jason and the forest. Jason was incredibly cold, some of his extremities were numb, and his fine motor skills were stiff and awkward. He had spent the night unconscious in the snow. The vegetation and cliff around him provided shelter from the wind and cold, but not much.

Bleeding, cold, and in pain, Jason was in a perilous situation. So far, he had survived the life-and-death struggle with this shape-shifting demon, but he was still in the woods. Far from his cabin, far from society, and far from safety.

Jason brought himself to his feet and assessed his surroundings, using the rifle as an aid to help himself stand. The winter snow blanketed the forest's dead, barren trees and covered the ground with enough snow to reach Jason's knees. With determination, Jason limped forward, hoping to find a way out of his environment.

"Where are you going? Get comfortable, Jason. Why bother putting yourself through this pain? Lie down and sleep, and it will all end," the demon's voice advocated from above.

"What are you? Why have you come after me?" Jason questioned out loud as he trudged his way through the thick snow.

"Come after you? You still don't understand, do you? I haven't come after you, Jason. I have always been with you. I AM you." The demon's guttural voice roared throughout the trees.

"None of this makes sense. You speak in riddles. I don't have the time for that bullshit." *Have I lost my mind?*

"Always the impatient one, eh?" the demon jeered. "I'm not surprised. You've never taken the time to understand yourself. You've been so wrapped up with the outside world and its misgivings that your soul has rotted away. I am the result of that, Jason. You created me."

Jason leaned against a tree to catch his breath. Lifting his shirt in pain, he inspected his wound. The dark red blood had begun to dry around the puncture, but some blood was still seeping out. *I need to do something, or I'll bleed out.*

"You like to judge me, eh? What do you know about what I've been through?" Jason shouted. "You don't know anything about me."

The demon let out a sinister laugh. "Ignorant fool, spare me the self-pity! You are not the man you used to be, due to your own doing! It has been your own decisions that have brought you here to me." The voice came from a different location each time it spoke, causing Jason to look in all directions as he continued to walk through the trees.

"I'm just your inner voice—the voice of truth and reason. I won't spare you any mercy to please your fragile ego, Orion. I will tell you exactly what it is you need to hear. You just need to start listening."

"And what do I need to hear? More of the bullshit nonsense that you've been spouting?" Jason questioned, pushing branches out of the way.

"That it is time, Orion. It's time to give up. You have no family, and you have no friends. You are not happy and have lost the joy in life. You can't even complete simple tasks like going to a grocery store without an emotional breakdown. I'm here to tell you it is time to let go and give in." The demon continued to persuade Jason.

"I have my faults. But I think I showed you up on that cliff that I am not giving up. I still have some fight left in me. If you want to finish this, then show yourself! Stop hiding from me!" Jason shouted out into the air.

"I am not your enemy, Orion. I am your friend. I just want what's best for you. The best thing for you is to find peace, and the only way to find that is to end your life. If you don't choose that path, you choose a life of misery and torment! Haven't you had enough of that already? You're not happy, and that's exactly what you deserve. To never be happy."

Jason again stopped at a tree, placing his hand on it to hold himself while clutching his rifle in the other. He spat on the ground to painfully clear some blood from his airway. While observing his surroundings, he noticed small dark figures adorning the branches above. Hundreds of ravens sat in silence, staring at him. Feeling even more uneasy, he placed his weapon into his shoulder.

"I've had enough of you, is what I've had! It'll make me happy to see you gone."

In the distance, Jason could hear the sound of moving water. Thirsty and tired, he moved toward the sound, hoping the water would help him gain some idea as to where he was.

"Of course you've had enough of me. I am the voice of truth! That's something you've never wanted to face, so I have followed you everywhere you go, and I will continue to follow you for the rest of your life," the voice echoed.

Noticing tracks in the snow, Jason took a knee and inspected them. *That's a big bear.* The paw prints were massive and made their way east and parallel to the sound of rushing water, which now grew closer.

"Well, let's finish this! You want me to die? Then come on out and kill me! You keep trying to convince me to end my own life! Why is that? Are you too weak to do it yourself?" Jason was shouting at the top of his lungs. His eyes were wide with a mix of fear and anger.

"Is that what you want, Orion? You don't know what I'm fully capable of. You may regret this decision." The demon tried to persuade Jason once more.

"Why don't you reconsider taking the easy way out? No more cold, no more sadness, no more anger or frustration … no more fighting and no more pain …" The demon's voice became more profound and inhuman as it spoke. "You have one more bullet left. Put it to good use."

"I'm done with this shit! I'm not running away from you anymore! I'm making my stand right here, right now! You want me gone so badly, then come on out and do it yourself, bitch!"

Silence filled the forest. The demon's voice no longer answered. Jason could hear nothing but the wind blowing through the trees and the rushing water in the distance. He looked around for any sign of the demon but could not find any.

"You've had so much to say to me, yet now you've become silent? Who is hiding from who now?! Who is afraid now?! I'M RIGHT HERE!" Jason screamed as he held his rifle at the ready, scanning the forest.

Still, no answer came to him. *Is he gone?* Jason was chilled to the bone. His adrenaline was no longer giving him the warmth provided by his rushing blood. Standing still, Jason waited for the demon to show itself.

"I'll never get rid of you, eh? It seems like I just did! Who's the coward now!?" Jason shouted triumphantly.

"WHO'S THE COWARD NOW!"

Hundreds of ravens burst from their branches and flew off into the sky as if scenting danger. The ground began to tremble, and branches snapped in the distance. Far off in the forest, Jason could faintly make out what looked like swaying trees, as if something was pushing them out of the way. Puffs of snow flew up above the trees into the sky. *My God …*

Fear gripped Jason. His eyes widened as he awaited what might come from that direction. His heart raced, and his breath became heavy. His fight-or-flight instinct began to kick in, but he wasn't sure which one to choose. Aiming his gun in the direction of the chaos in the distance, he awaited his fate.

Erupting out of the dense crop of trees, a large black creature knocked over a tree to make its way forward. It stood six feet tall with two pincers and six legs. It had five red eyes and a menacing tail that reached over its body, its stinger at the ready. Its oily black skin was hardened as if made of ebony armor. The giant Scorpion was much bigger than anything Jason had ever seen before.

The Scorpion stood on its back feet and made a forceful screech that bellowed throughout the forest. Its open mouth had razor-sharp teeth and was as black as the abyss it came from. Its pincers clapped the air, cutting down a tree in its way. Showing off its strength, it struck the ground with its stinger causing snow and dirt to fly up into the air, leaving a crater where it hit. The strength and power of this enormous monster were on display, showing Jason its full capability and intent.

FIGHT!

Jason fired his remaining round at the massive Scorpion, striking it in its face. The bullet ricocheted off its hardened outer shell and struck a tree behind it. The creature released a rageful roar and began pushing toward Jason, its six legs clacking with each movement.

RUN!

Jason turned and ran in the direction of the rushing water. He hobbled as fast as possible, pain shooting up his calf and into his side from his injuries. Turning his head, he could see the Scorpion closing the distance, knocking over trees as it got closer. *My God!* Jason threw his empty rifle on the ground to lighten his load, hoping to gain more speed.

A horrible screech arose from behind Jason, closer now than before. Too terrified to look behind him, Jason continued his escape from death. *Run! Run! Run!* Sticks flew in front of him, caused by the Scorpion chopping through trees with its pincers. The fog from his breath blew like a steam engine as Jason desperately tried to escape.

With a mighty blow of its tail, the Scorpion ripped a tree out of its roots, causing part of it to hit Jason in the back. Jason stumbled and fell forward onto a large rock boulder. Rolling onto his back, Jason leaned against the rock, facing his doom. The black death stood in front of him, massive in size, and let out a gigantic, bloodcurdling screech. Its stinger struck down toward Jason.

Jason rolled off the rock at the last second, causing the stinger to penetrate the boulder. Lying in the snow just underneath the creature's mouth, Jason froze. Its blood-red eyes stared deep into his soul. Seconds felt like hours as they scrutinized each other. Its gaze hypnotized Jason. He could feel the strong pull of the abyss.

"You will come to me, Orion." The voice spoke telepathically to Jason as the Scorpion moved its face closer. *"You will come to me."*

Attempting to strike Jason again, the Scorpion struggled to remove its stinger from the boulder. It had struck the boulder so hard its tail was now trapped in the rock. Jason's face was filled with horror and dread as he gazed deep into the eyes of the monster. What he saw within them was darkness of the purest form. Evil incarnate. Death.

The Scorpion let out a frustrated screech as it struggled to free itself, causing Jason to snap out of his trance. Seeing his chance to escape, he rolled out from underneath the Scorpion and began running toward the sound of rushing water. The frustrated screeches behind him grew with each step he made.

A considerable cracking noise came from behind him. Jason turned to see if the creature was still stuck in place. It wasn't. With a mighty roar, rocks blasted up into the sky as the creature freed its tail. It began trudging faster and faster toward him, making a white cloud form around the monster as snow and dirt kicked up from the ground. Its determination to kill was absolute.

While sprinting through the forest, flashes appeared within Jason's mind. Combined with the audible sounds of drums beating, the visions filled his universe. He saw his own rageful face staring at him. The background behind his face switched with every beat of the drum. The parking lot where he almost shot the innocent father switched to him sitting on the couch watching the news of dead soldiers. He was lying in his hospital bed, staring at the ceiling, and then seated at the bar in a drunken rage. He was sitting on a log holding an axe staring at the fallen tree, then driving in his car with one hand squeezing the wheel in a death grip. Sitting in the cabin, staring at a wall and then in the mirror, peering deep into his own eyes.

His face looked the same in every flash. Angry. Rageful. Visions of his face from the past were filled with hatred for himself and all life around him. The drum beat faster and faster as Jason saw every moment in his life when he was angry or upset. The vision of his face wrinkled in rage as tears of bright red blood dripped down his cheeks from his bloodshot eyes. *Pain. So much pain.* It enveloped his entire being, ripping through his soul. The images flashed in his mind faster and faster with his face in the foreground. Repeating every moment that Jason was taken over by hatred and shame.

The forest reappeared in front of Jason. He could now see the rushing water through the trees. The river's width was massive, and the swift current was too strong to cross safely. He would undoubtedly be swept away. Jason broke through the tree line and made it to the shore. The creature came closer and closer, breaking through trees and bushes.

Stuck on the river's edge, Jason was trapped. Out of breath and in pain, he could no longer run. The Scorpion roared, echoing throughout the wilderness. Jason stared into its blood-red eyes and saw his fate within them. He turned to look at the rushing white water, its rapids promising a cold, cruel, chaotic death. A feeling of the inevitable overcame him, and he thought of Jack's words and contemplated if he was right about everything. *Maybe it would be better if it all ends.* An intrusive voice disrupted Jason's thoughts as the sound of the Scorpion grew close.

If things get tough or you feel lonely, always remember that you're never alone. Always remember that.

Always remember that.

Always remember that.

Jason closed his eyes as the voice of his father echoed within his heart. Jason turned his back on the Scorpion and peered into the rushing water. Both staying or jumping promised the likelihood of death, but with the Scorpion, it would be absolute. Jason leaped into the rushing water. The Scorpion halted at the river's edge and watched as the water swallowed its prey.

The cold water shocked and took the breath out of Jason's lungs, causing his heart to skip. In shock, with numbness taking over his body, he was dragged downstream, water rushing over his head and tossing him side to side. He could feel his legs strike rocks underneath the water as wave after wave dropped over his head. Darkness and white water obscured his vision. He could not see where the river was taking him. His senses were overwhelmed; he was unable to hear anything except the roaring current and his gasping breaths.

Jason's body became cool. The cold attacked his muscles until he could feel nothing at all. He felt no pain and heard no sounds. The current continued to take him to nature's chosen destination. No longer in control, Jason stopped struggling against it and prayed the nightmare would end. *Please. I don't want to die. I want to live. Please. Please.*

The foaming white water turned to black as his head slipped under.

Chapter 12

Knowledge without spirit is like finding yourself on a cold winter's night
with all the wood in the world, and no flame to light it.
—Guy Finley

The River's Edge
Present Day

Jason's hand dug into the soft wet sand, rocks slipping through his fingers as he crawled on his hands and knees. Frozen and numb, it took resilience to use his stiff muscles to drag himself onto the shore. The current had swept him a mile downriver. He had repeatedly sunk under the ice-cold water, pummeled by the turbulent rapids. It wasn't until the whitewater subsided that he was pushed onto the shore.

Exhausted, Jason collapsed onto the dark gray sand. His lips blue and pale, he made short, shallow breaths. His wet black hair, draped over his face, blew with each exhale. *Help me.* He felt a warmth rise within his chest and could no longer feel his extremities. Reaching a hypothermic state, his body was beginning to shut down. The late stages of hypothermia began to set in as his body used all its energy to protect its vital organs. *I'm dying.* A great peace blanketed his soul. *So this is what it's like. This is what it's like to die.*

He had always heard that people who froze to death became warm and filled with an enduring peace before they died. Accepting his fate, Jason did not attempt to move from his position on the shoreline. No longer having the will to go on, he closed his eyes and let death come for him.

The sound of gravel and sand crunching under a weight grew prominent over other noises. The crunching pattern was familiar, like the sound of shuffling footsteps. Jason tried hard to open his eyes but could only do it briefly due to his weakened body. *It's come to finish me off. Just do it. Get it over with.*

Jason's blurred vision began to focus on the origin of the sound. A figure in the distance, dressed in thick dark clothing made of animal skin, walked toward him on the shoreline. Jason's eyes shut again. *This is it.* The sound came closer and closer until he heard the footsteps stop in front of his face. Jason gradually opened his eyes to see a pair of feet dressed in furry brown and white moccasin boots with a rope tied around the ankles. He heard a stern voice speak in an unfamiliar language, and his eyes closed again.

"Help … me …" Jason pleaded in a weak voice to the unknown man, not knowing whether he was a friend or foe.

The man rolled Jason onto his back until he faced upward toward the bleak morning sky. Wet sand encrusted Jason's clammy skin; cold and struggling to stay awake, he was in a perilous condition. The sound of drums beating began to echo softly through his head. Unsure if this was a sound made by somebody or if it was something created by his mind, he opened his eyes once again.

Above him stood an older man dressed in winter clothing made entirely of animal skins. Squirrel backs were sewn together to create the majority of his tunic. Decorative beads and porcupine quills hung from different parts of the material. A hood adorned his head, lined with thick gray wolf fur, the inner lining consisting of the hair of a wolverine.

Peering into the hood, Jason could not see the man's face. The man mumbled something Jason could not understand and grabbed him by the wrists. Jason felt himself being dragged further up the shore and into the forest. The crunching of snow and the sound of his body pulling across the ground was all he could hear. He was too cold to feel anything.

Jason's eyes would close and open sporadically. Each time he opened his eyes, he saw something different above him. The bleak open sky turned to the tree-covered canopy above. Diluted sunlight moved through the branches as he was pulled deep into the forest. Jason felt himself being hauled onto a blanket of some sort. The blanket was thick, padded, and lifted a few inches, supported by sticks and branches. It began to push forward.

Jason presumed he had been placed on a sled by how he glided across the ground. Whoever this man was had pushed him to an unknown destination. Powerless and unable to keep his eyes open, Jason fell asleep for what he believed could be the last time, never to awaken again.

He was awoken from his sleep by the man dragging him off the sled. Jason tried to assess his surroundings. They had halted near the shore of the river. Its width stretched over one hundred yards and was calm and softly flowing. This part of the river was unlike its rapid white water further upstream. Small rocky islands pockmarked the shallow river throughout its width. The gray stone inlets reached the shore, and fallen trees and dark driftwood were scattered throughout the water. Jason turned his head to see where the man was pulling him.

He could see a small hut made of thick animal skins propped up by a contraption of sticks and branches. Beside it was a drying rack with fresh-cut deer skins suspended on it. The man pulled Jason into the hut and laid him on a bed made of fur. The mysterious figure piled blankets on top of him without saying a word. He began to light a fire in the middle of the hut, using a primitive method of creating fire. He smacked the hard edge of a flint rock against a piece of iron pyrite. Since leaving his cabin, Jason began to feel the first semblance of comfort. He succumbed to the warmth the blankets and fire provided and fell asleep.

Hours passed, and Jason was awoken by pain shooting throughout his limbs as his body began to thaw. Nobody else was in the hut except for Jason. The man had disappeared. The fire still burned in the middle of the hut. Judging by the darkness outside the hut entrance, he had been asleep most of the day as it was now nightfall.

Jason found himself naked as he lifted the blanket to inspect his wounds. His wet clothes had been removed while he slept, and somebody had patched up his injuries. The bullet hole in his abdomen was packed with a dark, dirty substance and stitched together. The hide of a squirrel had been placed on top to act as a bandage. The same went for the wound on his calf caused by the Scorpion upon the cliff. It was packed with a dark substance and wrapped with squirrel hide. Jason placed the covers back on.

He could tell the room resembled an old native hunting hut. His father had shown him something similar in pictures long ago. There was no flooring inside, just the earth's gravel on the river's edge. Across from his bed lay a stack of animal furs consisting of moose hides, wolf skins, and others. A pot was beside it, along with a knife. A makeshift bench was placed across the room, with some furs and leaves forming a temporary bed. A small hole adorned the top of the hut to let the smoke escape. Through that, Jason could see thousands of bright stars shining down from above.

He was lost in the beauty of the night sky, wondering how he had been able to live another day to once again see the magnificence of it. So much had transpired in such a short period. Jason's head rang with confusion.

The hooded man entered the hut and stood in the doorway. He held pine needles and other vegetation in his hands. Dressed in his animal fur clothing, he stared at Jason and then made his way to the other side of the hut. The man picked up the black pot and threw the vegetation into it before sitting on the bench, facing Jason.

"Who are you?" Jason whispered in a hoarse voice.

The man sat in silence as he placed the pot onto the fire. The oversized fur skin hood concealed his face in the darkness. The orange glow from the fire danced around the hut as Jason stared at this silent man, pausing for an answer. Reaching up, the man withdrew his hood. The firelight revealed an older Native American man of Athabascan origin. The bottom half of his face was painted red from the middle of the nose. A black stripe ran horizontally across the top of the red paint. His long black and gray hair was split down the middle and tied into a ponytail at the back. He had high cheekbones and a square jawline. His darkened, weathered skin gave him a hardened appearance—the appearance of a man who had spent much of his life in the wilderness, bearing the elements. His dark, sunken eyes made contact with Jason.

"Do'int'a segena`," the man replied. *Hello, my friend.*

Jason heard the words in another language but somehow understood everything the man said. It was as if he was fluent in the man's native language, a tongue he had never actually heard before today.

"How can I understand you?" Jason asked, lying confounded on his bed.

"We all speak the same language," the man replied, adjusting the black pot on the fire. He took a waterskin from his tunic, poured water into the pot, and began mixing the needles and vegetation to a boil.

"I don't understand." Jason's voice was still hoarse and weak every time he spoke.

"That much is clear," the mystifying man said while mixing the pot with a knife.

"Why did you save me?"

"You looked like you could use some saving." The pot gave off an aroma of pine and wild juniper, filling the hut with a pleasant odor.

"Well … thank you. And I take it you also helped patch my wounds? Thank you for that as well. If it weren't for you, I'd be—"

"Dead." The man finished Jason's sentence in his native tongue. Yet somehow, Jason understood it fluently.

"Yes … thank you." Jason shifted onto his side, grimacing in pain. "I still don't understand. I don't know your language, so how can I understand what you're saying to me?"

"We all speak the same language. It matters not where we are from, as we are all the same." He placed the knife on the ground beside the pot, allowing the water to stew. "What caused those wounds on your body? How did you end up in the river?"

"If I told you, you wouldn't believe me. I can barely believe it myself." Jason replied. *I already think I'm crazy, so you definitely would.*

The expressionless man sat in silence and stared at Jason. Uncomfortable with the quiet, Jason told the man about his hunt, shooting the deer, and coming face-to-face with the Taliban fighter. How the fighter turned into himself and the fight that ensued. His encounter with the wolves and the younger girl. His fall off the cliff. Being attacked by an enormous Scorpion, and the choice he made to jump into the river to escape being killed. None of these details appeared to surprise the native man.

"You are strong to have survived such encounters." The man spoke in a deep, monotone voice. Light from the fire cast shadows across the hut and lit up his painted face.

"I don't feel strong." Jason sighed.

"True strength comes from when you feel the weakest." The fire crackled, and the soft sound of moving water could be heard from the river outside.

"Don't any of those things seem crazy to you?" Jason asked, irritated by the man's lack of surprise at what he had just shared.

"No, they do not." The man spoke earnestly. He made no facial expressions, continuing to stare at Jason.

"Who are you? What is your name?" Jason asked.

"My name is Charging Bear. I have lived in these lands for many years," the man responded as he lifted the warm pot of water and needles. "Drink this. It will help you." Charging Bear brought the pot to Jason's lips. Hesitant and untrusting, Jason placed his hand out to stop the man. "Trust is hard for you. A person must go to great lengths to enter your heart, as saving you from death seems not enough?"

Contemplating the man's words, Jason lowered his hand. Charging Bear brought the pot to Jason's lips and assisted him in drinking. The warm pine water soothed Jason's throat as he gulped it down. The heat filled his insides, providing a powerful relief.

He was grateful that this man had given him such hospitality and saved him from certain death. Jason, though, was still cautious and untrusting toward people. He wanted to leave. "Well, Charging Bear. My name is Jason, and I am very grateful for your help, but I gotta get going." Jason wiped his mouth with his hand and painfully began to sit up until he remembered he had no clothes. "Um, could I have my clothes?"

"They are hanging outside and are not yet dry. I recommend that you stay here tonight. It is cold and dark outside. I have some clothes for you that are better suited for this weather when you're ready to continue your journey."

Accepting the man's truth, Jason lay back down. He was still frail and hurting. Entering into the darkness of the night could only end badly. The blanket covered the lower half of his body, leaving his chest exposed. The scars on his chest were plain to see. Caused by the explosion in Afghanistan, it was a chaotic map of deformities on his pale white skin.

"How did you get those wounds?" Charging Bear inquired, pointing at his own chest and face in reference.

"I was injured in a war. A blast caused it." Jason spoke while looking down at his scars. "That was a long time ago." *But it feels like yesterday.*

"You have been through a lot, haven't you, son?" Charging Bear offered him more of the brew, which Jason readily accepted.

Jason gulped more of the warm water and then lay back down. He gazed up through the hole in the hut and toward the stars. "I guess you can say that." Jason did not like it when people asked him questions about his history. He felt like he was some object of others' amusement. The people who inquired about him only cared to hear an exciting story. Yet Jason did not feel that way toward Charging Bear. For some reason, whether it was the way he spoke or his presence, Jason felt reassurance from the man. A comfort that he could not explain.

"What has brought you to this place, Jason? You are far from home." Charging Bear began to warm his hands by the fire.

"I'm from Nebraska. I traveled out here a while ago. To be alone."
To find peace, he thought to himself. "I have a cabin many miles from here
that I live at. It's peaceful."

"So, it is peace you seek? Have you found peace?" The shadows
danced across Charging Bear's face.

Jason's weary eyes continued to stare up through the hole. He
recollected how he had been about to end his life in his apartment. "I
thought I did, until recently. I left society behind to be alone. It was the only
option I had left."

"What are you running from?" Charging Bear inquired.

"I don't know. Everything? Everyone? As of recently, a giant black
Scorpion? I thought I'd be happier out here." Jason let out an exhausted
exhale.

"Peace comes from within, Jason. You should not seek it without."
The hooting of an owl rang out in the distance. "You cannot outrun your
demons. They will follow you to the ends of the earth until you choose to
face them. At which time it may be too late."

"I have been facing my demons, old man," Jason replied, upset at the
man's assumptions. "I've had to face many of them since coming back. You
will never be able to understand."

"Have you? Or were you running from them? Suppressing them?"
Charging Bear drank from the pot. "I found you on the shore of this great
river like an exhausted elk. You looked like you had been running for a
while."

"I was escaping!" Jason spoke forcefully.

"Escaping from what exactly? Your demons?" Charging Bear placed
the pot on the ground and leaned in toward Jason. "Spirits roam this great
land. Some are good, and some are evil. The evil spirits will gather strength
from those whom they see as weak. A broken soul is like easy prey to them.
Your soul is wounded."

"What do you know? You know nothing about me." Jason reacted,
angry at the man's speculations.

"I know more than you think, Orion." A gust of wind rushed
through the tiny hut, causing the flames to dance.

"Why did you call me that? How did you learn that name?" Jason
was bewildered at this man's knowledge. "Tell me what is going on. Now!"

Charging Bear grew stern. "What you have encountered is the
manifestation of your own demons. Your own negative inner voice is
embodied in the man you fought. Those encounters are representations of

all your fears and guilt. Your soul is wounded, Orion, and you permit your demons to torment you. This is why you have not found peace where you seek it."

Jason shuffled in his bed. "So none of this is real?"

"Wrong. It's all real. More real than you could possibly understand."

"But if I've manifested them, I can just … unmanifest them, right? Ignore them?" Jason was puzzled at what the old man was telling him. "They can't kill me if it's something I only created in my mind. I can just ignore it and make it go away. Right?" Jason's head began to throb with the information he was receiving.

"No. Ignoring them is what brought you here." Charging Bear stood up, looming over Jason. "Make no mistake. They can kill you, Orion, and that is what they are trying to do." The glow of the fire illuminated his painted red face.

"You have not found peace. You are vulnerable, and those demons will take advantage of you. Your shame and guilt are aiding them in their purposes."

"How do you know this? Listen, I've made mistakes. I killed innocent people by accident. I lost friends because I wasn't fast enough to respond. I wasn't there for my father when he needed me. I've caused nothing but trouble and heartbreak for those back home." Jason felt a lump in his throat begin to grow, making it harder for him to breathe.

"Peace, for me, is an elusive dream." Tears began to well up in his eyes and roll down his cheeks. He could see the star constellation of Orion's belt up in the sky through the smoke hole. "I'm angry, old man … I have hate in my heart for everything and everyone, including myself. Nothing makes me happy anymore. I'm tired … I'm so tired."

"Do you need to be *made* happy to achieve happiness?" Charging Bear brought out a pipe and began to pack it with tobacco.

"What do you mean?" Jason rubbed the left side of his face.

"Happiness comes from within. If you wait for something to *make* you happy, you will not find the true meaning of it. It will not last. Happiness can be the fresh air filling your lungs in the morning cold. It can be the true acceptance of who you are and who you aim to be. Happiness is seeing the beauty life brings." Charging Bear continued lighting his pipe.

"When a child plays, he can pick up a flower and admire its shape and colors. The child could spend minutes staring at this simple object, appreciating all the beauty it has to offer. The child is entirely in the present.

The child is mindful of the present, examining life's beauties and mysteries. At that moment, nothing else matters to the child except for the beauty of being conscious in the present moment. That is happiness in its truest form. A skill set that many men lose as they go through life."

Jason wiped the tears from his eyes. Crying made him feel vulnerable, but something made it seem okay to be vulnerable in front of Charging Bear. The presence of this man and how he spoke brought a quietude to Jason's heart.

Jason had no rebuttal to what Charging Bear had just told him. "We will speak more, my son. You must get some sleep to build your strength." Charging Bear laid his hand on Jason's forehead and turned to walk out of the hut.

"You will need it for what is coming."

Chapter 13

We can only be what we give ourselves the power to be.
—Native American Proverb

The River's Edge
Present Day

Morning broke with a fresh breeze blowing into the hut, waking Jason from his prolonged sleep. The previous day's exhausting events had caused Jason to fall into a deep slumber. He had no dreams, nor did he remember tossing and turning as he usually did during sleep. The young veteran had been out cold throughout the entirety of the night. He awoke feeling stiff and sore but refreshed.

The firepit had turned to ash with some tiny burning embers providing slight heat. Stretching, Jason looked around the hut. Charging Bear was not there. A pile of clothing had been laid out in front of Jason's bed. A hooded tunic made of animal skins, moccasin boots, and brown seal fur pants. A drawstring was fastened at the waist. *Hmm.*

Jason sat on the edge of his bed, the blanket covering his waist. *Well, I guess that'll do.* Dressing, he felt great comfort in how the attire touched his skin. It was warm and breathable, much better than the expensive jackets he bought from his hunting and fishing stores.

Jason exited the hut, shielding his eyes from the morning sunlight. The stony river extended wide underneath the blue sky before him. The tree line on the other side of the river was covered in beautiful white snow. Jason spotted a beaver waddling into the water.

"You've awoken!" Charging Bear cried out. He was standing on top of a rock on the river's edge with a spear in his hand. The spear had a wooden shaft and three prongs made from bone, crafted for fishing. Behind him was a drying rack for the fish, complete with five pink humpback salmon hanging from it. Jason walked toward Charging Bear, who stood staring vigilantly at the river below, his spear at the ready.

"Thanks for the clothes." Jason's voice felt much smoother than it did yesterday. *The tea must have helped.*

"They suit you well." Charging Bear said as he thrust his spear into the water, piercing another salmon. Leaping from the rock, he retrieved his bounty; the fish flailed at the end of the spear. "The great spirit has been kind enough to provide us with a generous breakfast this morning."

"So it seems." Jason eyed Charging Bear as he removed the fish from the spear and began cutting it with his knife. The man ripped eggs from the pregnant fish and consumed them. Clutching more, he held his hand toward Jason, gesturing for him to eat. Although Jason had never liked fish eggs, he was in no position to turn them down, having not eaten for quite a while.

"How are you feeling this morning? How are your wounds?"

"I'm doing better. The pain isn't as sharp as it was; I'm more comfortable now. My leg is what pains me the most." Jason spoke, trying to ignore the bitter taste of the fish eggs.

"It will take time. Time can heal all wounds." Charging Bear sliced the fish and offered a piece to Jason. Grabbing the fish meat, Jason ate it raw. In desperation, he devoured the food like a starved wolf. Jason knew his body needed to replenish nutrients. His hunger was overwhelming, and he needed energy. "Do not be so quick to eat. Enjoy the taste and texture of this creature that the great spirit has gifted us. Every bite is a blessing."

"I'm starving. I could eat this whole river," Jason replied, continuing to shove pieces of raw fish into his mouth.

"A man should take only what is necessary to sustain himself." Charging Bear stood and looked at Jason with judging eyes. "You have a lot to learn, my son, and if you are patient, I can teach you."

Jason paused. "Last night, you said I will need my strength for what is to come. What did you mean by that? What is coming?" he asked, devouring the last of his meal.

"I told you. You cannot escape your demons … you will have to face them." Charging Bear walked past Jason without saying another word. Confused, Jason turned and pursued him.

"Hey, wait up! What do you mean? Do you know something I don't? Who are you? Why do you seem to know more than you're letting on?" Jason caught up with the strange man.

"I know many things that you do not know." Charging Bear walked back toward his hut. "You ask many questions, but have you considered asking the right ones?"

"What is with people speaking in riddles to me? First that guy who tried to kill me and now you? Why can't you speak plainly to me and answer my questions?" Frustrated, Jason continued to follow him to the hut.

"You must find the answers to your questions yourself. It will do you no good for me to solve all your troubles." Charging Bear entered the hut, followed closely by Jason. "A child most effectively learns from their father's guidance when he is at a distance, with a watchful eye. It would provide no benefit if the father did everything for the child. If he prevented them from failing or choosing unwisely, the child would have no mistake to learn from. It would impede the child's ability to grow naturally with strength and wisdom."

"I'm not a child." Jason stood, irritated at the man. Charging Bear bent over to grab something.

Standing, the man turned to face Jason with a look of displeasure. He held two spears and slung a waterskin over his shoulder. Charging Bear gave Jason the second spear by forcefully pushing it into his chest. As soon as Jason clutched the spear, Charging Bear exited the hut. Jason looked down at the wooden tool he now held. It had a sturdy wooden shaft with twine bound around its base for grip. At the tip of the spear was a hunting knife. It had been tied tightly onto the end with rope, completing a formidable hunting spear.

Admiring the tool, Jason thought of his current situation. *Well, what do I have to lose? I'll see what this man is all about. What the hell.* Exiting the hut, Jason chased after Charging Bear. "Nice spear you made here. I like it."

"You will need it for where we are going." Charging Bear spoke as he trekked down the shoreline.

"And where are we going?"

"Hunting."

Hours passed with Jason and Charging Bear advancing through the forest. They had been stalking an elk for the past half hour, its tracks zigzagging through the woods. Fresh droppings left by the creature signaled it was not far away. Not much conversation was had between the two men.

Being experienced hunters, both kept their talking to a minimum, keeping their senses alert. Jason had never hunted with a spear before. He wasn't sure how he would fare once he encountered his prey. Yet he remained confident in his ability to make the right decision. Hunting, after all, was his passion.

Charging Bear raised his hand to signal Jason to halt and slowly lowered himself to one knee. They stopped in a part of the forest with wide-spaced trees. Dead brown pine needles covered the forest floor in areas not concealed by snow. Charging Bear pointed in the distance and grasped his spear with both hands.

Jason could see what Charging Bear had spotted far through the trees. A large elk was grazing alone in a bushy area. Tan, with a dark brown head, the elk was crowned with a twelve-point antler. The animal would provide more than enough meat for the two of them. In different circumstances, it would have made a great wall hanging. *Beautiful creature.*

Charging Bear signaled to Jason to stay put as he retraced his steps backward. Once far away, he began to stalk widely around the area to get behind the elk. The men spoke no words between them. The silent maneuvers and hand signal communication reminded Jason of his time in the military, where he had to use similar skills. *A tale as old as time, I guess.*

Jason had an idea of what the man was doing. Charging Bear was preparing to conduct a hunting strategy often used by two hunters. He would drive the elk out and chase him in the direction of Jason, and Jason would be the one to bring the animal down.

Good thinking, old man. Jason clutched his spear tightly and waited behind the tree. Minutes went by that felt like hours. All he could do was admire the elk from a distance as he waited for Charging Bear. There was something peaceful about seeing the animal conduct itself in the wild. All it seemed to care about at that moment was eating and staring off into the woods. *It's in the moment. Nothing else matters to it except for the present moment.* Jason was reminded of what Charging Bear told him about being mindful. About being in the present. *It seems so peaceful.*

The elk stopped eating. It turned its head behind it, standing still like a statue. *It heard him.* Charging Bear sprinted toward the elk, raising his spear above his head. A mighty scream broke through the forest. The elk, terrified, flew in Jason's direction. Charging Bear had driven the elk toward him, just as Jason thought.

OK, here we go! Jason tightened his grip on the spear, waiting for the timing to be correct. Once the elk was close, he would jump out from behind the tree. Grunting and panicked, the elk was only concerned with what was chasing him. Petrified, it ran straight toward Jason's tree. *Now!*

Jason leaped out from behind the tree with his spear pointed toward the animal. He let out a cry and thrust the spear into the elk's chest. The force of the elk's run violently knocked Jason to the ground. The elk flipped over Jason with a thud and clumsily tried to get back to its feet. Having the wind knocked out of him, Jason groaned on the forest floor as he strained to get back to his feet.

The elk made it to its feet and began running away. *No!* Jason then felt a spear whip past the top of his head and watched as it penetrated the elk's heart. The elk ran a few more steps and fell. Running, Charging Bear stopped, took a knee beside Jason, and placed a hand on his shoulder. "You are supposed to hunt the elk, Jason. Not fight it." Charging Bear smiled and moved toward the downed elk, leaving Jason to catch his breath. *Well, no shit, thanks.*

The two spent the rest of the day gutting and quartering their prey and making many trips to the hut. Dragging the remnants of the elk back to their camp was exhausting. Having strung up the meat to dry, the two men, drained from the day's events, sat down at the open fire by the river's edge.

It was nightfall, and a thousand stars painted the open sky. Elk meat roasted on the fire, emitting an aroma that had Jason salivating. Filling their stomachs, the two men ate in silence. Jason began to cherish every bite of the juicy meat. Starved, he felt like wolfing down the entire meal as fast as he could. Following Charging Bear's advice, Jason focused on each bite, chew, and swallow. He concentrated on being mindful of each sensation. The way the juices seeped from the meat, how tender the texture was, and how grateful it made him. *Who is this guy?*

The hunt made Jason forget the events from the days before. He felt a sense of normalcy in this part of the woods. Although it was anything but normal.

"You have a fighting spirit, Jason." Charging Bear broke their silence as he swallowed a mouthful of food. "Have you always been a fighter?"

"I've been getting into fights since I was a young kid." Jason unconsciously rubbed the left side of his face. A reminder of what scars fighting could bring. "Certain things brought that side of me out during childhood."

"You are experienced. But good fighters learn how to adapt to their enemy. They learn to adapt to what they are fighting. Sometimes they need to adjust their methods and tactics to what they are facing." Charging Bear's painted red face grew stern in the fire's glow. "You must adapt to your troubles, Jason. You are losing your fight."

Up in the sky, the northern lights danced below the stars. The shimmering lime-green and purple rays flowed like a majestic river above. Casting its light down below, it reflected its magnificence off the snow. Admiring the view, Jason paused and thought how much his dad would have liked to see it. *I wish you were here with me. I miss you.*

"Did your father teach you about fighting?" Charging Bear asked coincidentally, causing Jason to study his eyes.

"He did. He taught me lots of things." Jason gazed into the fire and watched its red-hot coals glow under the burning logs. "I miss him. I wish he were here with me now. He would have loved this." Jason's heart weighed heavily. *I'm sorry, Dad.*

"He is here with you." Charging Bear's comment caused Jason to pause and make eye contact. The firelight lit up his face in an orange hue; the red paint glowed on the bottom half of his face. He looked wise beyond his years, with a feather in his dark black and gray hair. It was as if this strange man had experienced hundreds of years on this earth. As if he knew secrets about this world no one else knew. *Who is this man ...*

"A father's influence never leaves his son." Charging Bear pointed at Jason's chest. "A part of him lives on within you." Pointing to the sky, he continued, "It is said those lights above are spirits of the animals we have hunted. Even in death, they remain in our lives." Charging Bear leaned toward the fire.

"The spirit of your father is here too. We are blessed with this beauty and should remind ourselves of what the great spirit has provided us. To show gratitude toward the good things in our lives. Nature, family, and peace."

A massive, bloodcurdling screech broke the silence. It roared in the distance across the river through the pitch-black wilderness. The dark trees shook across the riverbank, and wolves began to howl. *That sound!* Panicked, Jason grabbed his spear and stood up, awaiting what might come. *The Scorpion? The wolves? The Taliban?*

"That's the same sound the Scorpion made! It's coming! Grab your spear!" Unfazed by the dreaded noise, Charging Bear focused his gaze on the fire.

"What are you doing? Arm yourself! Grab your fucking spear!" The creature wailed in the distance. En masse, ravens began to fly across the river. Like a living black cloud, they landed on tree branches above them. "Charging Bear! It's coming! Get up!"

Closing his eyes, Charging Bear motioned for Jason to sit down. "Do not be afraid. Those demons cannot cross this river." Grasping his spear, Jason ignored him and awaited the attack, knees bent and scared, with a racing heart.

"So long as I am here, they will not come close." The creature's screams faded into the distance, moving upstream along the tree line. The dark trees swayed, providing a glimpse of the beast's path. *It's huge.* Perched on their branches, the ravens peered down at the two men below.

"The hell are you talking about?" Jason took a knee, still maintaining a watchful eye on the forest across the river. "Are they afraid of you or something?"

"Demons are limited in their power and influence. They can only be what you give them the power to be." Charging Bear grasped a handful of sand and let it slip through his fingers. "My presence frightens them. And if you open your mind and heart, eventually, yours will too." Charging Bear pointed to the ravens above. "Do you see those ravens?"

"Yes," Jason quickly looked and brought his attention back to the river, fearful of what might come from the other side.

"It is believed that the raven stole light and brought it to the earth. They symbolize helping people and shaping the world. My people have many stories about the raven. He represents rebirth, recovery, renewal, and healing. He signifies moving through transitions by casting light into darkness."

Jason paused and looked at the ravens above. They stood on the branches, stoic in their posture, gazing down at the two men. "You are lucky to have a raven watch you from above. I hope it brings light into your darkness."

Jason sat down, pushing his hair back as he addressed Charging Bear. "I think I'll need more than just a raven to light my darkness and fight my demons." Charging Bear's words were beginning to make Jason question his presumptions, but he could not shake his cynical instinct of questioning the validity of it all. *You have no idea, old man.*

"This is true, Jason. You will need much more than the raven. Every man goes through transitions, and it is time for you to go through one as well."

Chapter 14

We are twice armed if we fight with faith.
—Plato

Plattsmouth, Nebraska
Spring 1994

In the spring of 1994, Jason was a youthful twelve-year-old starting to find his way through the challenges of growing up. Mostly, he was a quiet kid who was subdued and focused on his schoolwork. Jason had friends in his class and peers who were not so friendly toward him. Skinny and quiet, he was an easy target for those wishing to wield negativity. He became a target of the cruelties that juveniles often commit while still youthfully ignorant.

For his age, Jason was very composed in these situations. He controlled his emotions when he felt angry and brushed off any insults with a thick skin. Jason managed to not let the other kids see how their words and actions affected him. He ignored their insults and practical jokes. Jason's ability to control his emotions became like a shield he held in front of him. He honed this skill throughout his youth, increasing his capacity to persist through hard times.

Growing up without a mother hardened him. He was never exposed to his mother's love, the type of love that can soften men's hearts. He cried tears for her at night when he felt lonely, which he often did. Jason sometimes wondered what his life would be like if his mom were still alive. Would he see his mom and dad hug each other in the kitchen? Would he get random kisses on the cheek from her? What kind of adventures would they go on together as a family? Unfortunately, fate forbade him from knowing those answers when cancer took her after he was born.

Jason relied intensely on his father; he was the only role model he knew. His father devoted himself to teaching Jason and ensuring he was raised in a way his mother would have been proud of. He took as much time off work as possible to spend with his son. They would play catch in the backyard, catch up on homework, play board games, and wrestle. His father tried to take on the burdens of a mom, a dad, and a friend all at once.

Years later, Jason greatly appreciated what his father had done for him in those influential years of his life. Holidays were not that eventful in their home. He didn't understand some kids' hype for Christmas, Thanksgiving, or Easter. For Jason, Thanksgiving dinner was just a typical dinner with his dad, except it involved a nice homecooked turkey they hunted. The large family gatherings were something Jason could not relate to, as the only family he had was his dad.

Springtime in Plattsmouth Elementary brought about hundreds of excited kids during recess. Having persevered through the cold winter, they were able to play with more than just snow. Seeing the basketball courts filled, the soccer fields bustling, and children playing catch in the yard brought the nice feeling of knowing that winter had broken. Summer was on its way. The potential to be filled with friends and adventures yet unknown hung in the air.

With a smile, Jason walked across the schoolyard pavement toward a group of friends standing by the fenced perimeter. Jason wondered what kind of games they would play today. "Hey!" Jason raised his hand and called out to his friends.

Smack!

A blow to his head made Jason fall to the ground as the force of a basketball escaping from the court made contact. Rubbing the left side of his face, Jason stood up, embarrassed but no worse for wear. Children laughed from all directions as a larger boy strolled over to Jason to retrieve the ball.

"You shouldn't catch things with your face, loser," Tommy White said, laughing. He was one of the regulars who would choose Jason as a target for their insults. Larger than other kids his age, he often used his size to intimidate.

"Yeah, thanks," Jason replied sarcastically as he ambled off to his group of friends. Reaching them, they all had their eyes on Jason. His friends were quick to try and cheer Jason up.

"Ignore that jerk, Jason," his friend David quipped as the others voiced their agreement.

"I know. I'm getting tired of him. Tommy and his buddies are always doing something like this to me." Jason glared at the boys playing basketball. "I bet he's not as tough as he acts, though."

"Why don't you ever stick up for yourself?" Leah, the petite brunette girl, asked. "You can't let him keep doing stuff like this."

"I can take it. I've got thick skin, and Tommy's insults are nothing I haven't heard before." This was quite true; Jason was often on the receiving end of insults. Mainly insults from his negative inner voice that criticized everything he did. Being called a loser didn't affect him because Jason had called himself that many times, along with being weak, skinny, and pathetic. There was no shortage of words he used to describe his shortcomings. Jason was very hard on himself. During his life, this negative inner voice grew louder and louder.

It was not until Jason joined the military that the voice would become muted. The army ended up giving Jason the confidence he needed with the respect and friendship of his fellow soldiers. His father's teachings and the military became the core foundation of his conviction. Never had he felt so sure of himself and his abilities. It was not until his tragic return from Afghanistan that this negative voice returned. It came back more vociferous and more potent than ever before.

His father taught Jason to know when to fight and when to walk away. When faced with making that decision as a child, Jason always chose to walk away. The thought of fighting scared him. He questioned his ability to fight, and his self-doubting thoughts interfered with his confidence. His dad was not aware of Jason's confidence issues. Although they were close, Jason kept his feelings near his heart. He kept them guarded, wary of opening vulnerabilities and showing weakness.

"Dad, have you ever been in a fight?" Jason asked at the dinner table, the two of them eating leftover pasta.

"Yes, son, I've been in a few. Why?"

"Just wondering." Jason buried his eyes into his meal.

"I once got into a fight in school because I was tired of a kid bullying people. There was a jerk named John who would constantly pick on other kids for their looks and other things. One day I had enough and confronted him. We fought, and I got suspended, but he stopped behaving like he did."

"Were you scared?"

"Well, of course. Getting hit in the face isn't fun. I was scared of getting hurt and getting in trouble, but I felt in my heart that it was something I needed to do. I believed in myself."

"Oh, OK ..."

"Jason, if something or someone is bothering you, you can always tell me. But my advice for you would be to avoid fighting at all costs. It should only be a last resort. Sometimes, however, it is necessary." His father put his fork down and continued. "You need to understand something, though."

"What's that?" Jason paused, curiously looking up.

"If you ever get into a fight, you need to believe in yourself. You need to have faith in your ability to win and persevere. If you don't believe in yourself, you've already lost your battle." His father interlocked his hands together, leaning in toward Jason. "Remember that, Jason. Always believe in yourself. Never quit and never stop fighting. Not until you know you've won the battle." It was advice Jason put a lot of thought into.

Jason's confidence issues in this matter would be tested in the spring of 1994. He would be forced to decide on his way home from school—a decision that would have him choose between acting or doing nothing.

In late spring, the kids were let out of school for the day; they scattered into the wind to make their way home in hordes of various groups. They traveled home on buses and caught rides. They got picked up by their parents or walked like Jason every day. It was a short walk home through the neighborhood. For most of his commute, Jason stayed on the sidewalk. He spent his time admiring the dogs in people's yards that he would pass along the way. Today, however, things took a turn from the everyday routine.

While walking home, his attention was grabbed by a pack of kids on the other side of the street. Loud, obnoxious laughter erupted as the group threw a bag around in the air. It wasn't until he got closer that he could see what was happening. On the other side of the street, his friend Leah was in the middle of four boys. They appeared to have stolen her backpack and refused to return it. They tossed the bag back and forth as she pleaded with them to stop. Jason could hear the frustration and helplessness in her voice. *Assholes.*

Jason felt a wave of outrage boil up inside of him. He was content with being the target of their harassment; he could deal with it. But when he saw it happen to somebody else, someone he cared about, it sparked something in him that could not be contained. Jason's heart began pounding as a million thoughts raced through his mind.

Could you do something about it?
They'll kick your ass; you're too skinny …
Think about how she feels right now!
You're pathetic; you can't fight …
Are you just going to walk away and leave her?
Don't be a coward.
Believe in yourself …
Always believe in yourself.
Do something!

On one side of the road, he was safe. On the other, fear, danger, and pain awaited him. Jason had to resolve what to do. Cross the street? Or stay where he was? Remembering his father's words was the incentive Jason needed. His dad's dinner-table advice acted like a force, helping guide him to the other side of the road.

Jason began crossing the road. While walking, Jason was completely aware of the consequences of his decision. He knew that he would be faced with a brutal confrontation. *There's no going back now.* Jason armed himself with his father's words. *Believe in yourself.*

"Hey, dickheads! Leave her alone! Shouldn't you guys be pulling wings off flies or something?" Jason shouted out at the group, his heart thumping like a racehorse.

"Jason? You don't have to." Leah was cut off from speaking as the backpack was thrown into her chest by Tommy White. "Ow!" She fell to the ground.

"Look who it is. What are you going to do, Jason? Run to your mom? Oh … that's right, I forgot." Tommy now stood, staring at Jason, along with the other three boys. Leah collected herself and made her way to Jason.

"You're a real asshole; you know that, Tommy?" Leah spoke up. Jason was still frozen in anger and apprehension. He stood there, never breaking eye contact with Tommy. *I want to hurt you so bad.*

"How do you hang around that loser? He barely talks!" Tommy laughed.

"Well, I'm talking now, and I suggest you back the fuck up." Jason's face became flushed as his blood began pumping with adrenaline.

"Do something about it, bitch!" Tommy stood with his arms wide open, inviting Jason to a fight. The other boys behind began tossing insults and taunting Jason, provoking him to fight.

The rage boiled over. Jason sprinted toward Tommy and tackled him to the ground, unable to control his fury. Cheers and yelling could be heard from all around. The two of them struggled on the sidewalk as any child within earshot came rushing to see the commotion.

"Fuck you!" Jason screamed as he mounted Tommy and began raining punches down on him. The feeling of his fists connecting with Tommy's face brought about great pleasure. *I'm winning! I'm actually winning!*

Tommy reached up and hugged Jason down toward him. He rolled over until it was Jason now being mounted. Punches hammered down on top of him, repeatedly hitting his face and chest. All Jason could do was cover his head and try to prevent the blows from connecting. Jason felt a crunch as a punch smashed through his defense and broke his nose.

Blood began streaming down his face, and Jason started to panic. *My nose! I'm stuck!* Shifting onto his belly in desperation, he tried to crawl out underneath Tommy. In vain, he scraped his knees and elbows to escape, but he wasn't strong enough to break free. Tommy's arms wrapped around his neck, choking Jason as he was pulled backward. Jason was now facing the sky with Tommy attached to his back in a chokehold. *I can't breathe! I can't breathe!*

He felt like his head was going to pop from the pressure. Unable to breathe, he saw nothing but the blue sky above him and some kids standing in a circle. Time seemed to slow down for Jason as every sensation and vision heightened. He saw Leah standing with her hands on her mouth in horror. He saw a mass of kids standing wide-eyed, watching the events occur. He glimpsed an adult from across the road racing toward them. A grinning boy was standing over them, wearing a black hoodie with an image of a scorpion.

Jason flung his hand over his head and poked Tommy in the eye. Screaming in pain, Tommy released his grip as Jason rolled onto his knees, gasping for air. Both boys were on their knees, Tommy holding his eye in distress and Jason his throat. Blood flowed out of Jason's nose as he reached his feet.

Jason wiped his bloodied nose with the back of his hand, causing a bright red smear to drape across the lower half of his face. The blood made him appear like a wild animal, like a bear about to charge at his prey.

With an extensive wind-up, Jason kicked Tommy in the face, causing him to fall back to the ground on his back. Standing over him, Tommy held his face, crying in pain. Jason had won the fight.

"You shouldn't catch things with your face, loser!" It was a satisfying thing to say, using Tommy's words against him.

An adult eventually broke up the commotion and notified the school of what had occurred. Word of what had happened traveled throughout the school. Officials notified the families of those involved, issuing discipline for both kids. Jason was picked up by his father and brought home.

"What were you thinking?" his father asked as Jason sat at the table, holding an ice pack to his face. Dried blood smeared the lower half of his face.

"He was picking on her! He was being an asshole!" Jason's face looked like a collage of injuries. With two black eyes and a broken nose, it looked like he'd lost the fight rather than won.

"I told you to avoid fighting at all costs. You shouldn't have done that …" Jason's father stood at the other end of the table, arms crossed with concern and disappointment.

"You also said that you got into a fight to stick up for someone when you were a kid! You told me to believe in myself! You said you felt in your heart like it was something you needed to do! I felt this was something I needed to do in my heart! He made fun of me for mom being dead!" Jason was yelling now, angry and bewildered as to why his father was lecturing him about this.

"Listen, Jason. I understand. I can only imagine what you must have been feeling, and I would probably have done the same … I don't want you getting into fights again. I don't want you getting hurt and in trouble because of some jerks at school. I love you, son. You're my boy, and I don't want to see you hurt." Jason stared down at the table, his eyes watering with tears.

"But, listen. I'm proud of you, son. I'm proud of how you stuck up for your friend and yourself. The fact that it took one of your friends to be in danger for you to act shows how big your heart is. You have a good moral backbone, Jason. You should be proud of yourself. Your mom would be proud to see how her son stood up to those devils."

Jason's heart filled with comfort, and his shoulders lightened. That night, the two of them went to a restaurant and ordered a large pepperoni pizza, talking the night away. Jason would never forget the time he spent with his father that day. It was a special moment that was born out of troubling times.

Chapter 15

The mind creates the abyss, the heart crosses it.
—Nisargadatta Maharaj

The River's Edge
Present Day

A month had gone by since Jason was rescued from the clutches of death in the icy river. Since then, Jason had camped out on the river's edge with Charging Bear, a mysterious, spiritual Native American whom Jason had grown fond of.

Under the open sky, they spent their days hunting, fishing, creating shelter, and making tools. Living within nature and learning from Charging Bear gave Jason a feeling of peace—a peace that he had desired for a long time. He first came to Alaska looking for that peace, hoping to find it alone and in the vast outdoors. He'd made that decision in desperation—a last endeavor to persist in living.

All he found in Alaska was anguish and despondency. He had been besieged by the demons that plagued his mind. They pursued him everywhere; no matter how hard he tried to run or hide, they would still be with him. It wasn't until he met Charging Bear that he began to feel unburdened by the overbearing harassment of his demons.

According to Charging Bear, the river they camped at acted like a barrier, a border that Jason's demons could not cross. They frequently heard the demons' frustrated howls and screams from the other side. But no matter how loud they grew, they never crossed. Jason felt safe with Charging Bear. He could take advantage of his life while feeling free from the misery that tortured him. It was something he hadn't been able to do for many years.

Charging Bear spent these days teaching Jason the importance of mindfulness. Of blocking off negative thoughts by treasuring the moment at hand. Whether it was the smell of fresh air or snow crunching underfoot, all moments were to be cherished. They spoke for many nights, with Jason opening up more about himself. Charging Bear guarded his history closely, never revealing too much about himself no matter how persistent Jason was in his questions.

The camp they settled in had grown to two huts, one for each man. There were more tanning racks for the animals they skinned and a collection of crafted hunting tools. Charging Bear helped Jason hone his spear and hatchet-throwing skills. He guided him in his teachings and strengthened him mentally and physically.

Jason kept up with his assigned exercises while he had the time. He would sprint through the forest to strengthen his stamina, jumping over fallen trees and bounding over bushes. He would lift logs and rocks and do push-ups and sit-ups at the river's edge. He felt like he was training for war again.

Charging Bear continually emphasized the importance of maintaining a healthy fitness level. "You must have a strong body to complete a strong mind." That was what he would say. The more consistent Jason was in being physically active, the more hardened he felt in his mind. *I can almost feel the difference in my head.*

Charging Bear walked up to Jason at the river's edge, interrupting him as he did push-ups. Jason was in fantastic shape. He pumped off several push-ups with his hands positioned in the water, his bearded chin striking the water with each repetition. The extra fat he'd had on his body, caused by poor diet and drinking, had withered away.

Noticing Charging Bear, Jason stood, wearing only his tanned animal skin pants. His abdomen and chest had become defined and toned, and he looked healthy, strong, and alive. Being in the woods for an extended period had allowed Jason to grow a thick black beard, accented by hints of gray. His dark black hair had grown lengthy. He slicked it back while rising to meet his friend.

"Tonight, you will embark on a journey. You must save your strength. Drink water and eat food." Charging Bear stood in his usual outfit, the bottom half of his face painted red.

"OK. Sure thing, Cee Bear. What is it this time? Another hunt? Fishing? A nice walk in the woods?" Jason stretched his arms behind his head, smiling. Something he had not done in quite some time.

"No, my son. This will be a journey that cannot be described in words. But it will be one with profound meaning." Charging Bear moved past Jason and began walking into the woods. "Set a fire at sundown. I will meet you then."

"Profound meaning? Wait! What does that mean?" His question was not answered. Charging Bear disappeared into the forest, leaving Jason to stew in his curiosity. *This guy and his cliffhangers.*

Hours passed with Jason anticipating what Charging Bear was referring to. He could not decipher what he meant by a journey with profound meaning. *One that could not be described with words? What does that mean?* He ate fish and elk for his evening meal and drank as much water as possible. The sun began to dip behind the horizon, casting a beautiful pink sky cut with thin white clouds. Jason had started to notice the beauty in it all, more than he had done before.

As directed, Jason set up the fire and waited for Charging Bear. He sat cross-legged and gazed into the fire. Alone, he reflected on his journey so far and the events that had brought him here. He began to reflect back on his childhood. His thoughts drifted to the people in his past. Like a snowball, the memories came. His dad, his school friends, Brad, Sergeant Bass, Rodriguez, Tommy White, and his dad again.

His dad on the floor, alone, in agony. Afghanistan, the three fighters he killed in the ditch, the little girl, her dead mother, body parts, blood, screams, anger, horror. The wolves, the Scorpion, the Taliban, the Taliban changing to himself. He was covered in blood. His demon. He was the demon. His demon's face, his own face, stared back at him. *Come to me.*

Jason shook his head and took a deep breath. Rubbing the left side of his face, he grabbed a waterskin and took a big drink. A terrifying roar came from across the river. Wolves began to howl, and a rageful scream cracked through the air. The trees across the river shook as if something was caged behind them. *You cannot escape your demons ...* Jason remembered Charging Bear's words, a constant reminder of what was waiting for him on the other side.

"I see they have become unsettled." Charging Bear spoke as he appeared through the darkness. "They can sense fear. What were you thinking about?"

"I was just enjoying the sunset, but my mind drifted to the past, the bad parts." Jason eyed the other side of the river, fully aware his journey was only beginning.

"But they also fear their own weakness, Jason. You are their weakness, and as you become stronger, they will become more dangerous to you. It is their last attempt to win the battle of your mind. They will not stop. So you must be cautious."

"I see." Jason stared back down at the fire. After all his work with Charging Bear, there were still seeds of doubt about his abilities. Jason feared confronting his demons and what that would entail. He had almost died multiple times in his previous encounters with them and only imagined what threats awaited him if they were more dangerous. Even if Jason made it back to the cabin alive, he still had doubts about himself and whether he could carry on with life outside the wilderness. Would he revert to the same Jason who had almost ended his life in the apartment? *I don't want to go back.*

"I like staying here with you, Cee Bear. I like the life you live. I'm perfectly content not to cross that river ever again and stay here with you." Charging Bear ignored the nickname Jason had ended up giving him.

"Unfortunately, you cannot stay on this side of the river forever, Jason. It is not your time." Jason stared across the river toward the dark wilderness. "I have brought something for you."

Charging Bear placed a pot on the fire and filled it with water. From his tote bag, he removed a handful of different items. He threw some tree roots into the water, along with pine needles, berries, and a dozen wild mushrooms. He stirred the pot with his knife. The firelight painted his face; the lines on it were like the fingerprints of a long life.

"It is time for your journey, Jason. This is a journey that only you can go on. You may not find all the answers you seek, but you will find something." Charging Bear removed the pot from the fire. "The earth is connected with us. All things, all animals, all trees and insects. From the dirt to the sky, there are secrets that the earth keeps. The land can speak only to those who are willing to listen. Now, drink."

With hesitation, Jason followed Charging Bear's instructions. Analyzing the contents of the warm pot, he gently placed it to his lips and drank the concoction of bitter earth and liquid. The warmth flowed into his belly as Jason finished the entire serving. He put the empty pot back into the fire and wiped his lips. It was not the most tasteful thing he had consumed, but what it lacked in flavor, it made up for in its soothing heat. Jason and Charging Bear sat staring at each other in silence.

Charging Bear began to speak to Jason, but Jason had a hard time understanding what he was saying. Charging Bear's words were being spoken in his native language, but Jason's ability to interpret them had vanished. Confused and disjointed, Jason began to feel light-headed. *What's happening? What are you saying to me?*

A hand appeared in front of Jason's face. Looking up, he saw Charging Bear extending his arm toward him, signaling Jason to come with him. Jason's movements felt like they were in slow motion. Blurriness began to take hold of his sight as he reached out to hold Charging Bear's hand.

Charging Bear stood Jason up onto his feet, helping him keep his balance. The two strolled toward the hut; Jason's entire body vibrated. He squeezed Charging Bear's hand tightly as fear began to creep in. *I feel so strange. What is happening to me? What did you give me?*

Charging Bear laid Jason onto the animal skin bed and knelt beside him. Jason held on to his hand for dear life, afraid to let go. Charging Bear spoke to him in words he could not understand. *What? What are you saying?* Loud drums began to beat from somewhere within Jason's mind. *Those drums, I remember them. I'm scared!*

The vibrations within Jason grew more assertive. Although near his face, Charging Bear appeared to sink backward away from him. The drums beat faster and faster, growing louder with each percussion. Jason could see the stars through the hut's smoke hole. They grew brighter and brighter until they elongated like strings hanging from the sky and reached down toward Jason. *Wait! I'm not ready!*

Jason felt himself being ripped from the Earth and shot into the depths of the unknown.

Chapter 16

Whoever fights monsters should see to it that in the process, he does not become a monster. And if you gaze long enough into an abyss, the abyss will gaze back into you.
—Friedrich Nietzsche

Purgatory
Unknown

A kaleidoscope of colors encircled Jason's world. It was the most beautiful thing he had ever seen—glowing shades of green, blue, red, and yellow. Geometric shapes floated among the colors, morphing into different sizes and formations. The outline of a face grew within the colors. It enlarged itself until it took up a prominent center among the forms.

The face smiled at Jason. Its reassuring grin began warping into a grin, then a scowl. It grew horns from the top of its head and began to open its mouth in an intense expression of rage.

The kaleidoscope exploded. The face, colors, and shapes scattered into the darkness; the scowling head was no longer visible. A million stars painted the night. Galaxies were visible and swirled like time was passing at light speed. The stars danced and flew like a universal blizzard. Jason felt one with everything. Everything that ever was and ever would be on this planet and elsewhere. Jason felt like he was the embodiment of life. An all-encompassing feeling of oneness and peace radiated from the universe.

The stars smashed together and merged until they formed two recognizable constellations. Orion and Scorpio. More stars emerged from the darkness until a galactic outline was made. The stars showed the entire image of the Greek hunter Orion and the Scorpion that the gods had sent to defeat him, Scorpio.

The two figures advanced toward each other, vaulting to attack their sworn enemy. The stars crashed together and swirled around in chaos, mixing until the image of the celestial foes was obliterated. The stars continued to spin until they all combined into one tiny light.

Jason was surrounded by darkness and could only focus on the one source of light, like a light at the end of a tunnel. It was blinding white and came with a feeling of euphoria as he stared into it. The once-small light grew vaster as it floated toward Jason. He felt like he was moving toward the light and into God's open arms. An incredible peace blanketed his soul.

The growing light began to emit the sound of a rumble. The rumble grew louder and louder. Jason had heard this sound before. Mesmerized by the glow, it began to blur. It formed into a semirecognizable form, but Jason couldn't decipher what it was. The feeling of peace he had within him withered away.

Horrified, Jason was immobile and fixated on the approaching object. The blurriness gave way to a clear image of what was coming—a white Toyota Corolla being driven by a dark figure. Panicked screams and gunfire reverberated through the darkness. The engine roared like a lion, speeding toward him. *NO!*

BOOM!

The car bomb exploded in front of Jason, destroying the universe. He felt himself falling into infinity, tumbling through the dark unknown. Terror and panic gripped him. Jason tried to reach for anything as he fell, but there was only darkness. He could feel the increase in speed as he plummeted downward.

The fall was stopped abruptly when he smashed into a wooden floor. Jason panted heavily, lying face-first in a room, only able to see a wall and doorway in front of him. He tried to get up but could not move, stuck as if his brain and body were disconnected. He could give it no commands.

Hyperventilating, Jason moved his eyes around the room. He could only see the faded gray walls, a white door, and the wooden floor below him. *I'm at my dad's house …* Jason was mortified. He lay in the same spot his dad had when he collapsed. He was incapable of moving and all alone. Scared, helpless, and panicked, Jason tried to scream but could not open his mouth.

Dad! I'm sorry! I'm sorry! Jason's soul felt frail as he was placed into the same situation that had befallen his father.

Slowly the white door opened. A burst of white light blasted out of the entrance and filled the room. A dark silhouette stood within the entryway in contrast to the blinding light behind it. The figure stepped toward Jason, who remained incapacitated, face down on the floor. As it reached closer, it took the form of a woman. Jason's panic became subdued, and his breathing slowed. He lay there, eyes wide open, as this dark female figure came closer.

She stood in front of the immobile Jason and knelt, making eye contact with him. An overwhelming sensation of love reassured Jason's soul. Tears welled up in his eyes, and he tried to reach toward this woman with all his might. Her face was now becoming clear. The woman's beautiful white face stared at Jason with a loving smile and the calmest regard. *Mom?* She placed her hand on Jason's head and kissed him on the forehead. She was the most beautiful being Jason had ever laid eyes on. *Mom! I love you!* Jason closed his eyes and drank in this feeling of absolute love and acceptance. A feeling that could only be felt through a mother's love. *I love you!*

Jason opened his eyes to find he was no longer on the floor. His mother was gone, and he was now lying in the pale brown sand of a desert. The light-colored dust and rocks were scattered for miles with nobody around except himself.

Jason stood, now able to control his body. There was a feeling of loneliness as he looked around. It was just him in this vast arid unknown. He felt directionless and lost. He wiped the tears from his eyes and shielded them from the blistering hot sun above, which was now ten times its normal size. It was a massive ball of fire that covered half of the sky, blazing its heat down upon the earth.

The ground began to rumble as the earth rose on two sides beside him. Two giant mountains formed, reaching the heavens and leading into the distance. Jason stood between the corridor that had now assembled around him. The sand plastered the ground like a river of tanned dust. In the distance, he saw something rising out of the sand from the other end of the corridor, massive in its size.

Jason had an overwhelming sense of trepidation. The sand fell off the gigantic black Scorpion that rose from the sand. Its deadly features were revealed. There was no escape. The mountains were too steep on either side and reached infinity in their length. The Scorpion dashed toward Jason, its six legs clacking with each step. Jason wanted to run, to hide, to cry. He was frightened and frozen. *Brace yourself!* Weaponless, Jason widened his stance and held his fists up, knowing there was nowhere to run. It was all he could do. *Fight!*

The enormous Scorpion shrieked as its tail struck down on Jason. The strike detonated everything around him, creating a storm of sand and rock with hurricane-like force. Jason shielded his eyes from the onslaught of flying debris. He could no longer see the giant Scorpion in the zero-visibility storm. Pieces of white snowflakes began to mix with the sand in the air. Leaves and sticks also flew by. The storm's strength began to weaken and dissipate as the remnants floated softly to the ground. Jason was now standing in the middle of a forest.

It was daytime, and animals ran past. Elk, beavers, eagles, and deer all appeared as if there were hundreds of them. All were racing in every direction together. Jason felt the magnificence that nature emitted. Their actions and how they behaved seemed unnatural. Jason looked all around, interpreting their movements as hunters often did. He saw how many there were and how they acted. The sun shone down from the sky above, painting the forest with beautiful light. The sun's rays shone different colors as they penetrated the trees overhead. The forest was alive.

Jason spotted another small animal break through the bushes, approaching him toward his front. *My God.* The animal was no animal at all. A little girl was covered in dust and holding her stuffed bear. She stood staring at Jason with no emotion on her face. Jason's heart sank as a sense of despair filled his gut. *I'm sorry! I'm so sorry!*

Glancing around the forest, the little girl shouted out as if she were lost. "Moor? Moor?" She sauntered closer to Jason, looking around her, clutching her stuffed bear. "Moor? Moor?" There were no more animals; the magical colors of the sun's rays had become regular, everyday sunshine. "aMoor? aMoor?" Jason's eyes were fixated on the little girl as she stood before him, looking up. "Armoor? Armoor?" Her words were blending.

Making eye contact with Jason, the girl reached up to hand him her stuffed bear. Staring at the old, beaten-up stuffed bear, Jason was reminded of Charging Bear and everything that man had taught him. How protective he had been of him, shielding him from the brink of death. Jason reached down to receive the bear, her innocent face peeking up at him. As he grabbed the stuffed animal, she said one word to Jason without letting go. "Armor."

The sun smashed down into the forest. Sunlight blasted through the trees and faded away into darkness. The girl had disappeared, and Jason now stood alone in the dark forest. Confusion and anxiety arose once again within him.

He could hear drums beating in the distance through the trees ahead. *That sound.* Jason trekked forward toward the noise. Pushing through the dense forest, he ducked under branches and stepped over logs. Jason broke through the tree line and into an open field. An enormous bonfire had been lit in the open.

Jason stopped in the field before advancing toward the fire. The drums were deafening now. He could see many dark figures standing behind the fire, beating on what appeared to be drums made from animal skin. Louder and louder, their cadence filled the open field. Jason could feel a sense of danger radiating from this fire.

A lone figure stood in front of the blaze. The figure's silhouette cast a dark shape in front of the flames. It stood stoically, staring at the fire with its back to Jason. The man wore a helmet of a wolf's head and antlers; its pointed antlers reached up like insidious fingers. He looked like he was half-man, half-beast in the shadows. Jason clenched his fists. A feeling of peril spread within him.

The man turned around to face Jason in a standoff that felt like the entire universe observed. Jason knew who he was staring at. It was his demon. The man he battled in the forest. *You ...*

The demon raised his arms in the air, and the tree line around the field erupted into flames. There was a forest fire all around, encircling the area. The fire reached miles into the sky, and the heat was unbearable. Jason began sweating profusely but refused to take his eyes off this man.

The light from the forest fire now illuminated the horned demon. It was Jason. The top half of this demon-Jason's face was painted in blood, looking the opposite of Charging Bear's. The demon stood gazing with a look of rage on his face. "COME TO ME!"

He screamed at Jason, provoking him to walk toward the fire. "COME TO ME, ORION!" The drums were so loud now that they sounded like thunder. Tornadoes made of fire ripped through the forest behind the tree line. Lightning struck overhead again and again. The dark sky above flashed, illuminating clouds of death. Jason clenched his fists, concentrating on the most significant threat he had ever faced. Himself.

He abruptly felt the presence of people behind him on either side. These people stepped out of the inflamed tree line behind Jason and stood on either side. Next to him, Jason could see Sergeant Bass, Brad, and Rodriguez on his right. Turning to his left, he saw his dad, Charging Bear, and mom. None of them looked at Jason. They all kept a razor-sharp stare toward the demon in front.

Jason looked forward along with them. He felt he had the power and strength of all warriors who had ever lived. He stared down at his demon. "I'm ready" he whispered to himself. *Believe in yourself.*

Like a warrior, Jason dashed from the line and sprinted toward his demon. He screamed at the top of his lungs; adrenaline and determination fired through his body. His loved ones stood where they were, but Jason did not need them; he could feel them. The demon charged toward Jason with a spear in his hand, roaring. The two Jasons crashed into each other, creating a fireball brighter than a thousand suns. A blinding white light encompassed the universe. Jason could not feel anything. He could not sense anything. The blinding white light flickered and faded, turning to complete and absolute darkness.

Chapter 17

The real voyage of discovery consists not in seeking new landscapes, but in having new eyes.
—Marcel Proust

Anchorage, Alaska
Summer 2016

A bell rang through the cabin as the airline stewardess began speaking over the intercom. "Ladies and gentlemen, we are just about to make a landing at our final destination, Anchorage, Alaska. Please ensure your loose baggage is stored under your seat or in the overhead compartment above. All tables and chairs shall be upright, and all window shades will be open. We hope you enjoyed your flight with us. Thank you for choosing American Airlines."

Jason awoke, his neck sore from the cramped economy-class seat. Rubbing the left side of his face, he opened the window shade and peered out the airplane window.

The snow-capped mountains extended far and wide, reaching up from the earth as if trying to escape into the atmosphere. The dark green trees encircled the bottom of these enormous monuments, dissipating the higher they climbed. No life could reach the top. The vast wilderness surrounded the city of Anchorage below. A society built aside the frigid Bering Sea in the harshest of conditions.

This wasn't Jason's final destination. He had bought a remote cabin in an isolated part of interior Alaska, so secluded that only a float plane could reach it, but Jason was not planning on using a plane. He would travel there on foot. The cabin's owner had recently passed away, leaving the dilapidated wooden structure cheap and ripe for the taking.

It had been almost six months since Jason put his handgun underneath his chin. He had been at the end of his rope and could see no way out, no escape from his chaotic situation. Jason's unhinged emotional outbursts, paranoia, and crushing depression had made him feel like an outcast in his hometown. Before making the spontaneous decision to end his life by pulling the trigger, he spotted an old magazine. It featured the vast wilderness the state of Alaska had to offer. The picture of the pristine boreal forest promised a life of solitude and isolation. It was the only thing that prevented him from pulling the trigger.

The idea of fleeing Plattsmouth and living alone in the wilderness came to him as a final option. He could use his skills to live off the land, and he would not be exposed to the triggers that society dealt him. *And if I die out there, no big deal. I was going to kill myself anyway.* It seemed like the ideal last-ditch effort to keep on living. He would either find peace or death. He was okay with either one of them.

The plane landed and pulled into the terminal. The passengers disembarked, grabbed their belongings, and headed through the security checkpoints. Surrounded by strangers on their journeys, Jason felt alone among them. The only items he brought were his large Osprey pack and hunting rifle. It was packed with survival items and clothing. The gun had been secured lengthwise to the side of the bag. He planned to make a few stops along the way to pick up essentials like preserved foods and other necessities he would require.

Leaving the airport, Jason quickly hailed a cab to take him to the nearest hotel. Resting for one day seemed like the best option before he made his journey north. Considering the trek he had waiting for him, it might be a while until he had a mattress, shower, and other comforts.

Jason made the most of that night in his hotel. Figuring it would be quite a while until he slept in such luxurious conditions, Jason soaked in all they had to offer. Running himself a bath, he watched TV late into the night. Jason was on a mission, focusing his thoughts on the journey ahead. Concentrating on what he needed to do prevented him from getting sucked into his negative inner thoughts. Virulent reflections were always waiting in the shadows of his subconscious.

The future ahead was unknown and filled with unknown dangers. Jason could be killed or maimed, or succumb to the elements. The potential risk the Alaskan frontier brought and how he prepared for it gave Jason a sense of déjà vu. It made him feel like he was training for war again, not knowing what the future harbored.

Jason took his last morning shower before heading out. Soaking in the hot steam as he placed his hand against the wall, he let the warm water flow over his head. Jason inhaled the humid air and let out a sigh. He prayed that he was making the right decision. *I'm so scared.* He imagined the hot water dripping down his body like a baptism, cleansing his soul with the hope of a new beginning … or end. Jason moaned as his naked body received its last soothing shower, perhaps for months. The scars on his body were the contours of a physical map, a testament to all he had been through. None of those scars, though, were deeper or more profound than the ones he had in his mind. *I hope I'm doing the right thing.*

After leaving his hotel, he stopped at a few supply stores. With little money, Jason attempted to hitchhike north along the highway. He was forced to be as frugal as possible throughout his journey. He had been walking for some time with nobody stopping to give him a ride. *I'm in for a long walk if this keeps up.* The gravel crunched under his feet as he sauntered down the side of the road, lost in his thoughts, the cool Alaskan air blowing against his face.

He had walked for hours until, ultimately, a purple Jeep pulled over to the side of the road ahead. Jason strolled up to the driver's side window to witness a beautiful middle-aged woman. Wearing a black T-shirt and jeans, she sported a white baseball cap with her brunette ponytail sticking out the back. Jason was instantly attracted to her.

"Where are you heading, hon?" she asked while chewing gum. A black Molossian hound sat in the backseat scrutinizing Jason.

"I'm just looking to head north, ma'am," he said, pushing his hair back. *She's cute.*

"Well, I'm heading to Fairbanks if that's good enough for you. Throw your stuff in the back, sweetie. I'll give you a lift."

"Sure thing, ma'am. Thanks." Jason tossed his pack into the Jeep's trunk and jumped in the passenger seat. The black hound sniffed him and licked the left side of his face, causing Jason to kink his neck in its direction.

"Hey, big guy!" he said with a laugh. The dog stared intensely at Jason, evaluating the wounds on his face like he was studying his history, reading Jason like a book.

"Don't mind Trigger there. He doesn't do that to many people, so he must really like you." The woman put the Jeep into drive and pulled back onto the highway.

"I guess so." Jason wiped the drool off the left side of his face and gave the dog a pat on the head. *Not sure why'd you'd like me, but I'll take it.* "He's a beautiful dog."

"He sure is." The woman gave a smile. "My name is Artemis, yours?"

"Jason." He immediately felt an attraction to her. There was something about her presence that made him feel instantly comfortable.

"Well, nice to meet you, Jason. We've got a long drive ahead of us, so don't be afraid if you want to fall asleep. It looks like you've been walking for quite a while." The woman's voice was soft and kind; it alleviated Jason's usual suspicions of strangers. "You don't sound like you're from here. Where are you from?"

"Plattsmouth, Nebraska. It's my first time here."

"I could tell by your accent. If you don't mind me asking, how did you get those scars on your face?" Jason instinctually touched the left side of his face and remembered the car bomb.

"Wounds from when I was in Afghanistan." Jason felt uncomfortable and awkward, like he normally did when people asked him those questions.

"Oh, I'm so sorry." An awkward silence filled the car. This was something Jason was used to, however. He often made people uneasy when he brought up his past. It made it a difficult conversation to avoid, having it painted on his face for everyone to see. No one ever knew what to say to him or how to react, but he knew exactly what she would say next. *Thank you for your service.*

"Well, thank you for your service. That must have been very painful. I'm glad you're still here with us." The woman watched Jason with kind eyes.

"Yeah, me too. I guess. Thanks." Jason felt like a liar. He said he was happy to still be here, but truth be told, Jason wasn't sure if he was or not. *I wish I was with you guys,* he thought, remembering his lost friends.

"Well, what are your plans here in Alaska?" The woman drove, looking over to Jason each time she spoke.

"I bought a cabin up north. I plan on living there. Figured I'd get away from society for a bit, enjoy nature, live off the land, and do some hunting."

"Fancy yourself a hunter, eh?" Artemis smirked.

"Yeah, I've hunted most animals. Big game hunting, like moose, is my favorite. It's so satisfying to finally get your prey after a long day. So I'm looking forward to getting out there, catching that feeling again." Jason's mood was uplifted as he got caught up speaking about his passion, one of the only things he still felt excited about. He recalled the many times he had a successful hunt with his father.

"Well, it can be difficult out there. Hunting in Alaska brings its dangers with the terrain and the type of game you intend on hunting." The woman spoke with concern on her face. She could sense Jason was holding something back.

"I shouldn't have a problem," Jason spoke with arrogance and brushed off her uneasiness.

"Confident, eh? Be careful with that bravado. Have you ever gone bow hunting? That's my favorite." Jason looked over toward Artemis, assessing her.

"It's not my go-to. I usually use my rifle." Jason felt a strange feeling of butterflies in his stomach each time she made eye contact with him. A sensation he had not felt in many years.

"Ah, you see, you're not the finest hunter out there. You can always improve yourself. It would help if you learned bow hunting. That's how hunting was done back in the day, with bows and spears. It'll bring you a new challenge. We all need those in our life." The woman laughed.

"I've got enough challenges in my life … ."

"Do you have the right ones, though?" Artemis raised her eyebrow at Jason. "You never want to become stagnant, even in things you enjoy, as they can become stale. They'll lose the power they had over you and the joy they brought. Always try to add something new, a goal or a challenge. Something that you can accomplish and be proud of." It was an interesting suggestion that Jason had never put much thought into. He watched her as this beautiful woman stared at the road ahead. *She's lovely.*

"By the way, what kind of name is Artemis?" Jason was quick to change topics.

"That's probably a question I get asked as much as people ask you about those scars," she said with a laugh. "My parents were Greek, so they were into Greek mythology and that sort of thing. They were also avid hunters. So, they named me Artemis, after the goddess of the hunt, the wilderness, and wild animals. Imagine me growing up with that name. My middle name is Diana, so I also go by that if you want."

"Ah, I understand." Jason thought back to when Brad gave him the nickname Orion, bestowing it upon him after Jason used his grenade-loaded belt to end an attack by the Taliban. *Orion's belt* … "Naw, I like the name Artemis. I'll call you that."

The two spoke for a while until Jason fell asleep. He felt a growing connection with this stranger as they bonded through their conversation. She gave Jason some sound advice regarding the Alaskan terrain and seasonal weather.

The sun had dipped below the skyline as they approached Fairbanks. "Wake up, blue eyes. We're here." Jason shuffled in his seat and gazed at the approaching city lights. "Well, hon, where do you want to go from here?"

He was unsure exactly how he should leave. Jason only knew he needed to start northeast in the direction of the cabin. "You can drop me off here at the side of the road. I'll start walking from here."

"The side of the road? Now? This late? Nu-uh, honey, not happening." Artemis paused and analyzed Jason as he sat in the passenger seat, looking worn out and tired. "I'll tell you what. I've got a spare room at my place, and it's just north of the city. You can spend the night there and leave in the morning. It'll beat walking around this late at night."

Jason stared out toward the blackened tree line. He considered the difficulties he would have departing at night in unfamiliar terrain. "I would very much appreciate that, ma'am."

"OK, fine, but there's one rule. You have to stop calling me ma'am."

"Yes, ma'am, I mean Artemis … or Diana … ?" Jason sighed in embarrassment.

They arrived at her home, a tiny two-bedroom bungalow surrounded by birch trees. It was a peaceful little house tucked in amid the wooded countryside. Artemis cooked him a salmon and vegetable dinner and opened a wine bottle for the two of them. Jason felt drawn to her. They shared a common bond, and their conversations flowed just as quickly as the wine they drank.

"So, Jason. Do you have any family or close friends back home? What do they think about you taking off to the backwoods?" They were both seated close together on her gray felt couch.

"Nope. I'm alone. I've lost a few loved ones in my life, but I've learned to live with it." Jason shrugged his shoulders as if he were trying to downplay the trauma.

"Sorry to hear that." Artemis placed her hand on the headrest of the couch, almost wrapping it around Jason. "Well, I don't think it's good to be completely alone. I hope you'll be OK when you get to your cabin."

I will be. Because it can't get any worse than it already is. Jason thought of his disdain for the society he was leaving behind.

"I'll be fine. I'm a big boy." He chuckled as he had another sip of wine. "You know what's funny?"

"Your accent?" Artemis giggled.

"No," Jason replied, laughing. "You said your family was into Greek mythology, and that's why they named you Artemis. Well, my friends overseas gave me the nickname 'Orion,' after the mythical hunter. Like the constellation in the sky, Orion's belt."

"No way, that's so cool! I love that story! It's one of my favorites." She beamed with joy. "Well, you better be the best hunter on the face of the planet if you want to live up to that name!" Artemis chuckled as they continued their conversation.

Having someone act so caring toward him had Jason feeling strangely relaxed. The way Artemis spoke with her soft words and genuine consideration had Jason captivated by her. *God, she's beautiful. I'm gonna miss her.*

They continued to drink throughout the night, and eventually, their infatuation with each other turned into desire. They spent the night in her bed. The feeling of human contact was not something he had expected to feel upon his journey to the backwoods, but it was a welcome experience.

Her warm body was serene. Having Artemis's arms around him made Jason melt into her. The emotions he felt were foreign to him. Having been so used to pushing people away, he had inadvertently turned his back on love. *I wish I could stay here forever.* Artemis looked into his eyes as they lay in bed together.

"You seem sad." She caressed his face.

"I'm happier than I've been in a long time, Artemis."

"Are you running to something or away from something, Jason?"

He gazed into her beautiful face, just inches away from his. "I'm just looking for some peace and quiet. That's all." Artemis looked deep into his eyes, studying Jason as if she were reading his soul. She continued to caress Jason's scarred face until he fell asleep, the two of them entwined in her warm bed.

When morning broke, Jason could not remember the last time he had slept so peacefully. He awoke in the morning to the smell of bacon and eggs. Artemis had awoken early to prepare breakfast. He was sleeping so well that he barely noticed her get up. The sun broke through the front windows and lit the bungalow with a yellowish haze.

"Good morning, sunshine. How'd you sleep?" Artemis was flipping bacon on the stove, wearing nothing but shorts and a sports bra.

"I had a fantastic night. Thank you. It's going to make my trip to the cabin that much harder, though." Jason sat at the table, skeptical about the journey ahead of him.

"Well, hon, you know where I live." She smiled at him.

"I'll head out after this if you don't mind." Jason felt an oncoming sense of loss thinking about leaving this woman he had just met. He also had an impulse to go as quickly as possible, mitigating the risk of him growing closer to her. She was beginning to profoundly affect him, and he'd already lost enough people he cared about in his life. *I'd only cause her trouble anyway* …

"OK, I'll drive you a bit north from here, and you can be on your way. Just don't forget about me, Jason! Or I'll be the one hunting you down!" Artemis laughed, placed the food on the table, and the two had their last meal together.

They drove north for an hour until they were on a very secluded road surrounded by woods. The thick green trees reached the sky, creating a forest wall that spread for miles. The tree-lined wall gave off energy as if it had another world on the other side. The car stopped.

Jason turned to Artemis. "Thanks. You've been very kind. I won't forget you." Jason exited the truck and leaned into the window to kiss her.

Artemis placed her hand on the left side of his face. "Listen, Jason. I know you're searching for something. Or escaping something. I'm not sure what it is, but I want you to be careful out there. These woods are dangerous; it's another world out there …" Jason saw genuine concern in Artemis's eyes. "You may not find what you are seeking …"

"I'll be careful." Jason placed his hand on top of hers.

"I'm serious, honey. Many people who seek a new beginning have never finished with their past. I hope you find what you're looking for." Jason grabbed his pack, stepped back from the vehicle, and watched as she placed the Jeep into drive.

"Happy hunting, Orion!" Artemis made a U-turn and drove off down the dirt road waving her arm out the window as a last goodbye. Jason's heart grew heavy as the truck disappeared in the distance, amused that she called him Orion. He smiled as she disappeared.

Jason stood on the road alone. He was so close to his final destination. All that awaited him was a few days' trek through the woods. *Focus, Jason. She would have just caused you heartache. You don't need anybody. You just need to get away.*

Facing the tree line, Jason stepped into the forest and disappeared into the wilderness.

Chapter 18

A person often meets his destiny on the road he took to avoid it.
—Jean de La Fontaine

The River's Edge
Present Day

Jason awoke with the crisp morning air filling his nostrils. He felt like a different person, as if a burdensome weight had temporarily lifted off his shoulders. After his celestial experience, Jason supposed he knew a secret about life, fate, and the universe that no one else did. The tea Charging Bear gave him produced a vivid experience that rejuvenatingly impacted his soul. *What a rush. I've gotta tell Charging Bear.*

Rolling out of his furred bed, Jason threw on his animal skin clothing. His lungs could sense the sharp, fresh air with each inhalation of the chilly morning atmosphere—a sensation he had never noticed before, as if he was breathing for the first time.

A calm white mist floated above the river, giving the morning a beautiful yet ghostly vibe. All the trees were coated in glistening white snow as if painted with shining diamonds. *It's beautiful.* There was a heavenly brilliance to it all, laid forth as a testament to what beauty the world was capable of.

Jason admired the flowing river and brought his attention to the other side. His chest tightened as he thought back to his experience. It was something he had never encountered before. The visions that came to him brought about a mix of emotions. Fear, love, happiness, and sadness mixed into one undefinable sensation.

While Jason immersed himself in the world before him, he thought of his mom and dad. He thought about the demon who spoke to him, the same one that Jason believed was waiting for him on the other side of the river. He remembered the confrontation, the forest fire … and those who were by his side during the battle.

"Good morning, Jason!" Charging Bear called out as he sat by his hut, whittling a piece of wood. "How do you feel?" Jason hurried over to the elder Native American, eager to speak with him about his visions.

"Charging Bear! It was unreal. It was the most beautiful yet horrifying thing I've ever experienced. I've never felt anything like that before!" He spoke at rapid speed, his excitement getting the best of him. "I feel so different." Jason was having a hard time describing how he felt. The experience was like a dream or a memory he had trouble recollecting, reminiscent of the type of dream that partially dissipates, with the remnants leaving an impact in your gut that you carry around all day.

"Well, you are not so different. You are the same person you were yesterday and the same person you will be tomorrow. You are the same as you have always been." Charging Bear continued to sculpt the thick stick, the knife sending pieces of curled timber to the ground.

Jason sat on a log and leaned forward earnestly, placing his elbows on his knees. "You wouldn't believe what I saw. Or where I was! There was a forest fire. I saw my mom! I saw my dad! And …" He hesitated.

"I saw him …" Jason looked across to the other side of the river.

"What you have seen, Jason, is for your interpretation only." Charging Bear interrupted him abruptly. "Do not try to understand it with a common language; you must feel it." Charging Bear didn't look up while speaking, focusing on the object in his hand.

"I mean, I get it. I'm not sure I can accurately describe it anyways." Jason rubbed the left side of his face. "The words I have for it escape me. Like … like … gold dust slipping through my fingers." Jason stared at his calloused hands, weathered from years of manual labor.

The sound of a wolf howling in the distance brought his attention to the other side of the snow-covered river. Jason's heart sank as a dreaded feeling overcame him. *I'm not dreaming anymore* … The anxiety punched him in the gut with what awaited him in the future. The darkness on the other side of the river was looming over him.

"It's waiting for me, isn't it?"

"Indeed it is."

"I'm still scared, Charging Bear. I don't think that drink you gave me fixed that. I don't know if I'm brave enough to cross back over that river …"

I'm not sure I even want to …

"That is good … you should be scared." Charging Bear placed the object on the ground. "Being scared is the only time someone can be brave, Jason. That drink was not meant to fix your problems or cure your mind. It was a message from the universe, the great spirit, and mother earth. Only you can understand its importance and meaning." Charging Bear stood. "You must decide what that means for yourself."

Jason watched as Charging Bear walked to the river's edge. The man knelt and washed his face, pouring the cold water over his skin. Grabbing a handful of wet sand, he stared intently at it, rubbing it between his fingers. Jason watched as this older man knelt by the river. *What does he think about … what is his history?*

This native elder appeared graceful and at peace in every movement he made. It was a far cry from some people in the rushed, modern world he had come to loathe. His admiration for this man had grown immensely since being rescued from the water. Charging Bear had treated him like a wounded bird, mending him back to health.

I wish I could stay and live like him.

"What if I don't cross the river?" Jason shouted out.

Charging Bear stopped and stared at the water. He provided no answer. Standing up from the log, Jason repeated himself. "I said … What if I don't cross the river?" His voice echoed throughout the wilderness.

The man stood, gazing across the river. Still, he provided no answer to the question, leaving only his back to Jason. "Hey! Listen, Charging Bear. I've listened to you, followed your instructions, and done everything you've asked of me! I've opened up to you like I haven't done to anyone else. Yet every time I ask you a question, I never get an answer! Why is that?" Jason's voice was rising in frustration. The fear of crossing the river and not having Charging Bear by his side caused the stress to pour into other emotions.

"I said, why is that?! Who are you!? What is your story?! Why can't I stay?!" Jason's anguished cries were reverberating among the snowy trees. Shouting in frustration, he strode toward Charging Bear.

"Please! I need to know. You've told me nothing! I've told you everything!" Charging Bear pivoted, and his painted red face gave Jason a rugged look.

"Why can't I stay here!? What if I don't cross!? You said these demons can't get me on this side, so why on earth would I cross over to them?" Jason's voice was cracking with emotion.

Charging Bear remained stoic in the face of Jason's questions, causing him to erupt in anger. Jason shoved Charging Bear, causing him to take a step back. There was no reaction.

"Answer me! Who are you!?" Jason delivered another firm push into his chest. His heart was beating rapidly, and his breathing was shallow.

"Tell me!" The cold mixing with his distress was causing Jason's muscles to stiffen. Tears began to roll down his face and his throat closed, gripped by his emotions. "I don't want to go ... I don't want to go back ..."

The two men stared at each other in a muted standoff. Jason noticed how weary and worn-out Charging Bear looked. He seemed older than before; something appeared different about him, but Jason couldn't decipher it. Looking deep into his gentle eyes, Jason hung his head in shame, covering his face with his hands. "I'm sorry." His muffled voice protruded from his shield of embarrassment. *I'm an idiot. Pull yourself together.*

Charging Bear placed his hand on Jason's shoulder with a firm grip. "My son, my history, and who I am, matters not. You do not need to hear my words to know who I am." His eyes gazed deeply into Jason's soul.

"You can feel it already in your heart; that is the only language you should listen to." Charging Bear brushed Jason's hair back with his hand, as a father would do to his young son. The caress brought Jason a familiar sensation of a love he felt long ago.

* * *

Jason stood in front of the mirror in his suit, attempting to tie a Windsor knot for the fifth time. *God! I'm so stupid. Can't even get this damn thing right.* His father walked up behind Jason and inspected him.

Jason was dressed in the new black suit his father bought him for high school graduation. Fitted and pressed, it made him look older than he was. His young face grew frustrated with his failed attempts at tying a tie.

Jason's father placed his arms around him and began to tie it for him. "Don't stress about the little things. It's just a tie." With a few motions, he fixed and adjusted Jason's tie.

"See? Good as new." His father beamed with pride, staring at his son, who was becoming a young man, growing each day. "All it takes is a little practice. Just like everything in life." Jason admired himself in the mirror. *I look pretty good.*

"You look great, son. You're all grown up." The smile on his father's face was a mix of pride and apprehension. The realization that his young boy was turning into a man gripped his heart. His soft, radiant eyes spoke as if he wished time would freeze and allow his baby boy to stop growing. Jason's father cleared his throat as he began fixing his son's hair.

"Thanks, Dad."

"No problem, son. If Mom could see you right now, her heart would melt." The two men smiled.

"You're becoming a man, Jason. You're starting a new journey now. It's a new beginning with many different opportunities." Jason turned around to face his father.

"It's a big world. It will be filled with all kinds of challenges, failures, and successes. Only you decide how those things will affect you. They can change you for the better or eat at you like a disease." His father placed his hand on the left side of Jason's face. "Only you have the power to carve your own destiny."

Jason placed his hand on top of his father's. "Thanks, Dad, for everything you've done for me."

"I love you, son. Life can be scary, but if you trust yourself and love yourself, the path you take will lead you where you're supposed to be."

* * *

"Jason, tonight we will have a nice meal, a celebration for all you've accomplished these past months." Jason was pulled back from his memories.

"I also have a gift I would like to give you." Charging Bear sat and picked up the stick he was carving. "I would like you to go forage for some berries; I believe they would make a nice dessert for our meal. You can set out in the afternoon, and I will prepare our food."

With obedience, Jason did as he was instructed that afternoon. Charging Bear's words played over in his head repeatedly. *What does he mean I can feel it? I wish he would just be straight up with me.* Jason had many questions that he was sure would not be answered.

The evening approached as Jason returned to see Charging Bear standing over the fire with slices of elk and herbs roasting. The aroma made Jason salivate, reminding him of backyard barbecues he and his dad would have in the Nebraskan summers. *God, that smells so good.*

"Have a seat, Jason. Let us celebrate the first steps you have taken."

"First steps to what?" Jason asked as he sat, admiring the sizzling meat.

"The first steps to reclaiming your mind." The fire caused shadows to dance across Charging Bear's face. "A seed cannot grow if it does not receive the care it needs.

"You have been given that seed. It is in your soul now, in your mind and body." The crackling of the fire provided a soothing background.

"That experience you had was a gift. A gift from the great spirit. You must hold on to what you felt and understood from that journey. That is your seed.

"If you care for it with love and affection, it will grow within you."

The two men sat and ate around the fire, discussing life, fishing, and other topics. Jason was enjoying the moment with his older friend. He peered into Charging Bear's face, admiring the old man. *I wish this moment would last forever.* Jason tried to soak in every moment he could. Charging Bear reached down and grabbed an object from behind him.

"Jason, this is a gift I have made for you." Charging Bear handed Jason a handmade tomahawk; it glowed with the firelight. The shaft was a white oak with various markings and symbols carved into it: a wolf, a bear, the sun, and stars. The star pattern seemed to form the constellation of Orion. The head of the tomahawk was a dark Damascus steel. It had white designs that mimicked the lines you would see on fingerprints. A small line of beads and two feathers hung from the neck of the shaft.

"This is amazing. Thanks so much." Jason was in awe of the intricate design of the weapon. It was evident Charging Bear had put in a lot of time and effort to create this gift.

"It is but a tool. The real weapon is here." Charging Bear tapped Jason on the head with his finger. "And here." He tapped Jason's chest near his heart. "Those two things are all one needs to fight his battles and live a happy life." The fire's light danced upon Charging Bear's face. "You will meet your demons again, Jason. They will always be with you, and it is up to you to deal with them."

Jason brushed his fingers along the head of the tomahawk. Admiring its sharpness, he thought of the demon across the river. "I think I'm ready, but I'm not sure." Jason lifted his head to meet Charging Bear's eyes.

"You will always have doubts, Jason, just as you had doubts about jumping into this river.

"Jumping into this river was a decision you made based on faith. A leap of faith can only be made in the shadow of doubts.

"The river brought you to me for a reason, and I'm lucky to have met a fine young man like yourself, Jason.

"The scars on your body do not compare to those in your heart." Jason looked up from his tomahawk.

"When I found you, you were in great pain. You will always feel the pain of loss. But behind that pain is the footprint of love. The love you have for your friends, your father, your mother. That is something you will always feel as well.

"But you must be kind to yourself. You must rid yourself of the negative inner voice that feeds your demons." Charging Bear had Jason's complete attention as he spoke.

"Hating yourself. Hating others … it is what opens the gates for those demons. You must keep them out of your heart. You must never stop fighting them.

"Never stop fighting them …"

The men continued to eat and converse throughout the night. The stars painted the black canvas above, and the northern lights danced throughout the sky. A green glow shone down upon the river's rocky edge. A full moon brought light to the darkened forest, and no sounds were made across the river. It was a peaceful night filled with laughter, love, and friendship.

Morning came with a sharp chilliness. The temperature had dropped, and Jason began to awaken, the cold air causing a chill to roll down his spine. In his hut, he could see overcast clouds blanketing the sky through the smoke hole. *Man, it's cold.* Rising out of bed, he put on his clothes and grabbed the new handcrafted tomahawk. Admiring the tool, Jason sauntered into the frigid morning.

However, when Jason stepped outside his hut, his heart sank. Snow had fallen, creating a pristine white blanket on the river's shore. But that's all there was. Charging Bear's hut was gone. There was no trace of him. No footprints, no trail, not even markings where his hut had been for the past months. It was as if he had never existed. Vanished into thin air.

"Charging Bear?" Jason called out to the wilderness for his friend. "Charging Bear?" *God, no, please.* Desperation gripped him as he began running along the shore to see if he could find any trace of his friend. "Charging Bear!" *Please, don't leave me too.* "Charging Bear!" In vain, Jason continued to shout, desperately hoping his friend would walk out of the woods.

Jason's throat began to tighten, and his chest grew heavy. With tears in his eyes, he returned to the spot where Charging Bear had camped. Kneeling to examine the ground, he found fresh footprints in the soft white snow where the hut used to be.

Huh?

The prints were large in size and created by a bear. They led from the spot of the former hut and disappeared into the forest. The tracks, massive in their size, appeared to have formed out of nowhere.

They did not show the animal's arrival at the site, only its exit toward the forest. Jason stood up from inspecting them and gazed into the woods where they led. His heart broke as if he had just lost a loved one, but inside, he knew he hadn't.

What do I do now ... ? Jason asked himself as he hung his head, feeling more alone than he had in years.

Jason sighed and examined his tomahawk. With its marvelous inscriptions, the oak handle emanated a sense of assertiveness and hope. *Never stop fighting ...* Jason traced his finger over the engraved constellation of Orion and looked to the other side of the river.

Chapter 19

I have come to lead you to the other shore; into eternal darkness; into fire and into ice.
—Dante

The River's Edge
Present Day

A cold breeze blew through Jason's hair as he assessed the other side of the river. The moment had come, and he knew it; there was no escaping it. Charging Bear was gone. This mysterious man had emerged from the wilderness and rescued him from the brink of death. Yet as mysteriously as he appeared, Charging Bear had vanished back into the wild, leaving Jason alone and isolated. The man taught him things he never understood: how to find peace, stability, and hope in times of darkness and despair with the wisdom of a spirit he could not fully understand. With Charging Bear gone, Jason was alone yet again. His fate lay solely in the decisions he would make from here on out.

He admired the irony of it all. He had come to this place to escape people by finding solace in isolation. That was the whole purpose of his journey. Yet the shocking events that led him to Charging Bear had contorted his mentality into something that had a foundation of hope. Now Jason stood in the snow, alone and cold with no human around for miles, and it saddened him. *I miss you already.*

Thousands of large snowflakes shrouded the air. They smeared the open river with a stunning mesh of white, providing a thick veil of beauty in the ambiance of the precipitation. With a deep breath, Jason walked over to his hut and reluctantly began dismantling the shelter and packing his belongings. He rolled up the furs he'd utilized along with some dried meat.

Jason secured the handmade snowshoes to his back and slung his waterskin, one of the many items Charging Bear had assisted him in crafting. He picked up the long wooden spear designed for him on his first hunt; with a knife attached to the end, it was a formidable tool he had become quite versed in. Admiring it, he thought back to the many hunts he had participated in with the old man. *I'm going to miss you.* Jason tied it to his pack.

Eyeing the ground, Jason lingered and gave deep thought to the object that lay before him. He picked up the last gift Charging Bear ever gave him. The beautifully engraved ivory-white tomahawk stood out among any other item he had. Snow dropped onto the head of the weapon as Jason admired it and its personalized aesthetics. Holding it tightly, he raised his head to the overcast sky. *Thanks for everything.*

The tomahawk had Jason feeling like a part of Charging Bear was with him. The protection, guidance, and wisdom that the man demonstrated profoundly impacted him in a way that possibly pushed him onto a better path in life. A course that was symbolized in the tomahawk he now held. A powerful reminder of everything he had learned about faith, sorrow, and persevering through trauma. Now, the challenge was to retain all he had learned. A challenge that Jason was still skeptical he could overcome.

He walked toward the river's edge and stopped before his feet touched the water. The trees glistened with a captivating shimmer of sparkling white as the fallen snow coated the thousands of branches before him. Nothing could be seen behind the tree line as darkness provided a cloak for what was behind the trees. A foggy haze spread across the river at knee height, creating an illusion that he was standing on a cloud. *It's time.*

Jason felt a familiar feeling within his chest that brought back a vague memory from his childhood. He recollected having to decide whether he should cross a road and confront the school bullies antagonizing his friend. He remembered how apprehensive and frightened he was, yet determined all the same. *Just like I feel right now … Believe in yourself.*

"Come to me," a faint voice whispered in the wind.

Jason paid it no heed. He was not going to cross the river because the voice told him to. He would cross it of his own accord, under his own willpower and determination. Looking down into the shallow water, Jason made his first step toward the tree line.

The water sloshed around his ankles as he traversed from the rocky shore, wading into the shallow river. Each step he took in the icy water felt like a barrier was being broken down. His heart pounded with tension, but Jason kept his chin held high. Anxiety made him grip his tomahawk tighter as he concentrated his steely eyes on the other side.

Halfway through the crossing, Jason looked down the length of the river. It seemed to stretch for miles upstream as if it was directed by the white trees surrounding it. He knew the river's temperament further up was rough, as that was where he almost drowned in the rapids.

Rocky islets spread throughout this section of the river, making crossing easily achievable. All that was required was perseverance and a will to step to the other side. *Keep moving forward. Keep walking,* he thought to himself. *Keep your chin up and shoulders back. Believe in yourself. You can do this.*

Jason stepped out of the cold water and onto the other side of the river. Having crossed the icy water that had acted as a barrier for these many months, Jason had now crossed the terminus into the domain of his demons. Looking back with a deep-rooted feeling of nostalgia, he examined the area where he and Charging Bear had spent the past few months. Heavy snow continued to fall onto their vacant campsite, creating a white shroud between the two shores. *Thank you, old man.*

All the conversations, the training, the hunting, and the fishing were now memories of his past. All the impactful advice and spiritual lessons he had received took place on that shore. To Jason, staring at the other side of the river where he spent so much time was like looking at a hallowed ground of an unassailable world. A sacred place that would have a special place in his heart until the end of time.

Jason turned to eye the tree line that now stood in front of him. Dense and thick, it gave no hint about what lay beyond it. *There's no going back now.* The thick bush stood as a white wall with a spattering of green pine needles. Nothing could be seen behind the tree line.

"Come to me," the voice whispered again. Jason grasped his tomahawk in suspense. His heart was pounding as he thought back to his vision of the terrifying fires. Jason shut his eyes. *"The only time you can be brave is when you are scared,"* Charging Bear's voice echoed within his heart. Jason took a deep breath of the crisp winter air and stepped into the dark forest, leaving the river's edge behind him. His Rubicon had been crossed.

The forest was murky. Dead branches hung from the trees like deformed fingers reaching down from above. The forest floor was a mix of dead leaves and patches of snow. Jason first noticed an oddly shaped animal carcass lying dead on the ground. He knelt to inspect it.

Assessing the carcass, Jason made out a half-decomposed stag. Its insides were ripped from its stomach in a fashion made only by a monstrous creature creating an empty cavity in its torso. The body had been mutilated, but it did not look like animals caused it; all the inner organs were missing. The head was decapitated, and the skull's skin had been peeled back to create a horrifying look of bones breaking through the skin, making a frightening grin on the deceased animal. *What in the hell did this?* It was as if someone had placed it there for him. A welcome gift for the world he had now crossed into.

A drop of blood landed on Jason's hand from above. Unnerved, he peered upward and witnessed dozens of inner organs hanging from branches. The stag's insides had been ripped away and hung from the branches like macabre ornaments of flesh. Jason grew even more anxious with the environment he was now in. Standing up, he took one last look at the skull and tightened his grip on his tomahawk. *Keep moving, Jason.*

He planned to follow the river upstream, hoping that would be the best way to lead himself back to his cabin. Jason was unsure how long the journey would take; he could not tell how far he had been swept downstream, and the forest remained unfamiliar to him.

Walking through the forest, he ensured he could always hear the sound of the water in his left ear. He would know he was walking in the right direction if he could listen to the flowing water. *It's the only guide marker I've got right now.*

An imminent sense of depravity never left him during his hike. Jason felt like a million eyes were observing him at all times. Paranoia was spreading throughout his body in a way that ran the risk of becoming overbearing. *Breathe, Jason. Take some breaths and keep your eyes open. Keep. On. Moving.* Jason reiterated this to himself, attempting to settle his nerves.

The forest eventually thinned out to an area not as thick as the part he'd been walking through. The trees were tall and spread out, creating long lanes with dead brown needles on the ground. The branches stood high at the base of all the trees, obscuring the sky and leaving rows of bare trunks below. Jason noticed something odd about them as he trekked through this section of the woods.

The trees had oddly shaped objects placed onto their trunks. As Jason got closer, he froze in horror at what he saw. Decomposed human skulls were embedded into the trunks of the trees. Some had holes in the cranium, and others had crushed orbital bones and broken teeth. Their jaws were agape as if screaming in pain from a torture they were eternally subjected to. They covered every tree in front of Jason, creating menacing timbers of despair. Readying his nerves, he ambled through these monuments of death.

"Come to me," the voice whispered in the wind again.

His heart pounding, Jason was at risk of having paranoia infect his judgment. With hypervigilance taking over his mindset, he spun around, looking for who was speaking. Casting his eyes in all directions as he walked, he held his tomahawk tightly.

"Orion! Bud, how have you been!" A familiar voice came from behind the tree a few yards before Jason.

"I've missed you, man!" Brad Redman stepped out from behind a tree. Dressed in his desert camouflage uniform, a large smile illuminated his pale face. "It's so good to see you, bud!" He stepped toward Jason with open arms.

"Don't come any closer!" Jason shouted, pointing his tomahawk at Brad. *My God. Brad … This can't be.*

"What's with this? I thought you'd be happy to see me." Brad stood, confused, throwing his hands in the air.

"This isn't real. It can't be." Jason's eyes were wide with suspicion. Conflicting emotions ran wild within him. On the one hand, seeing Brad standing there in the flesh made him want to run and hug him, embracing his old friend who he missed so much. On the other hand, he knew this was another mind game being played on him. It was so real that Jason was in danger of believing it.

"You're always so negative. Just enjoy the moment, man! I'm here! We're back together, even if it's just for a little bit. Isn't that what the old man at the river told you to do? Be in the now? Be in the moment?" Brad placed his arms down on his hips and stood ghostlike, awaiting Jason's reply.

It's not real, Jason. It's not real. Brad is dead and never coming back. Don't be fooled.

"You're not Brad. Brad's dead." Jason kept his tomahawk pointed at him, his eyes unblinking.

"I mean, this isn't exactly DC's Waterhole, but we can make the most of it. Let's sit down and catch up! You got any beer in that sack of yours?" Brad laughed.

The thought of catching up with his old friend was a powerful proposition. Jason had prayed to have just one more day with his old friend many times since his death. Now here he was in the flesh, standing in front of him.

"You're not Brad. Brad died in 2010. I was standing right beside him when he died! Brad's dead, and you're not him. No matter how hard you try, you'll never be what Brad was." Jason pushed down the conflicting emotions that risked fissuring his resolve.

Brad sighed in disappointment and stared down at the ground. "You're right." Silence filled the forest as the two men stood feet apart from each other. "I am dead." Brad looked up, his dark sunken eyes meeting Jason's. "Because of you, Jason." Jason's heart sank as he vividly remembered the car bomb and all the shots he fired that missed the driver. Survivor's guilt began to set in once again.

"You know, Jason, you were the best shot out of all of us. We all looked up to you. But you were too busy with your head in the sand to react when we needed you the most. You let me die!" Brad's face twisted in pain.

The words Brad spoke stuck Jason like a knife in his gut. Hearing this from his best friend lit a fire deep in his consciousness, threatening to torch his grip on reality. His survivor's guilt rose within his heart, the same shame he had lived with for the past decade.

"That's bullshit! We were both talking together, and the vehicle came out of nowhere! I tried to react as fast as I could. All of our shots didn't stop that vehicle, not just mine! All of ours! It's not my fault." Jason's voice boomed through the forest. Jason felt strange as he responded to Brad, refuting his accusations. These were the same accusations Jason blamed himself for, but now, for the first time, he was disputing them.

"It is your fault, and you know it!" Brad stepped closer to Jason, pointing at him in rage. "I counted on you, and you let me die. Now here you live your life while my corpse lies in the ground rotting. I hope you're enjoying your life ..." Brad's face twisted with hurt and irritation.

"I will no longer blame myself for your death, Brad. I'm done with it." Jason stayed steady with his tomahawk by his side. Brad sighed, and his eyes began to well up.

Jason desperately wanted to hug his old friend. He wanted to hold, sit with, and talk to him for hours on end. Jason desired to tell Brad how much he loved and missed him, but he controlled himself from these temptations. He struggled hard to keep his emotions from taking over his grip on reality.

Brad dropped his face into his hands and began to weep. "I wish I was still alive. To be able to experience all the things you still experience." Brad wept as he spoke into his hands, hiding his face from Jason.

"I thought you'd be ashamed of yourself for your failures, yet now you don't even feel guilty for letting me die? What kind of friend are you, ORION?" Brad's head snapped up to reveal a decomposed skull. No eyes were in the sockets, and flaps of skin dangled from his face. The terrifying sight made Jason gasp in shock and step backward.

Brad kicked the white tomahawk out of Jason's hand. Thinking quickly, Jason pounced and tried to retrieve it but was tackled by Brad before he could get off his feet. Jason attempted to crawl toward the weapon, but Brad adjusted to put his total weight on top of him, trying to restrain him. As Jason realized going for the tomahawk was hopeless, he flipped over and attempted to push Brad off. With a powerful grip, Brad pinned Jason's arms to the ground. The two came face-to-face.

Brad looked him in the eyes and released a horrifying high-pitched scream of pain. His skin started to melt away on his body. It dripped off his face, neck, and chest as his insides fell onto Jason's body, covering him in organs, blood, and flesh. The desert uniform Brad wore began to spontaneously ignite, burning away in a fire that brought the smells of burning flesh and sulfur. The scream was deafening, louder than a human could ever scream. Brad was in unimaginable pain. His voice resounded with the feeling of a thousand souls being tormented in the most horrendous ways. Horrified, Jason persisted in breaking from his grasp.

The screams echoed throughout the lifeless forest. All the skulls affixed to the trees began shrieking, creating an orchestra of terror. Jason slipped out from underneath the decomposing version of Brad. The rotting man fell face-first to the pine-covered ground, screaming into the earth in terrible pain. Jason crawled on his hands and knees to reach his tomahawk. Retrieving it, he arose from the ground and watched his friend decay and burn in front of his eyes.

Jason's stomach twisted inside of him. The horror of what he witnessed brought the taste of vomit to the back of his mouth. What he saw next shook him to the core.

Brad slowly stood up. What was once Brad had now become a bloodstained skeleton. A pile of burned skin and inner organs lay in a pool below the skeletal figure. The dark red blood was caked onto this creature's bones, with skin and pieces of uniform falling off it. The grotesque skeleton unleashed a brutal scream of despair and fury, looking at Jason. The skeletal creature began sprinting toward him.

Jason widened his stance to defend against the oncoming charge. Jason dropped to his knees as the skeleton neared and swung with all his strength. He shattered the creature's femur with his tomahawk. The monster tumbled to the ground, continuing its terrible scream of agony.

Regaining his composure, Jason hesitantly advanced toward the prone soulless creature and observed its flailing bones. *That wasn't Brad. That wasn't Brad. That wasn't Brad.* He tried with all his might to control the direction of his mind. Jason raised his tomahawk with two hands and quickly smashed its skull with a crushing blow.

The screaming ceased. All the skulls on the trees stopped shrieking simultaneously and the forest became silent. Jason breathed heavily, adrenaline and fear still coursing through his veins. He examined what was once Brad, now a pile of broken and burned bones on the forest floor.

"You weren't Brad." Jason stood and stepped backward.

In some sense, he felt he had lost his friend yet again. "You weren't Brad, and it wasn't my fault." Jason remembered his actions that day of the car bomb. *The real Brad wouldn't want me to blame myself. That wasn't Brad.*

Jason used the forest floor to wipe the remnants of crushed bone and blood off his tomahawk. He listened for the sound of the river, hoping to regain his bearings. Its flow had become louder. The whitewater current was strong when he jumped in many months ago; Jason hoped he would close in on that spot. He started following the sound of the river, walking in the same direction where he'd had his encounter with the Scorpion.

The open forest gave way to a denser section of dark trees. Not finding any animal or man-made trails, Jason had to push branches out of his path to make his way through. He trudged over fallen trees and rocks, carefully traversed down steep tree-covered hills, and climbed up rocky embankments. The land's contours and the elements that the Alaskan winter brought were punishing his aching body.

After hours on foot, he was unable to ignore his hunger. *I need to eat. I'm starving.* Jason found a large rock to rest on and took out the only food he had from his pack, dried meat from his many hunts with Charging Bear. Staring at it and brooding about the encounter he had just had with Brad made him nauseous. The image of Brad decomposing in front of his face was a difficult vision to ignore. Jason had to force himself to eat, pushing the disturbing images from his mind.

After a few silent moments, thirsty, Jason removed his waterskin and drank the cool water from its leathered body. Consuming the refreshing water, a feeling of dread overcame him as if he was being watched by someone or something. Out of his peripheral vision, he spotted something walking from behind a tree. It had moved from behind one tree to another, causing Jason to gaze in its direction. *Someone's there.* Again, he saw a figure moving from one tree to another. This time he captured more detail. It was a man. He seemed large in stature, and antlers adorned his head.

He stayed in his position for some time, but no matter how hard he searched, Jason could no longer spot this person. He chose to secure his tomahawk to his pack and remove his spear. At least with this weapon, it could provide him with more standoff distance compared with the shortened hatchet. Standing, he scanned the forest but could see nothing. His chest felt tight in anticipation as the crisp Alaskan wind blew through the barren, snow-covered trees. He knew somebody was there but could not see him. Spinning with his spear, Jason could hear no sound except for the flowing water of the river. *Alright, alright, calm down.*

Maintaining his vigilance, Jason determined it was no longer wise to remain in this spot and resumed his journey south along the river. Walking with the sound of flowing water to his left, he held his spear with two hands as he walked, in preparation for the worst. *Damn, I wish I had my gun …*

Jason had traveled most of the day, and the sun was dropping below the horizon. The forest grew darker, and he set up camp for the night before it was too dark to see. Jason used his furred animal skins with sticks and vegetation to create a shelter. The forest was pitch-black by the time he was lying on the makeshift bed. He chose not to make a fire so as to not draw anyone or anything to his location. Jason slept with his spear close to his chest. No sounds came from the forest except for the occasional hooting of an owl and other nocturnal wildlife that called the forest home.

Closing his eyes, he thought back to Charging Bear. *Where are you?* It had been years since he missed the company of another person. He would give anything to have that old man by his side just one more night, especially one as cold and threatening as this one. The day's journey had taken a physical and mental toll on him. His body ached. The forest was quiet. Nothing but the flow of the river could be heard in the distance. From the darkness, the silence was broken by a voice shouting out in distress.

"Moor?"

Chapter 20

Cerberus ate my heart. Hell awaits me. As night approaches, the thoughts come like hounds chasing me, relentless. I descend into this. This place called wrath.
—Melissa Jennings

Backwoods, Alaska
Present Day

It was a sleepless night. The troubled calls of the young girl had continued throughout all the hours of the night. Jason heard the tormented sobbing, whimpering, and pleas of "Moor" repeatedly wailing from the darkness, plaguing his consciousness. Despite the repeated calls for her mother, he did not venture out. Jason stayed underneath his animal skin tarp and clutched his spear, cradling his weapon as a frightened child would hold a teddy bear.

The teddy bear ... He recalled the image of the little girl holding her teddy bear while weeping over her mother's deceased body. That night Jason cried uncontrollably; his heart grew heavier with each call the child made. An uncontrollable surge of emotions swept over him. Fear, despair, regret, and loneliness encapsulated his heart.

The memories of what had happened to her family were a burden he could not push himself to overcome. Tears ran down his cheeks like a rainstorm of guilt and shame. He had orphaned that child, and no wise elder, no kind woman or great spirit would ever change that. *I'm so sorry.*

That night Jason was at a breaking point. He felt like giving up on this never-ending struggle and surrendering to death to have those dreaded memories permanently wiped from his soul. His heart was shattered, and his soul felt depleted of substance. *Maybe if I fall asleep, I won't wake up …* He wished the darkness would peacefully take him away from his existence.

However, Jason's hope of dying in his sleep did not come true. Sheer exhaustion made him pass out, and it wasn't until morning that he awoke to the sound of ravens above him. The caws of a singular raven sang out like a fit of laughter, with its low croak hollering from above in three loud bursts.

Jason gradually opened his crusted eyes and peered above him to see hundreds of ravens silently sitting on the tree branches. The only sound came from one raven on the lowest branch, which continuously looked down upon him, trumpeting its song to Jason.

Dammit. Why couldn't I have just died in my sleep? Jason, who was still cuddling up to his spear, rolled out from underneath his tarp onto his knees and looked around, his spear laid across his lap. There was nothing: no girl, no monster, no human, only a snow-covered forest and the unkindness of ravens. Unkindness was a fitting name to call the group of ravens, as unkindness in this forest ran deep.

A foreboding sensation washed over him as he felt the eyes peering down at him. As he looked up, all the blackbirds persisted in gazing at Jason, motionless in their pose apart from the one emotive bird. The sight brought chills down Jason's spine, and dread began to fill his core. They sat covering the canopy above, assessing, judging, gaping into his soul. Then he recalled back to when he had arrived on the river's edge many months ago and what Charging Bear had told him regarding ravens.

"It is believed that the raven stole the light and brought it to the earth. They symbolize helping people and shaping the world. My people have many stories about the raven. He represents rebirth, recovery, renewal, and healing. He signifies moving through transitions by casting light into darkness."

Jason's dread seeped away, and his shoulders felt lighter at the knowing words of his older friend. "Well, I hope you guys have some light for me," he expressed to them, gratified.

With a long journey ahead of him, Jason had a quick bite of his dried meat and packed up his shelter. *Keep moving, Jason.* He mustered up the determination to make it back to his cabin. *One step at a time, keep moving.*

As he wandered, Jason's thoughts were filled with the events that had occurred since crossing his Rubicon and his recent moment of weakness in the night. It wasn't the crying or the emotions of sorrow and guilt that constituted the weakness, but his thoughts of dying, wishing to not wake up, to not exist. That is what Jason now saw as a weakness. *Hold it together. I'm my own worst enemy. I'm my own best friend.*

The change in Jason's thinking was a testament to how far he had come in recovering his mind from the pits of ruin. While simple, it was a significant milestone for Jason to believe. *No matter how dark the night is, the sun will always rise in the morning.* Pushing through the thick forest vegetation, Jason broke through the tree line into an open field.

The field was large and over a few hundred yards in length. The entire valley was clad in pristine, untouched snow, glistening from the rays breaking through the overcast sky. Jason stepped forward and sank into the knee-deep snow.

Realizing how hard it would be to traverse the field, Jason elected to put on the snowshoes to make it more manageable. Charging Bear had taught him to create this helpful footwear many months ago. He tied the makeshift snowshoes tight to his feet, affixing them with twine and rope.

He began his trek across the field, making significant strides in his snowshoes. They were awkward to walk in, and the difficulty hindered his pace. Yet it was better than trudging through snow without them. Halfway through the field, he was beginning to feel exposed and vulnerable from being out in the open against the bare white canvas. It would be easy for anyone or anything to notice him. *Just make it to the other side.* He continued to push forward through his brooding anxiety.

Suddenly, Jason stopped in his tracks when he heard a familiar sound breaking from the forest behind him. He held his breath and listened harder, attempting to discern what he was actually hearing. *It can't be …* Again the animal-like sound made a noise in the distance. It was a distinct sound, not wild or feral, but akin to a domesticated animal.

Barking reverberated from the tree line behind him. *It's a dog!* Jason turned around and saw a lone black dog walking and sniffing the trees. He watched, astonished to see this domestic animal so far out in the wilderness. *What's it doing out here?*

The dog stopped and turned its black head toward Jason. Immediately it began to sprint toward him with excitement, leaping in and out of the snow and barking with zeal. As the black dog neared closer, Jason could distinguish its features. It was a large Molossian hound. *What the …* Its tail wagged fiercely as the giant dog vaulted on top of Jason, licking his face like he was a long-lost friend.

"Trigger? Is that you?" The dog barked in excitement and persisted in licking the left side of Jason's face. Jason laughed, happy to see this kindhearted animal. The embrace caused his heart to soften and lifted his spirits. "Are you out here alone? Where's your owner?" He was quick to remember her name. "Artemis? Where is she, boy? Is she with you?" The dog barked excitedly.

"Artemis!" Jason hollered, scanning the tree line for the Alaskan woman he'd met while hitchhiking. "Is she with you, boy?" he asked, scratching the dog behind the ear.

"Artemis!?" The hound barked and rushed back to the tree line it came from. Jason's mind was elevated, knowing that he might no longer be alone. His bout with loneliness and desire for isolation was a path well-traveled for him, but a path he no longer wanted to walk down. *If Artemis is here, she can help get me back.*

"Hey! Wait! Come here!" Jason awkwardly got back up to his feet with the snowshoes. *What if she's here? What if she came to find me?* Jason walked as fast as possible toward the dog, who stood at the tree line, barking at him. "Wait! Stay!" The snow kicked up around his wooden snowshoes. He desperately raced toward the dog, not wanting it to escape his sight.

As he approached the animal, it dashed back into the forest. *Fuck.* Jason stood at the tree line, panting, and began to unbuckle his snowshoes. *Don't leave, you stupid dog, stay!* Free from the constraints on his feet, Jason began to step back into the forest, scanning for the animal.

"Trigger? ... Trigger! ... Come here, boy!" There was no response.

Jason tried a different name. "Artemis? Are you here?" Nothing answered Jason's calls. All that could be heard was a soft breeze blowing through the trees. The unnerving silence made Jason pause and reconsider his options. *Just keep heading toward the cabin, Jason. Ignore this. You never know ...* Lingering in contemplation, he heeded his own advice. Jason turned to walk back to the field, leaving the animal to the wilderness, until a deep-throated growl rumbled in the distance.

It was loud, as if three dogs were growling at once. Its deep-throated rumble gave Jason the sense that he was not welcome. *Leave. Get back to the cabin ... NOW.* Jason strode backward, not wanting to turn his back on the noise that now grew louder and louder. Far into the forest, he saw a black dog heading toward him. *Trigger?* It grew more prominent as it neared, looking much larger than any dog he had seen. *That's not Trigger. What THE FU—*

Jason didn't stop to finish his thought. He spun and scrambled as fast as he could toward the field. The Molossian hound was massive, but that wasn't the most terrifying thing about it. It had three heads snarling and foaming at the mouth with razor-sharp gray teeth—a three-headed dog, like Cerberus.

Jason had learned about Cerberus in his Greek mythology class back in high school. It was the guardian of the gates to the Underworld. Its job was to ensure nobody ever left hell. According to legend, Hercules was the only person to ever escape Cerberus's wrath, and Jason was no Hercules.

"Fuck!" Jason shrieked as he ran away from the enormous beast. Leaving his snowshoes behind, he frantically waded into the knee-deep snow. The white powder sloshed around his knees and slowed him as if he was running in water in some bad nightmare. *Dear God! Please!* Jason was terrified.

The three-headed titan sprinted forward. Faster and faster, it leaped over mounds of snow with ease. The three heads foamed at the mouth and barked wildly. Closer and closer, it neared Jason. As he crossed the field halfway, Jason regretted tying his spear to his pack while snowshoeing. Weaponless, he continued to run in desperation.

"AHHHH!" Jason screamed in terror as he approached the far tree line. He could feel the heavy breath of the massive creature on the back of his neck. Its barking was thunderous, angry, and determined.

Jason smashed through the trees and tumbled to the other side. Flipping, he somersaulted down the steep hill that awaited him past the tree line. His body flailed like a rag doll. Over and over, his body smashed against rocks and trees. The steepness of the hill made his fall gain momentum with each tumble. Pain shot through his body with every blunt impact; it seemed like he would never reach the bottom. All Jason could hear were the painful sounds of his grunts as he smashed against the earth repeatedly.

With one last crunch, Jason came to a halt at the bottom of the hill. His backpack had broken his fall somewhat, but the damage was already done. His body ached, and his limbs throbbed. It felt as if somebody had hit him over the head with a hammer. Lying on his back, Jason stared at the top of the hill. No dog could be seen.

Agh, God … My head.

The bottom of the hill had arced, creating a leaf-filled ditch that Jason now lay in. Exhausted from the frantic escape, he listened for any sign of the beast. *What the fuck was that* ... Jason brushed the snow off his face and rolled onto his knees, grasping his shoulder in pain. *God dammit.* The fall had made him feel like he was on the receiving end of a beating by a gang of thugs. The hurt in his body quickly dissipated as he studied the mounds of snow, dirt, and leaves that filled the ditch. *That's not leaves ...*

To Jason's horror, dozens of bodies filled the ditch he was now sitting in. Their torsos were twisted in unnatural ways; some of their faces were flattened and caved in. Bullet and shrapnel wounds covered the corpses in all areas. The dead were all dressed in traditional Afghan clothing, some with a black turban. *Taliban ...*

Jason had a vivid memory of the fighters he killed in Kandahar. Their bodies were devastated similarly by Jason's assault, with his grenade launcher having a ruinous impact on his enemy. However, the number of bodies in this ditch far exceeded what Jason was accountable for. Weak with pain, Jason crept out of the ditch on his hands and knees, struggling to engage his muscles from their stiff, petrified state.

Jason was prevented from crawling further when he felt a dull smack on his leg. A hand had grabbed his ankle. "GAH!" Jason shouted in terror as he spun around. A dead Taliban fighter had grabbed ahold of his foot. Its face was flattened, with half of its skull missing in a grotesque, nauseating deformity.

The dead fighter salivated a black liquid and grinned, peering into Jason with its yellow, dried-out eyes. "Za niat ... akhes-tal ... zama ... badla ... !" The creature mumbled the foreign words that Jason had heard once before. *I will take my revenge.*

Screaming, Jason began kicking and punting the Taliban fighter in its mangled face, over and over. "GET! THE! FUCK! OFF!" he shouted with each thrust of his leg.

The decaying creature released its grasp as Jason's last kick crushed the other half of its skull. "God! Fuck!" Jason shrieked as he rushed to his feet and sprinted away from the trench, panting from the terror and exhaustion flooding his body. Jason ran while glancing back occasionally, checking if he was being pursued by the rotten corpse or Cerberus.

His escape from the undead was cut short when Jason turned his head. Before him, the giant three-headed dog was charging straight at him. Instinct made him stop, sliding through the leaves and snow. Jason scrambled to his feet and ran back toward the trench, desperately trying to evade Cerberus. *Oh my God, please, no! Fuck!* Running back to the ditch seemed like the lesser of two evils as the snarling bloodthirsty dog was more than he was ready to handle.

Run! Run! Run! Don't stop!

Jason could sense the beast getting closer to him as the rhythmic panting of the three heads grew louder. The foul stench of the culvert became more potent as he approached the ditch that appeared as if it was alive, writhing with limbs reaching in all directions.

What do I do? What do I do?!

Jason felt the warm moist gust of the dog's breath painting the back of his neck, and he did the only thing he could think of. *Duck!* Jason dropped to the dirt, hoping the sudden change of pace would catch the three-headed demon off guard, and it did.

Cerberus tumbled over Jason's prone body and rolled into the ditch. Lifting his head, Jason could see the confusion on all three faces of the hound as it stood and glanced down at the ground beneath it.

What followed next was an unexpected, horrifying sight of carnage and mutilation. In a blind rage, Cerberus began chomping at the moving corpses, ripping them limb from limb. Body parts flew in all different directions as the dog jumped from one place to the next. It was as if the corpses were trying to escape hell, and Cerberus was doing everything possible to prevent it—the primary duty of the once-mythological creature.

Lying prone and frozen at the grotesque sight before him, Jason pulled himself back from the horror he was witnessing and clumsily raced to his feet. *Go! Now! Get away!*

The sound of dogs growling and barking faded into the distance as Jason escaped from the preoccupied Cerberus. Running deeper and deeper into the forest, he didn't stop, no matter how fatigued he became. Jason had expected to encounter demons on this side of the river, but never one such as Cerberus himself. Reencountering it was something he hoped would never happen again.

Jason slowed to a walk until his legs gave out, collapsing to the leaf-covered earth. Lying on his stomach, his breathing was labored, working to push oxygen back into his worn-out muscles. Brown snow-covered leaves blew away from his face with each exhale, and his long dark hair lay across his face like oil streaks.

Unable to move, Jason examined what was before him, and although it appeared normal, there was a familiarity to it that he strained to recall from his memory.

The massive rock was split in half as if a mighty axe had swung down and chopped it in two, causing ragged pieces of stone to spread out all around it. It was the same rock that he had fallen into many months ago. The same one that prevented the Scorpion from striking him with its stinger.

Jason had been able to make his escape when the giant Scorpion struggled to pull its stinger from the rock, allowing him enough time to slip out underneath it and escape to the river—the river where he would eventually make his leap of faith.

In the vast Alaskan wilderness, Jason now knew where he was. *I'm close.*

Chapter 21

It is during our darkest moments that we must focus to see the light.
—Aristotle Onassis

Ramstein Air Base, Germany
Winter 2011

"Push, Jason! Push!" The physiotherapist shouted words of encouragement. "Keep going! Don't give up!" Jason collapsed onto the parallel bars, catching himself before falling to the floor. "Dammit!" He cried out in frustration.

It was the fifth time they had tried this exercise today. Wearing a weighted vest, Jason was learning how to walk again. The blast had caused devastating injuries to his legs, requiring rehabilitation.

He had been hospitalized at Ramstein Air Base for months now. His condition improved, but it allowed long days of exercise and rehabilitation. A personal physiotherapist had been assigned to Jason to support him through his recovery. The left side of his face no longer required a bandage. However, the scabs and scars ascertained how fresh his wounds still were.

The bodies of his teammates had already been flown home and buried. All were given full honors at their respective funerals. Their family and friends mourned, the news reported on it, and moments of silence were held at local sports games.

Then the world moved on as if nothing had happened. Jason's nights in the hospitals were long and lonely. Given his condition, there was not much to do, so he spent much of his time trapped within his own thoughts. He analyzed the incident with the car bomb repeatedly, straining to see what he could have done differently to change the outcome. He had begun to blame himself for not preventing it.

"I can't fucking do this! You might as well cut off my legs and put me in a wheelchair. I'm fucking useless now anyways …" Jason vented as he was helped into a chair.

"Jason, this is not going to be easy. You are going to have many days like this. You have made so much improvement since your injury, though."

Corporal Aceso, his military nurse and physiotherapist, tried to comfort him with her soft empathetic voice. "You should start looking at what you have done and not what you can't do."

"What the fuck is the point anyways?" Jason hollered, waving her off. "Even once I start walking fully, I'm being medically released. I'll be back in my hometown stacking boxes like a zombie at some grocery store." Jason pressed his hand against the left side of his face. It throbbed as the blood rushed to his head. "My friends are dead. I'm a gimp, and my future is about as bright as a black hole."

Corporal Aceso lowered herself and set her hands on Jason's knees, looking up at him. "We can't change our past, Jason. But we can decide how we approach the future. Please don't give up on it yet. There may be better things than the military waiting for you." Corporal Aceso looked into Jason's steely blue eyes.

Her delicate features brought about an air of innocence. Her brunette hair was tied back, and her eyes glowed a bright green. *At least I have a cute nurse.* Jason thought, trying to see the bright side of anything at all.

"Now, one last time. One last effort, and we're finished for the day, OK?" Aceso persuaded him, patting his legs.

"Alright, let's get this over with." Begrudgingly, he continued with his exercise.

Jason retired that night, his muscles aching from the exercises. His bed was in a shared room with other wounded soldiers recovering from injuries. It was a disheartening environment, but the attendants tried their best to brighten it up. Flowers and cards decorated the bedsides. Pictures of children's drawings adorned the walls; "Thank you for your service" was a common phrase written on them. When Jason examined the men in the room, all these words of thanks and well wishes meant nothing to him.

The soldier next to him had lost both of his legs. The stumps were wrapped in white bandages; he would spend his time reading, rarely speaking to anyone. Another soldier had been blinded by an IED and had frequent night terrors, startling Jason at night with his cries for help.

Jason's sleep was often disturbed by the sound of other soldiers weeping at night. A marine who had lost his arm. A man with a fractured spine. A young boy from Canada, looking no older than nineteen, had a neck brace and hardly moved. Everywhere he looked, there was pain.

Pain and thank you cards.

Fuck this place …

Jason gazed up at the outdated popcorn ceiling as he lay in bed. He thought of his friends, his dad, and all the other things that had been taken from him. Hopelessness was a contagion in that hospital. The only person he saw fighting against it was Corporal Aceso, and although Jason could get annoyed with her optimism, he was thankful she was assigned to him. Having such a caring nurse who wanted the best for him was pacifying.

As the weeks passed, Jason progressed from walking the parallel bars to doing bodyweight squats. He needed to be spotted if his legs gave out, but Jason could feel his muscles recuperating.

"Rise and shine, Jason, it's another day. Let's put that body to use, shall we?" Corporal Aceso pulled the covers off him and began preparing his outfit for the day. She handed him a water bottle, her radiant smile peering down at Jason.

"Yup. Another day …" Jason chugged the bottle and carelessly tossed it on his bedside table, causing it to tip over.

After picking up his bottle, she assisted him in standing up and positioned him in his wheelchair. He spent the day completing exercises to strengthen his calves, quads, and abdomen. Those areas were the focus of his recovery.

"One more! … TEN!" Corporal Aceso was ecstatic. "Ten squats! Jason, that's a new record! I can't believe how strong you're getting! You keep this up, and you'll be out of here in a few weeks. I promise." Jason flopped on his chair, wiping the sweat from his brow.

"Well, that's one thing that motivates me. Escaping this place." He rubbed his face as Corporal Aceso grabbed his water bottle.

"Escaping this place, huh?" She spun to face Jason.

"Yeah, escaping."

"Are you escaping from something? Or escaping to something?" Aceso pulled up a chair and sat next to Jason, handing him his water.

"Does it even matter?" Jason was annoyed again. *I'm sick of these conversations.*

"It does matter, Jason. If you're trying to escape something, you need to have direction, or your escape will be aimless. How will you know when you've truly escaped?" She placed her hand on his shoulder. "But, if you're escaping TO something, then you have a goal. A destination. It's much harder for chaos to seep into your life when you know where you are going." Jason felt her beautiful green eyes examine him.

"I guess you're right." Jason didn't care to comprehend what she was trying to say. He merely agreed with her so she would stop lecturing. It would be many years later, when Jason made his escape to Alaska, that he'd understand what she was trying to convey.

"Can we work on the upper body now?" Jason questioned. There was a moment of silence between the two as she studied Jason's eyes. She seemed to be peering into him, reading his thoughts and emotions, examining his soul.

She gave an affectionate smile and tapped him on the leg. "Sure, let's head to the chin-up bar." Aceso guided Jason to the black bar on the other side of the room. "Overhand grip, twenty pull-ups in total. It doesn't matter how long it takes, OK? Ready?"

"Sure, let's do it." Jason looked at the black bar dangling above him. At this moment, reaching it was the only goal he had.

"On three." Corporal Aceso placed her hands on Jason's hip to aid him in reaching the bar. "One, two, three, go!"

Jason vaulted and clutched the bar, grunting as he pulled himself up.

Chapter 22

Through every generation of the human race, there has been a constant war, a war with fear. Those who have the courage to conquer it are made free, and those who are conquered by it are made to suffer until they have the courage to defeat it, or death takes them
—Alexander the Great

Backwoods, Alaska
Present Day

Escaping from Cerberus and the others, Jason found himself in a familiar area. Collapsing near the shattered boulder offered him an indication of where he might be and helped direct him to the cliff he had fallen off many months ago.

Desperate to return to the cabin, Jason was not willing to risk venturing in a different direction only to get lost again. This left but one option, up. Although it was the more physically tricky option, it was the shortest and most familiar.

Jason moaned as he hauled himself up the rocky escarpment. "Ragh!" Grunting, he grabbed the last rock face and pulled himself onto the ledge. Jason collapsed, rolling onto his back, gasping for air, his muscles burning from overuse. Peering over the cliff's edge to the winter forest canopy, Jason thanked whichever god had been watching over him during his climb. *Jesus … How did I survive that?* The rock face was incredibly high, twice as tall as the trees below. It was a wonder that he had lived through the drop.

Jason rolled onto his knees and took a large gulp of fresh water from his waterskin. There was not much left of it, but he knew he was approaching the cabin. *Maybe a few more miles? I shouldn't be too far off now.* Jason poured the remnants of the water over his head, allowing the coolness to flush the sweat from his scalp.

With a deep breath, Jason untied the spear from his pack. *I'm gonna have you in my hands this time. You're useless to me, being attached to my pack.* Once his limbs no longer felt like rubber Jason stood and resumed his trek through the woods.

With all the walking, he had time to think about the future and his path forward once he reached the cabin. The cabin was a mere waypoint in his journey, and deciding what to do from there would be difficult. Staying there was out of the question. He knew remaining isolated would do nothing but deteriorate his mental health. Still, he could not dive back into the society he'd left. Jason missed his hometown, but he was unsure what awaited him there anymore.

Artemis … God, it would be nice to see her again.

Visiting Artemis again would not be easy, as he wasn't sure precisely where she lived or if he was still welcome. Jason was basically a drifter now in the literal sense. Many months had passed since his encounter with her, and although she now held a special place in his heart, he wasn't entirely sure it was mutual.

Regardless of his path, Jason was headstrong about moving forward in his life. Charging Bear had helped him come to terms with the reality he lived in. He made him see how his mind could be his worst enemy and that he could not survive this journey alone. Jason owed it to his friends and his dad to live the best life he could, to honor their lives by making the most of his own.

His demons, Charging Bear had told him, would always be with him. It was up to Jason to keep them from controlling him. The path beyond the cabin will be as difficult as the one leading up to it, but with a renewed outlook on life, it could be even more beautiful than he could imagine.

Jason pushed his way through the tree branches, stepping through dead leaves covering the forest floor with a spattering of snow. The area also seemed familiar; Jason felt like he was getting close. The thought of sleeping on an actual bed for the first time in months motivated him to keep moving.

Fatigued, Jason strolled with his head down, gazing at his feet as he pushed through the dead vegetation. His thoughts drifted. Jason recalled conversations he had had with his friends, their adventures, and the jokes they told. He laughed to himself, a smile breaking through his hardened face.

Jason remembered the random jokes Brad would always make and reminisced about past days.

* * *

"Always confident, huh? Does anything ever get away from you?" Brad spoke to Jason as they strolled along the dirt road.

"Well, of course. Never for long, though. I like the chase." Jason replied, smiling at his friend.

"Well, I hope poor Winnie the Pooh gets away. What the fuck did he ever do to you?"

* * *

"CONTACT!" The audible scream echoed throughout the forest and snapped Jason back into the present. It was not something he was thinking; it was something he heard. Not being able to tell if it was a whisper in his ear or a scream in the distance, he froze in his spot. Wide-eyed and uneasy, Jason glanced around the forest. *That sounded like Brad ...* It was their final conversation he was reminiscing about before the car bomb hit. Brad's last words were a warning that the enemy was approaching.

Grasping his spear, Jason scanned the forest for anything, but all he could see were barren trees. Their dead leaves lay on the ground below, covering the earth like a blanket of various shades of brown and white. Silently, Jason continued to walk, more alert than he had been before.

Suddenly, his attention was wholly transfixed by an unusual object in the distance. Too far away to understand what it was, a group of dead trees obscured the thing from allowing him to identify it. Unnatural in its shape, the angles and bends appeared man-made, and as Jason neared the object, it became clear what he was looking at.

Shit ...

It was identifiable now—a white Toyota Corolla in the middle of the forest. Abandoned in the thick bush, it would have been impossible to drive to this location. The car was rusted with flat tires and faded off-white paint. Its headlights were broken out, and it had no windows. The dilapidated vehicle looked as if someone had taken it from a junkyard and plopped it into the middle of the woods.

Examining the car from a distance, Jason dared not go near it. He had learned from his previous encounters that anything could happen in these woods. He was not about to go near the exact vehicle, make, and model that blew him up many years ago. Jason could feel blood rush through the left side of his face as his heart began rapidly pumping it through his body.

Suddenly, an insidious-looking head lifted up in the driver's seat and spun to face Jason. The top half of its face was painted in bright red blood. A decayed wolf's skull adorned its head like a menacing helmet. The boney headdress had antlers fastened to it, similar to the creature in his vision and the one he had spotted a few days ago.

Tightening his hold on the spear, Jason remained steadfast in his position. There was a silent standoff between the two. *Jack* … that was the name the demon gave itself when he first appeared to Jason. The devil had once shape-shifted into Brad, the Taliban, himself, and the Scorpion in an attempt to kill him. The first time it spoke to him, it shifted into a mirror image of Jason himself. The monster that had been plaguing him this entire time was now sitting in the vehicle of his suffering.

Jason's heart raced with fear, anticipating a possible confrontation with his most personal demon. His knuckles turned white as his iron grip squeezed the base of his spear.

"Moor?"

And then he saw it. Jason witnessed the little girl emerge from the forest a hundred yards in front of the vehicle. The demon slowly turned to face her, a vicious smile illuminating its face.

"Moor?" She wandered aimlessly, yelling for her mother as if not noticing either Jason or the vehicle. The man in the vehicle reached forward, and the car's engine turned to life. Slowly, he placed his hand on the steering wheel and shifted the gear into drive.

No … No …

"No!" Jason roared and ran as fast as he could toward the girl as the car started to creep forward. The instinct to protect this child was the only thing controlling his body. His muscles moved without cognitive thought as he sprinted through the forest, leaping over fallen branches and roots. *Don't let her die … don't let her die … you owe her that!* The engine revved, and the vehicle sped up, aiming for the child.

Jason pitched his spear to the ground as he approached the young girl. *He's going to kill her. It's going to explode!* The child continued to aimlessly look for her mother as the vehicle increased its speed. Jason witnessed the driver white-knuckling the wheel with an insidious grin.

Whether it was the guilt that plagued his conscience or a desire to atone for what he had done, Jason felt he had a duty to protect the girl from his demon's wrath.

Jason scooped the girl into his arms and dove out of the way of the racing car. With leaves and branches kicking up from its tires, the vehicle swerved, attempting to hit the two, missing only by inches and slamming into a nearby tree. The sound of crushing metal and splintering wood shot through the forest as the collision caused the car to turn sideways and lodge itself into the trunk, rendering it immobile.

Frantically Jason ran with the girl as quickly as he could. Knowing what would happen next, he tried to get as far away from the car as possible. Nearing the only suitable cover he could find, Jason dove behind a dense fallen tree, landing on top of the girl.

BOOM!

The car detonated with a deafening explosion that rattled Jason's entire body. His hearing went as the familiar high-pitched ringing noise returned. Branches and dirt rained down upon them as he used his body to shield her from the falling debris. The distance and the trunk's thickness had harbored the two from the brunt of the explosion.

As Jason peeked above the fallen log, nothing but a hole, scattered metal, and burned trees remained where the vehicle had once been. The little girl lay on the ground, terrified, hugging her teddy bear like it was the only thing left in her world.

Silence returned to the wilderness as Jason looked down upon her, her youthful face illuminated by innocence and fear. He could feel his heart swell and his throat tighten with emotion. As Jason looked at her, he said the only thing that came to mind. The foremost thing that he had desired to express for so many years.

"I'm sorry." He studied her frightened face and repeated the words. "I'm sorry ... I'm so sorry." Caressing her face, Jason wasn't sure she could understand him, but he needed to tell her. The guilt he was plagued with from unintentionally killing her mother was like a cancer that ate away at his heart and mind.

The girl's expression changed from frightened to a steadfast, motionless gaze. The child's eyes glossed over as she responded to Jason.

"Actus non facit reum, nisi mens sit re." The words that she spoke were not English, Greek, or Pashto, but Latin. A phrase Jason had heard before describing *mens rea*.

An act does not make a person guilty unless the mind be also guilty.

The powerful phrase, spoken by the child upon whom he had inflicted so much pain, had more impact than at any time he had heard it. The lump in Jason's throat became painful with emotion as he absorbed the child's words.

The girl's skin began illuminating bright white as she smiled at Jason. Her innocent, captivating smile started to dissolve before Jason's eyes. The child dispersed into the soil as every molecule of her body turned into glistening snow. The snow slipped through his fingertips as the young girl vanished, leaving Jason staring through his hands at the white-brown soil beneath, awestruck by what had just transpired.

"I'm sorry." In shock, Jason gazed down at the pile of snow and leaves before him. "I didn't mean to …"

"Bullshit!" the deep raspy voice bellowed from behind him, shaking Jason out of his mesmerized state.

"You know full well that's bullshit, Orion." Jason turned to see nothing behind him except the log he had been crouched behind and the dead trees above him.

"Do you think her little Latin phrase absolves you from what you've done? Do you believe you can now just move forward in life as if you never murdered her mother?" Jason stood, scanning his surroundings but saw no one. The voice continued to bellow from all around.

"I am waiting for you, Orion. Come to me, and I can end your suffering."

Jason unslung his pack and removed his ivory-white tomahawk, gripping it with anticipation. A cold breeze blew through the forest as the overcast sky darkened, giving the forest an ominous malevolent vibe. The evening was approaching, and Jason had to decide to either camp out or continue his trek for the next few miles to the cabin.

I'm not staying out here one more night. Keep going, Jason.

"You can try to ignore me all you like, Orion. But soon, I will not give you an option."

Jason stepped over the log and continued moving through the forest, walking past crumpled pieces of metal and burned timber. He eyed the massive crater as he strode past the place of detonation. The cavity was a black hole in the middle of a white forest, radiating death and destruction.

Bloodstained uniforms, helmets, and boots were scattered along the crater's edge, disturbing Jason with visions of his dead friends and bringing him back to the desert where he lost them.

Distressed, Jason stood still, closed his eyes, and took deep, deliberate breaths. *Snap out of it, Jason. Snap out of it.* He felt his heart rate subside and gradually opened his eyes, finding that the uniforms and military gear had disappeared from the crater's edge.

You can do this. Keep moving.

Jason moved past the crater in the direction he came from many months ago, clasping his tomahawk with determination.

"I have another Latin phrase for you, Orion," the voice roared through the forest. "Non enim misericordiae impius."

No mercy for the guilty.

Chapter 23

I guess darkness serves a purpose: to show us that there is redemption through chaos. I believe in that. I think that's the basis of Greek mythology.
—Brendan Fraser

Plattsmouth, Nebraska
May 1999

"Now, two other figures that are permanently ordained in the night sky are the constellations of Orion and Scorpio. Two eternal foes." The teacher stood at the front of the class, and the projection screen behind her flipped to various images of constellations.

"There are varying stories of Orion told throughout Greek history. But they all share certain commonalities." Artistic renderings of Greek gods and mythological figures flashed across the screen as she continued her lecture in the Greek mythology class.

"Although his father was Poseidon, the god of the sea, Orion was only mortal. Just like you and me. One version of the story has him falling in love with one of the Olympian gods, Artemis, who was also a huntress. A common bond they shared that made them fall in love." The students listened attentively at their desks as she continued.

"Things took a turn for the worse, however, when Orion angered Gaea." The teacher stopped as she noticed a hand raised in the back of the class. "Yes, Jason?"

"Ma'am, who was Gaea again?" Jason's attention was fully captured in his high school class. Now seventeen, he would soon graduate from secondary school and step out into the world. He currently worked part-time at one of the corner stores downtown, but he had bigger plans for himself, unlike the students who desired to attend university.

"Gaea was the goddess of the Earth, Jason. The personification of everything beautiful in the world. The mother of everything." Jason lowered his hand.

"Orion took everything around him for granted, including Gaea's most precious gifts, the earth's natural beauty." The screen flipped to a picture of Orion aiming a longbow. "On the island of Crete, Orion distanced himself from the earth's gifts and bragged that he was such a good hunter he could kill every creature on the planet." Jason watched as she spoke with enthusiasm, explaining the ancient myth to the class.

"When Gaea heard of this she was so outraged that she sent Scorpio, a giant scorpion, to kill Orion. The two enemies fought an epic battle and were both killed in the process." The screen switched to an image of Scorpio striking Orion in the leg.

"Artemis was so devastated by the passing of her lover that she asked Zeus, the supreme god, to place Orion in the skies. Zeus then decided to do just that and placed Orion in what we now know as the constellation, along with the scorpion that killed him. Scorpio." The teacher looked at the clock on the wall on walked back to her desk.

"Artemis, by the way, had a brother, Apollo. The God of prophecy, music, and all things beautiful. But that's a tale we can get into in another class." The bell rang throughout the classroom, causing all the teenage students to hurriedly pack their belongings and leave for the day.

"Remember everyone, tomorrow we will cover the goddess Aceso, one of the five goddesses who personified healing! We'll also dive into the tale of Cerberus and how he became the guardian of the gates of hell! A guardian that had the duty of preventing anyone from leaving!" She attempted to speak above the rushing crowd of students as they filed out the door.

Jason couldn't help but feel excited to learn more about the mythological stories. His Greek mythology class was his favorite elective, and his marks were outstanding compared to the rest of his grades. He found himself excelling in the things he had a passion for.

"Jason. Can I speak to you for a second?" The teacher waved him over to her desk as she organized the scattered papers in front of her.

"Yes, ma'am?" Jason stood with his black backpack slung over one shoulder.

"I just wanted to say that I loved your essay on Jason and the Argonauts. You really put a lot of effort into it."

"Oh, well, thanks. Yeah, I enjoyed writing it." He wasn't lying, either. Jason had spent the past week studying and researching his project every night.

"I wanted to ask. What made you choose that specific tale for your essay? Was it because you share the same name?" She let out a chuckle and smiled at him. Laughing, Jason replied.

"No, actually, I was really drawn to the story. The fact that Jason was given this seemingly impossible task to capture the Golden Fleece and the obstacles he went through to get it was fascinating." Jason subconsciously lowered his backpack to the floor as he continued his conversation, clearly sucked into the story.

"I mean, he didn't do it alone. Which is something I greatly respect about him. He knew he needed help, so he recruited the Argonauts for his journey. I liked the bond they made during their adventures. Fending off monsters, sirens, skeletons, and a giant bronze statue of Talos. It's an exciting tale."

The teacher replied to Jason with a look of pleasure painted across her face. "It certainly is, and I love how detailed you were with it. I enjoyed reading that one paragraph where you discussed the different endings of Jason's life. One has him killing himself, and another dying in a freak accident. I share your frustration in not having a firm answer in the story. It's comparable to Orion's ending. There are many different ways it ends."

"Yeah, it seems like that happens a lot in Greek mythology. There are so many versions of stories, it makes you wonder which one is the real one that was told so long ago."

"Well, maybe these differing stories are trying to tell us that life is not linear? Maybe it's a way to tell us that our own journeys can have different endings, complete with redemption or suffering?"

"I guess so." Jason enjoyed the metaphoric examples that she often threw at him.

"I also wanted to ask you. What are your plans after high school? College? University?" She looked at him curiously.

"Well, actually, I was thinking of joining the military." Jason spoke with a smile on his face. After much consideration, he was almost sure he would enlist after school. The outdoors, the rifles, the camaraderie, it seemed a perfect fit for his personality.

"Really now? Well. I wasn't expecting that answer. What does your dad think?"

"He's supportive. He thinks it'll benefit me and that I might even excel in it. We do a lot of hunting and camping, so he thinks it would suit me well."

"Well, that's good to hear you have a plan, Jason. We all need some semblance of a plan. It's the kids that leave high school with no plan or aspirations that are the ones I worry about."

"Well, that's not me, ma'am." Jason pulled his backpack off the floor and slung it over his shoulder.

"No, it certainly isn't. Hey, you never know. Maybe one day you will be the Jason of your own story, complete with a crew of Argonauts going on adventures and fending off whatever creatures the gods send you," she said with a sly look on her face.

"Well, as long as I'm as steadfast and unwavering as Jason and his Argonauts were, I shouldn't have a problem," he replied with a laugh. "I'll see you tomorrow!"

The teacher smiled at him as she watched him exit the classroom, wondering what kind of future was in store for her favorite student.

Chapter 24

Go down swinging. And I'll tell you: if you fight with all you have, more often than not, you won't go down at all. You will win.
—Jocko Willink

Backwoods Alaska
Present Day

Jason's time at the river's edge felt like a lifetime ago. Although it had been less than a few days, Jason's experiences on his pilgrimage back to the cabin were profound and at the forefront of his mind. He thought back to his friend Charging Bear and credited him with giving him the physical and mental weapons to combat the demons plaguing him. Weapons of patience, discipline, forgiveness, and self-confidence were all more valuable than a rifle ever could be.

Jason had leaped into the freezing rapids a broken man, hardly able to live in his own skin, and had returned as a revitalized individual with resolve and steadiness. He began to feel more confident in himself and his abilities to deal with adversity.

The warrior spirit that had once personified him so long ago was beginning to return. The last time he had felt this way was when he left for Afghanistan. His mentality was strong, mindful, and confident with goals for the future. He had pushed through adversity and grown with each burden he crossed.

However, the confrontations with his demons in this enigmatic forest took a significant toll on him. Crossing paths with the manifestations of Brad, the girl, Cerberus, the car bomb, and the continuous, never-ending torment of his predominant demon tested his resolve to keep a steady mind.

It will not be easy. Jason trekked through the woods as he remembered Charging Bear's warning. *And he was right.* Nothing had been easy about this journey. His heart had been drawn in a million different directions, muddying his mind on what was real and what was not. He had almost died a dozen times and struggled to push the traumatic memories from his mind. His journey through the Alaskan wilderness was a never-ending civil war of his mind, continuously fighting in the silence of his subconscious.

Jason walked through the forest that was now becoming more sparse. The trees spread out, as if giving each other space, not daring to get too close to one another. More and more snow had begun to cover the ground as the precipitation no longer needed to break through the covered forest canopy.

I'm close.

The slight change in the makeup of the forest brought about a familiar sensation for Jason. The vast amount of time he spent in the woods near his cabin helped develop an awareness of the area. Although not entirely recognizable, this part of the woods was as familiar as the one surrounding his cabin.

Jason carried the tomahawk in his hand, and his pack was lighter than when he first set out, empty of food, water, and his spear. *I can't wait to get a fire going in that cabin, I'm freezing.* Living in the outdoors for months on end gave Jason a new appreciation of the simple necessities of life, like a comfortable heated shelter.

Coffee, fire, and a comfortable bed.

Jason hoped the cabin would be a type of "home free" from the forest's darkness, but he knew that was probably wishful thinking.

Just get me there and I'll figure out what to do next.

A pack of wolves shook the ever-darkening forest with a bloodthirsty orchestra of howls. Pivoting to look behind him, Jason surveyed the vastness of the forest for the animals. *I'm almost there. Keep going, Jason.* Jason was now well-versed in mustering up the strength to control the restlessness of his nerves, something he had completely lost his ability to do months before.

The howling grew closer, compelling Jason to quicken his pace and glance around constantly. After recalling his last escape from the pack of wolves, Jason did not want to experience a similar encounter to the one when he fell from the cliff.

They were so aggressive, the way they jumped at me.

Abruptly, a ferocious growl ripped through the trees behind him. Jason could see a lone wolf fifty yards away, crouched as if it had finished stalking its prey and was ready to attack. *Fuck!* Jason did the one thing he had done so many times when faced with a greater danger than himself. He ran.

Fucking, God dammit! Shit! Shit! SHIT!

He was astonished that this cat-and-mouse game of trying to escape death had not yet concluded. He felt like he had been running and fighting his way through this dark forest for years. And in some ways, he had.

The snow kicked up from his heels as he sprinted through the rows of trees, leaping and swerving around the vegetation. Jason ran in a zigzag pattern as he attempted to outrun the ravenous wolf, but he knew full well that this was the wolf's domain and he was at a disadvantage.

A few rows away, Jason spotted two enormous gray wolves running alongside him out of the corner of his eye. Matching his pace, they ran with their tongues hanging out as they exerted themselves, boxing Jason in.

Jason began to run to his right, away from the wolves, when he once again witnessed another lone giant wolf running with him. *Shit!* Jason was now completely boxed in by these pack hunters. The same ones he had encountered after shooting the deer were now attempting to finish what they had started. He had a beast behind him and on both sides, funneling him in and directing him to run straight forward.

The breathing of the wolf behind him grew exponentially more frantic as the wolves to his sides gradually closed in as they ran. The dryness of the air was quickly sucking the moisture out of Jason's mouth. The cold air he inhaled into his lungs was becoming more painful than rejuvenating as the lactic acid built up within his leg muscles.

Before Jason knew it, the wolves were within arm's reach, racing right beside him. Running off sheer resolve, Jason swung his tomahawk at them as he continued to sprint, warding them away before they could bite him.

Undeterred, the wolves snapped at his ankles, trying to trip Jason up. He felt his hand vibrate violently as he blindly struck a wolf in the head with the back of his tomahawk. With a yelp, the wolf backed off for a moment and continued its chase.

What do I do? What do I do?!

Jason felt a searing warmth rip through his ankle as he suddenly lost his balance, throwing off the cadence from his sprint. Attempting to stay upright, Jason felt like the world had gone into slow motion. He lost his footing with each step, eventually tumbling into the snow and striking his head against a large, dried-out fallen log.

"Hnngh," Jason moaned in pain as he rolled onto his back, leaning up against the giant log. The snow turned crimson red around his ankle as it bled from the bite wound. The four wolves now stood before him, mouths agape, drooling and panting, catching their breaths as they examined the defenseless prey in front of them.

This is it. It's over. This is how it ends.

The wolves bent their legs, and the hair on their necks stood at attention as they snarled at him. Utterly exhausted from his attempted evasion, Jason didn't even have the strength to lift the tomahawk that now lay across his lap. He could hear nothing but the growling of wolves and the beating of his own heart.

Defeated, Jason accepted his fate and spoke to the encroaching wolves.

"Do it. Do it, you pricks."

In unison, the wolves halted and instantly looked to their right. A massive blur of brown tore through Jason's vision and encapsulated the wolves with an earth-shaking roar. Yelps, barks, and howls reverberated through the air as Jason watched, bewildered at the sight in front of him.

Before the wolves could finish Jason off, an enormous brown bear came charging from nowhere and knocked them down to the ground. Now a battle between the giant bear and the bloodthirsty wolves was occurring in front of Jason's eyes. All he could do was lie on the ground, exhausted, and watch this gladiatorial battle of nature in front of him.

The bear stood on its hind legs and bellowed a terrifying roar as the four wolves regrouped and made a semicircle around it. One wolf leaped toward the bear only to be swatted away.

One by one, the wolves probed their foe by risking an attack, seeking a weakness in the bear's massive defensive posture. A wolf, too slow to back away after its probing ankle bite, found itself pinned by the giant bear.

With a ferocious bite, the bear clenched its jaws around the wolf's neck, shaking the wolf violently. The frantic, hysterical yelps suddenly went quiet as its neck snapped, the body falling limp into the snow.

With the bear too focused on the foe within its jaws, the other wolves took advantage and all attacked in unison, jumping at the bear's back, side, and legs, frantically chomping at any part of its body they could.

Roaring in pain, the bear hurled two of them to the earth as it stood on its hind legs. Focusing its attention on the third wolf gnawing at its back leg, the bear dropped its entire weight on top of it, rendering the wolf immobile. Defenseless, the side of its face began to be torn to shreds by the bloodied teeth of the bear.

The sound resonating from this naked display of the most violent aspect of nature was a horrific thing to hear. Death, violence, and a struggle to survive played out in front of Jason as his muscles slowly began to recover.

Jason wiped away the blood that now poured from the wound on the left side of his face, caused by the head-first dive into the log. Still unable to move, Jason watched in astonishment as he viewed the battle through the fog of his breath.

Dispatching the second wolf, the bear shifted its attention to the remaining two. Blood painted the bear's bottom jaw, caking its brown hair with bright red. With one wolf limping, they attempted to spread out, forcing the bear to bounce from side to side, trying to keep them both at bay on either side of him.

The bear waited for the attack and then focused on one wolf. With a wolf lunging to bite its legs, the bear bit down on the back of its neck. The bear ripped and shook violently, trying to snap the wolf's neck as its companion jumped on the bear's back, endeavoring to stop it.

The wolf stood on top of the bear's back, desperately biting down in multiple spots, the attacks seemingly having no impact on the beast that was now obliterating its friend. The agonizing yelps from the wolf trapped in the bear's jaw suddenly ceased as its neck snapped in two.

The bear launched the last remaining wolf off its back, causing a cloud of white to fly into the air as it landed in the snow. The two animals now stood face-to-face. Three dead wolves lay scattered across the ground, their necks broken and their skin torn up. The bear stood on its two hind legs and roared in defiance. Assessing its fate, the wolf slowly backed up and ran away, choosing to live rather than continue to fight.

Silence now replaced the orchestra of nature's violence as the bear returned to all fours and began sniffing the deformed carcasses of the wolves. Jason's breathing became more shallow as he realized he was now the only living thing left besides the bear.

The bear shifted its attention to Jason, sprawled against the log. *God, no.* With panic flowing through his veins, Jason felt too terrified and exhausted to lift a limb, let alone try to escape. He observed helplessly as the bear closed in on him, stepping over the dead wolves, its eyes firmly locked onto Jason.

Jason winced as the bear neared. Helplessly, his legs flailed, softly kicking snow as his body did anything to escape the massive beast. The bear stepped closer to Jason, patiently making its way to the sprawled-out, impaired human. Its lips wiggled with each step. Its jaw hung open, laboriously respiring and covered in the blood of its dispatched adversaries.

Jason closed his eyes and contorted his face in preparation for the coming painful death awaiting him. He could sense the moist warm breath against his face, the odor reeking of iron and dead fish. Expecting the jaws of the massive beast to come crashing down on his skull, Jason closed his eyes. Anticipating pain, he instead began to feel a warm wetness tickling the left side of his bloodied face.

Jason opened his eyes and was frozen in fear and confusion as he watched the bear lick the blood off his face. *My God ... don't move ... don't move ...* His hands trembled as he held them up in surrender, hoping the licks would not turn into bites.

Soon, he found himself staring deep into the bear's eyes as it ceased its tonguing caress and studied Jason's face. The bear's eyes were dark brown, like large bloodshot marbles, their darkness gazing deep into Jason's soul.

The fear and panic seeped away from Jason as an overwhelming sense of ease coursed through him. It was as if he was staring at an old friend, personified in the form of an animal. Jason lowered his hands as his breathing slowed, the pain still ringing in his head from the fall.

"Charging Bear?" Jason spoke to the animal, unsure what he expected in return.

With heavy breathing, the brown bear turned and slowly walked away, stepping back over the dead wolves and sauntering deeper into the dark forest. The sun had now touched the horizon, turning the forest into a cold, dim wilderness. Jason watched as the bear faded away into the darkness.

What the hell was that? Was that you?

Jason rubbed the left side of his wet face and looked above at the sky. The dead branches hung like frail fingertips reaching down through the darkness. However, one of the branches caught his eye as being too close and unnatural to be part of a tree.

Then, Jason realized the object was no branch but the large handle of an axe hanging above him. Painfully, Jason rolled onto his knees and inspected the log he was leaning against.

The fallen log looked like it had been there for quite some time. Massive chips and cuts sculpted a curved divot in the middle of the trunk, where an axe stood embedded into it. *This is my log!* Before him, Jason identified the fallen log as the one he often used for a workout, aggressively chopping the tree to release stress and aggression and get exercise while doing it.

I'm here.

Jason stood and rolled over the thick tree to the other side. He limped in the direction of the cabin that he now knew was only a couple of hundred yards away. The wound on his ankle had stopped bleeding, but the pain continued to shoot through his leg.

The forest abruptly ended as Jason broke into a clearing at the bottom of a snow-covered hill. Alone at the top of the hill stood a lonely, isolated dark wood cabin. It stood just as Jason had left it.

A lump grew in his throat as he pushed his way up the hill, slowly dragging his feet. He could no longer hold the flood of mixed emotions streaming through him as he wept uncontrollably. Tears poured down Jason's face as he walked through the snow, gasping for air between his sobs.

When Jason first left the cabin, he was angry and tried to cool himself down by going on a hunt. He had never returned to that cabin, becoming lost in the woods for many months.

As he neared the end of his unexpected journey, Jason's experiences rolled through his mind like a film reel, reviewing everything he had been through. The revelations, sufferings, and triumphs passed through his mind, bringing a flood of emotions. He had labored painstakingly in these woods and persevered through many challenges to return to where he was. Now it was over.

Jason cried tears of relief, joy, fear, and pride.

He had returned to his cabin.

Chapter 25

Maybe the ultimate wound is the one that made you miss the war you got it in.
—Sebastian Junger

Plattsmouth, Nebraska
Winter, 2011

Jason stepped through the plane's door, feeling the cold Nebraskan breeze against his face. It was refreshing to be unburdened by the combination of the plane's sterile air and the body odor radiating from the hundreds of soldiers crammed into their seats.

Home. I'm finally home.

Stepping onto the tarmac, Jason bathed in the familiar climate of middle America until orders were hollered in a forceful voice, telling the soldiers to form up. As instructed, Jason and the rest of the two hundred and fifty soldiers lined up in formation on the black airport tarmac. Excitement resonated through the air among the anxious servicemen.

Jason felt more excited to be free from the plane than to arrive home. Walking across the tarmac, he lined up a couple hundred yards from the entrance to a large hangar filled with friends and family ready to greet their loved ones.

The flight home was bittersweet for Jason. As the jokes and conversations ran rampant throughout the plane ride, he could only think of how he was the only one from his platoon on this plane. The rest were still in Kandahar, fighting without him, and here he was, returning home without them. Jason was too injured to be allowed back to his platoon. His war was over.

I would give anything to be there with them again.

Jason had made a swift recovery from the majority of his injuries at Ramstein Air Base. Corporal Aceso was instrumental in the speedy rehabilitation, allowing him to hop on a flight with a returning unit of servicemen. He sat quietly throughout the flight, hearing a multitude of war stories, most of which had him shaking his head. Men who had spent most of their time inside the wire at the airfield would rant and rave about how they survived a measly rocket attack or brag about the one patrol they may have gone on.

Not all tours of duty are equal. I am not the same as you.

Even surrounded by his fellow uniformed soldiers, Jason felt he couldn't relate to them. Like a wounded alien, he sat quietly at the back of the plane, thinking back to his lost friends whose lives had ended on the desert road.

They are the real heroes. Not me. Not you. Celebrate all you want, and revel in your moment of glory. None of you compare to those we left behind, and you should all be ashamed to be so happy.

The wind whipped through Jason's short black hair as he eyed the hundreds of family members holding signs and flowers in the airport hangar. The black tarmac spread out before them like a welcoming red carpet. Smiles beamed from the soldiers around him.

"Forward! March!" The company commander issued the order for the men to march forward toward their families. Step by step, their boots pounded the pavement creating a rhythmic cadence he had heard so often. Swinging his arms, Jason looked straight ahead into the crowd, knowing full well no one was there for him.

A mother knelt by her daughter, holding a sign: "Welcome Home, Corporal Rigel!" Another older couple stood holding each other as they waved toward someone to the left of the formation. Two children jumped up and down uncontrollably, screaming, "Daddy! Daddy!" A woman stood alone with a sign saying, "Thank You, Corporal Saiph!" It was a crowd filled with loving anticipation for the returning servicemen.

Jason walked toward all this love and happiness, knowing he wouldn't experience any of it. As if on cue, the formation broke out into a run as the marching turned into a stampede of excitement. The soldiers ran toward their loved ones, and the crowds merged, spreading among each other with cries and shouts of joy. Women and children were lifted into the arms of their loved ones. Couples kissed, and parents hugged their grown children, who were now finally home, safe from war.

Jason stood still as he took in the atmosphere around him. He was happy for them but knew it wasn't a place for him to be. He was a stranger, and the only thing waiting for him was his lonely apartment near downtown Plattsmouth.

Jason stood awkwardly and rubbed the left side of his face. The numbness was still something he could not get used to. The nerves on the left side of his face were damaged from the blast that limited feeling and left pockmarked scars. Pain still ran through his legs as he walked, but it was not nearly as unbearable as it used to be. *I gotta get out of here.* Jason's desire to be away from the large crowd grew as it had him glancing at everything and everyone, his senses on overdrive.

Jason felt himself staring at everyone's hands and constantly surveying his environment. It felt like he could hear absolutely everything— everyone's conversations, the shuffle of their feet across the pavement, the laughter, and the hum of the plane's engine behind him. It was all so overwhelming.

Leaving the gaggle of people, he grabbed his rucksack from the pile of equipment and exited the airport hangar. *That's better.* The crowd's buzz could still be heard in the building behind him, but it no longer had a potent effect on him. Jason stood facing a vast parking lot with vehicles and people coming and going like ants.

Time to grab a cab and get home …

Jason eyed the long line of taxi cabs parked on the side of the curb across the parking lot, hoping to cash in on the returning soldiers who may not have a ride. Adjusting his pack, Jason stepped forth toward the yellow vehicles.

Suddenly a white vehicle came to a screeching halt beside him, startling Jason and causing him to drop his pack. Jason instinctively clenched his fists and turned to face the white Toyota Corolla that had almost hit him.

"Sorry, sir! Sorry! Welcome home!" The older gentleman driving had his wife in the passenger seat and two teenage daughters in the back. Just a family caught up in the excitement of a returning loved one.

Jason picked his pack up from the ground, eyeing the driver with a look of aggression, and gave the car room to drive forward. He stared the vehicle down as it passed him. A white decal of a scorpion was affixed to the rear window.

What the fuck. That scared the shit out of me. Just get me the fuck home. I'm done with this scene.

"Taxi!" Jason hollered at one of the stopped cabs and saw its trunk pop open. Tossing his bag in the rear, he entered the vehicle to see an older man with olive skin and a turban. Immediately Jason's body tensed up.

"Welcome home, sir! Thank you for your service! Where should I take you?" The man spoke broken English with a Pakistani accent.

"Seven Alexander Street, please. It's near downtown Plattsmouth."

"Absolutely, sir!"

Jason made eye contact with the smiling man in the mirror as he put the gear into drive and pulled out onto the roadway.

Jason viewed the familiar scenery of his home state as they drove through the freeway toward his apartment. Small patches of snow lay on the ground in various places, and the gray overcast sky prevented any sunrays from breaking through. About a mile away, he saw a forest outside his window. The familiar environment reminded him of the hunts he went on with his father as a child.

I miss you, Dad.

Focusing his attention inside the cab, he watched the pay meter numbers increase as they drove farther toward his town. The black leather seats were worn down with scratches, and he wondered how many people may have been in this vehicle before him. A rattling noise grabbed Jason's attention as he moved his attention to the pennant hanging from the rearview mirror. The banner pictured a bear with stars around the border, affixed to a string of beads that rattled as it swung.

Strange thing to have hanging on your mirror …

The vehicle abruptly stopped, snapping Jason out of his thoughts. The turbaned man twisted to face Jason, smiling. "We're here, sir! No need for payment. Thank you for your service and again, welcome home!"

"Thank you, sir." Jason quickly opened the door and grabbed his pack, happy to be out of the confines of the vehicle and away from the stranger. No matter how kind the gentleman was, he couldn't shake the feeling that he might have been a threat to him. Jason looked up at his apartment and took a deep breath.

Home.

Entering his home, he was welcomed to a sterile and bare one-bedroom apartment. Everything stood the way he left it so many months ago. *I'm home.* Dropping his pack by the door, Jason locked the deadbolt and kicked off his boots, making a beeline toward the kitchen.

Jason opened the fridge and saw the one thing he had been looking forward to since getting on the plane. He grabbed the bottle of Jack Daniels and shut the refrigerator, holding a glass from his cupboard. *You deserve this, Jason. Welcome home.* Jason opened the bottle of whiskey and poured himself a drink.

He spent his first few hours at home sitting on the couch and watching the TV. He felt a hollowness in his chest. Being stateside while other soldiers were still fighting overseas felt so wrong. The feeling of leaving something partially finished was the best way he could describe it. If he could, he would return to Afghanistan in a heartbeat.

Although it was tough overseas, it was also more uncomplicated than being home. There was something about the primitive way of life he had over there. Every day brought the chance of a violent death. He was in a community of soldiers bound by their experiences. Their only job was to keep themselves and their comrades alive. They were a tribe of warriors. By cherishing each day they were alive, they encountered the total weight of human mortality and the beauty and terror that could be a part of the human experience. Back home, there was nothing that could replicate what he felt overseas.

When the evening news came on, Jason watched as they reported on the return of another company of soldiers. He looked hard to see if he could see himself on TV but couldn't discern himself from the crowd. The happy news story was soon followed by the anchor speaking about five more soldiers who died in Afghanistan that day.

Unnerved, Jason immediately turned off the TV, leaving only his reflection on the black screen, his ghostly silhouette looking back at him like he was a person from another world. Jason looked like the same man he always was, but there was something different about it, something he couldn't quite put his mind to. He wasn't a stranger, yet he was not the same man he was when he left. His tired, sunken eyes were a testament to that.

Shaking off his reflections, Jason grabbed the half-empty bottle of Jack and poured himself another drink. Jason raised the glass to his reflection on the screen and toasted it.

"Thank you for your service, Orion."

With a large gulp, he downed the glass of whiskey and then poured himself another.

Chapter 26

But in fact, discipline is the path to freedom.
—Jocko Willink

The Cabin
Present Day

Jason stepped through the cabin door to find the barren wooden abode precisely as he had left it. Animal heads decorated the shelter walls, and the woodstove remained in the corner of the room, cold after having been neglected for many months.

Jason scanned the room for signs of intrusion but found nothing. The small kitchen seemed undisturbed, and the table in the middle of the cabin was unmoved, with two chairs on either end. Jason's breath turned to fog as it hit the cold air. His old jacket hung on the wall hooks where he had left it. Feeling comfortable enough that he was alone, Jason placed his tomahawk in the corner and began inspecting the cabin.

Peering into his bedroom across the way, he spotted his bed in shambles, pathetically unmade. The sheets were tossed chaotically on the mattress, just as he often left them. Something annoyed Jason about that sight. He couldn't exactly describe his sentiments, but he had the impulse to make the bed, to be rid of the disorderly leftovers of his previous self. Jason kicked off his boots and hung up his fur coat as he walked toward the room.

Jason made the bed with military precision, turning the disheveled linen into an orderly, respectable bunk. Jason stood with his hand on his hips, scrutinizing his handiwork. *Well, I didn't think this would be the first thing I did when I got here ...*

Jason ambled back into the main room and was frozen with concern as he spotted busted glass scattered across the floor at the back wall. *Someone was here.* He eyed the room to see if anything else was out of the ordinary but couldn't detect any other signs of intrusion.

Wait …

The glass scattered across the floor was nowhere near a window or any other entry point. *It couldn't have been a break-in … oh …* Jason had a moment of clarity as he recalled hurling his glass pot of coffee against the wall after burning his arm many months ago. Dried dark brown coffee stains were cast upon the wooden floor, a testament to the spontaneous and uncontrolled rage from a minor inconvenience.

Well, that's embarrassing.

Jason felt completely different from the man who once whipped the pot against the wall in anger. He felt shame and embarrassment from how easily he let his emotions control his actions. *Never again …*

Still cold to the bone, he strode toward the wood stove and lit a fire, endeavoring to bring warmth back into the wintry cabin. Jason thawed his frozen hands by the fire, admiring the dancing flames and soaking in the heat's comfort.

His stomach rumbled, reminding Jason how long it had been since he last ate. Starving, Jason opened a kitchen cabinet and grabbed some dried meat and water to satisfy his hunger before cleaning up the mess he had made. Jason tore into the dried venison with the vigor of a man who hadn't eaten a proper meal in days. He closed his eyes and savored every bite of the meat; the comfort of home was returning to him.

"Welcome home, Orion." Jason spun, dropping his water to the ground.

At the head of the table sat a man, a mirror image of Jason. It was the familiar demon that had been stalking him this entire time. The man, who referred to himself as Jack, sat in an all-black suit. The dress shirt and tie were black as night, and his jet-black hair was slicked back. He appeared as if he had just returned from a funeral. Or was about to go to one.

The temperature in the room dropped as the mirror image of Jason held a glass of whiskey in his hand and whirled it, eyeing the golden-brown liquid as it reeled in the glass. A half-empty bottle of Jack Daniels sat on the table in front of him.

"Honestly, I didn't think you would make it this far. I'd be lying if I said I wasn't impressed with your persistence. You should be proud of yourself, Orion." Jack placed the glass on the table and offered a sarcastic slow clap, mocking Jason with a contorted grin.

"Here, have a drink." Jack slid the glass across the wooden table toward Jason. "A celebration. Let's say a toast for you finally returning to this pitiful place you call home."

Jason eyed the glass of whiskey that had now made its way to his end of the table. Unmoving, he scrutinized the mirror image of himself. He scanned the cabin for any semblance of a weapon. His tomahawk lay by the front door, a fire poker next to the wood stove, and a spare hatchet against the back wall. All were out of arm's reach.

"And what a welcome you had! Nobody is here to greet you. No loved ones to say hi to and speak about your journey. Hell, nobody even cleaned up the mess you left before you ran out into the woods in a childish rage." Jack leaned back, interlocking his hands behind his head.

"It's almost as if you don't have anybody left in the world who loves you." Jason's heart began beating faster with outrage. *Keep a clear head. Don't let this guy suck you in.*

"Well, actually, maybe that's not true, Orion. I care about you. I've always wanted the best for you. We just never came to an understanding, that's all." Jack leaned forward and placed his elbows on the table, leaning into Jason with an insidious sincerity.

"I've only ever wanted you to find peace, Orion. You spent your time with that old man, and he taught you things that could help you. I'll admit that. But he never gave you any answers! I have the answers to your problems. Death, Orion. Death is the ultimate peace. No anger, loneliness, sadness and isolation, rage-filled, drunken nights—just pure, peaceful darkness."

The windows in the cabin had turned dark as the sun had now wholly set, casting the forest into darkness for another cold night. Jason rubbed the left side of his face anxiously.

"I've given you multiple opportunities to do this, Orion. Killing yourself would be the easiest way, but you were too much of a coward to pull the trigger. I offered to pull it for you, hell, I DID pull the trigger for you, but you were too cowardly to stand still! I'm offering you one more chance, Orion. Come to me. End this yourself, or I will." Jack's piercing blue eyes attempted to cut holes into Jason's soul.

"Have a drink, Orion. It will give you some liquid courage to go through with it all. Lord knows if there is one thing you need, it's courage."

Jason held eye contact with Jack and slowly slid the glass of whiskey off the table, busting it onto the wooden floor and scattering liquid and glass across the cabin.

Jack leaned his head over the side of the table and examined the broken offering. "Hmmph. Well, who's going to clean that up now? That wasn't very considerate, you know."

"I'm done with you," Jason spoke, his eyes shooting daggers at the man in black across from him. "I'm done with your mind games. I'm done with your tricks. I'm done taking your bait."

Jack leaned back and folded his arms in disapproval.

"I'm done with you. You will no longer control me. I've retaken my mind, Jack, and there's nothing you can do about it." Jason stood firm with his shoulders back and chin raised.

Jack spit on the ground beside him and frowned at Jason, undoubtedly displeased with what Jason had to say. "Bullshit. Even your creepy old friend Charging Bear told you you'd never be able to get rid of me. I'll be with you forever, Orion. FOREVER. And there is nothing you can do to get rid of me."

"Charging Bear was right," Jason responded, standing assertively at the end of the table. "He was right about a lot of things. I know full well I'll never be able to get rid of you, but maybe you have a hard time comprehending what I'm saying to you."

Jason placed his hands on the table and leaned toward the seated demon. "I will no longer let you control me. You will forever sit at the back of my mind and observe my new life. You will fade, whimpering into the night with your asinine words and directions."

Jason truly felt as if he were speaking to himself as he leaned closer to the demon with virtually identical features. It reminded Jason of the many times he leaned in toward the mirror and stared deep into his own eyes, questioning his path in life and who he had become. This time, it felt like he was speaking to an earlier, more immature version of himself.

"You will rage into the quiet recesses of my mind and forever be unheard, unacknowledged, and powerless. Yes, you will always be with me, but you will be MY prisoner, forced to watch as I reclaim my life from here on out."

Jack smashed both fists on the table, causing the bottle of Jack Daniels to tumble over. Enraged, Jack stood up abruptly, making his chair fall backward. Both men now stood staring at each other.

Jason, disheveled, unshaven, and dirty, was the polar opposite of the clean-cut and sharply dressed Jack. One man looked as if he had just come from a funeral wake, and the other from months wandering the woods.

"You can say that all you want, Orion. But it's easier said than done. You have many weaknesses, and I will be there to exploit them all. I will be there when you sit alone in isolation and doubt. I will be there when you get rejected and when you fail. When your face turns numb, and your legs throb with pain. I WILL BE THERE. I will be there to remind you that those are not scars of war. Those are scars of FAILURE. Failure to keep your friends safe. FAILURE to fulfill the duty you had. FAILURE to stop your friends from dying."

"I never failed. You made me believe I failed. I did what I could, but fate had other plans."

Jack bowed his head as he listened to Jason. Snapping his head up with a deformed face of anger, his eyes seemed darker and more sunken than before.

"You failed your friends, Orion, because they're all dead. Just like the little girl whose mother you killed. You failed her too. Now she lives a life somewhere without the love of her mother because of YOU."

Jason unconsciously stroked the left side of his face as the horrible memory of the event returned to him.

"You're right, Jack. I did kill her, but I never meant to. And if I spend the rest of my life in guilt and shame, I will be nothing but another casualty of war." Jason could feel the thump of each heartbeat reverberate in his chest as the emotions of the incident unwound within him. Throughout the flood of anger, sadness, and shame, Jason concentrated on keeping a clear mind, not permitting emotions to govern his actions or words.

"I've atoned for what I did, and although I will never be fully free from the guilt, I will not let it erode my mind any further. I paid the price, a price not as great as what the girl paid, but it was a price nonetheless. I am not a murderer."

Jack rolled his dark eyes and shook his head in annoyance. "Semantics, we all know who you are, Orion. Convincing yourself otherwise will only prolong the pain."

"That's right, we both know who I am. I am Jason *Orion*. I'm a soldier, a leader, and a loyal friend. I'm a loving son who is grateful for all his father taught him and misses the mother he never knew. I am not perfect. I have made mistakes and, like all humans, will make more in the future. I'm a fighter. I'm a fighter that has been to the brink of death multiple times, by my own hands and that of others, yet I have survived."

Jack's arms began trembling, and his lips quivered as he pressed his hands harder into the table with every word Jason spoke.

"I am a survivor. I am a soldier. And I have persevered through everything you have thrown at me and will continue to do so until the day I die, as an old man, peacefully in his bed surrounded by people who love him."

"DELIRIOUS!" Jack flipped the table in an unbridled rage, forcing the bottle of Jack to smash against the floor with a thunderous crash.

"You're delirious! That old man has poisoned your mind with false hopes and excuses! You let your father die on the floor alone, and you think that's OK? Do you think you can just live your life like normal and forget all the sins you have committed and the pain you have caused? All the death and devastation?"

Tears of jet-black oil began dripping from Jack's eyes as he continued to shout, enraged with Jason. His once-blue eyes were now fully flooded with black liquid.

"You don't deserve PEACE! You don't deserve HAPPINESS! Aargh!" Jack hunkered over and cradled his stomach in discomfort as if someone had stabbed him in the gut. Looking up at Jason with black liquid pouring down his face, his voice had changed into an insidious, deep-throated growl.

"You deserve to bathe in your GUILT! To soak in your SHAME! You deserve a death filled with PAIN and REGRET!" The hairs on Jack's skin began to darken and grow. Lumps of black blemishes sprouted across his entire body, merging and darkening his skin. Jason surveyed the room for weapons as he watched Jack's body transform.

"I don't care if you agree, ORION. I'm done with talking! It's time we put this to rest once and for ALL!" Black shards of organic armor tore through Jack's spine as he spoke in despair. His fingers broke and ripped as black pincer claws emerged from his forearms. A large, monstrous tail shot through his tailbone and rose painfully above him.

"I am the ABYSS, ORION!" Jason backed up into the kitchen counter, fear causing his muscles to weaken.

"AND YOU WILL COME TO ME!"

Jack's body exploded in a burst of blackness, his flesh and bones grotesquely scattering across the ground as the enormous beast ruptured from within him.

Scorpio.

Chapter 27

Throw roses into the abyss and say: Here is my thanks to the monster that did not succeed in swallowing me alive.
—Friedrich Nietzsche

The Cabin
Present Day

The Scorpion's stinger smashed through the kitchen counter, launching wooden splinters into the air, narrowly missing Jason as he dipped out of the way. The confrontation had turned physical as Jason's demon rid itself of its human form and burst into an enormous black Scorpion. Its saw-toothed pincers and razor-sharp tail were now attempting to accomplish what it had desired to do all along—end Jason's life.

The Scorpion let out a chilling, high-pitched screech that nearly burst Jason's eardrums. The creature drove its claw toward Jason, who stood with his back against the refrigerator. The appliance wobbled backward, denting the door's upper portion as Jason again evaded the strike.

Shit! Shit! Shit!

The confined space of the cabin filled him with claustrophobia and dread as he had little room to maneuver. Relentlessly the Scorpion used its pincers and tail to strike down upon Jason, who tried repeatedly to avoid the attacks.

Jason sidestepped a tail strike as the stinger punctured the cabin wall, giving him enough time to run around the monster and slide into his bedroom. *Weapons! Weapons! I need one!* Desperation turned to panic as the room lay bare of anything he could use to defend himself.

Jason heard the Scorpion's legs clacking like the engine of a locomotive as it turned to face the room. Panicked, Jason slid underneath his bed. He had never felt so helpless as he did at this moment. Like a child frightened by a nightmare, he rolled against the wall, hoping the Scorpion either didn't see him or couldn't get to him.

The creature was too large to make it through the doorway, but its tail was long enough to reach the mattress. A massive pointed stinger burst through the top of the bed and barely missed Jason's face, striking the ground with a dull thud. *Holy shit, that was close!* Jason pressed himself against the wall, trying to mold himself into the wall and away from the stinger's range.

Again, the tail pierced through the mattress above, hitting inches closer to Jason. *What the hell am I going to do?* A terrifying screech ripped through the cabin as the Scorpion shrieked in frustration. A black object abruptly obscured Jason's vision as he felt a warm, ripping sensation roll down his left shoulder. "AHH! FUCK!" he cried out in pain as the stinger withdrew from the bed. Blood ran down Jason's shoulder as he realized the monster had scratched him.

Desperately he pressed himself further against the wall and contemplated his options. *I can't stay here. I'm a dead man if I do. I need to get out of here, but how? What do I do?!* The stinger pierced the mattress again, closer to Jason's legs. *OK, OK, do something!*

Jason went with the first and only idea that came to his mind. As the stinger struck down and stabbed the wooden floor, Jason grabbed its tip as hard as he could, rolling onto his belly for support. With his arms firmly wrapped around the stinger, Jason used his back to push the mattress upward, forcing the bed to slide up the Scorpion's tail.

The monster retracted its natural weapon only to have its vision blocked by the bed wrapped around its tail. Jason rolled out of the way as the demon blindly stabbed the ground in frustration, unable to gain a precise aim through the mattress. *Go! Now!* Jason crawled as fast as he could through the doorway and underneath the monstrous Scorpion as it desperately tried to shake the bed stuck to its tail.

Breaking past the Scorpion, Jason rushed to his feet and raced toward the cabin's main door. *Get to the door! Get out now!* The world suddenly plunged from underneath him as he saw the exit door ascend above him. Jason fell flat on his face, sliding on the spilled whiskey and pieces of broken glass. He groaned as the wind was knocked out of his gut, momentarily paralyzing him. *Ugh, God! Go! Get up!*

Jason shifted to look behind him, witnessing the Scorpion pull back from the doorway, using the frame as leverage to free its tail from the mattress. With a roar, the Scorpion turned to regard Jason helplessly lying on the floor in a bed of broken glass.

He watched, momentarily mesmerized, at the black armored tail rising to the ceiling as an executioner would raise his axe. Swiftly the tail came crashing down, narrowly missing Jason's head as he rolled out of the way at the final second.

Jason rolled toward the back wall, farther away from the exit. The main door was no longer an option. He lay on his back and looked around, detecting all his trophies on the wall. All of the animal heads looked onward into nothingness. Their marble eyes were empty of emotion and life, fastened to their permanent resting place as a testament to Jason's accomplishments. Deer, moose, and wolves all looked on as the Scorpion turned to face its prone rival.

Injured, exhausted, and weakened, Jason struggled to get up. The inevitability of his situation ate at him. Mortality was all-encompassing as he felt the Scorpion's eyes fixate on him.

I'm going to die.

Defeated, Jason tilted his head backward in anguish, seeing the lone trophy mount he had affixed to the back wall. The head of the black bear looked directly toward the Scorpion, its jaws open in rage and fearlessness as if it were about to burst through the wall and attack. Just like it once did in his nightmare.

Charging Bear …

Memories of Charging Bear raced through his mind at lightning speed, brought on by the stoic deceased animal. All the words of wisdom, the faith he placed in Jason, the patience he had with him, the methods and skills he gave him … the love.

Jason thought of the journey that brought him back to this very place, the cabin. The long dark nights in the wilderness alone. The voices of his demons calling out to him from the darkness. The escapes from mythical beasts and battles with the manifestations of his friends and enemies. Everything came rushing back to him.

This is not how it ends.

As Jason lay facing the approaching Scorpion, pain needled into his back, sprawled out on the broken glass and dried coffee stains. *A fitting place to be.* The remnants of his previous self. After smashing the coffee pot against the wall, he left the cabin in an uncontrollable rage. Now he lay on top of his emotional destruction. Now, this was where he would die.

Not today.

Jason rolled, again evading the Scorpion's tail as it stabbed into the wooden floor. Rising to his feet, Jason could feel the blood rapidly pump through his veins. The sounds of drums began rhythmically beating throughout the cabin. The interior of his humble abode was utterly destroyed. Tables were flipped over, kitchen counters smashed apart, refrigerators busted, and glass and fragments of wood scattered across the floor. His once peaceful shelter of isolation and escape had turned into a war zone.

Breathing heavily, Jason slid toward the wood stove, the fire raging within its cast-iron belly. Seizing the fire poker, Jason shoved the iron bar into the stove pit and aggressively scooped out a log. With one swift movement, he flung the flaming log toward the Scorpion, striking it directly in its many insidious eyes. Embers and ashes dispersed past the creature as it wailed in pain.

"COME TO ME!" Jason screamed toward the creature, feeling as if a thousand warrior spirits had entered his soul. He no longer felt fear. He felt resolve. A desire to end this demon once and for all.

"This is what you wanted, isn't it?!" Jason stood screaming at the Scorpion as it flailed its extremities in pain. "Well, here I am! COME TO ME!" The demon unleashed a roar so loud it felt as if it had punched Jason in the gut. Jason shielded his face as his hair blew backward from the gust of wind roaring from the creature. Its legs clacked as it raced forward toward Jason. "COME TO ME!" Jason stood holding the iron poker like a baseball bat.

Jason ran and slid underneath the Scorpion as it thrust its saw-toothed claw toward him. With rapid speed, Jason stabbed the soft underbelly of the Scorpion's organic armor. Its light gray belly was pierced repeatedly, each thrust bringing a scream of agony from the monster.

"RRaaaaHHHGG!!!" Jason roared in furious anger. He raged toward the demon that had nearly persuaded him to end his life. The monster that had shadowed him everywhere he went. The devil that had waited until he was alone with his thoughts to pop up and poison his mind. Over and over, Jason stabbed the belly of the monster, dark red blood pouring down upon him, covering his face and chest. The demon withdrew and stumbled.

The Scorpion roiled in pain, flailing its legs, unable to reach its wounds. Jason stood and retreated slowly, hypnotized by the Scorpion's painful cries. Backing against the wall, he was startled by razor-sharp teeth materializing next to his face. The mounted head of the black bear looked ahead at the Scorpion as Jason peered into its empty marble eyes.

The cries of agony from the Scorpion ceased, causing Jason to divert his attention from the bear's head and back toward the demon. There it stood, its damaged eyes staring at Jason in pure hatred. Flames and smoke grew behind the creature as the burning log began spreading fire throughout the cabin. The odor of ash and sulfur filled the room, stinging Jason's eyes and making his lungs feel like sandpaper.

Jason witnessed the stinger rise and strike down toward him through the gray smoke. He slipped the strike, causing the stinger to miss and land within the mounted bear's jaws. The kinetic energy deformed its face and made the jaws clench down onto the tail.

With a scream, Jason raised his iron fire poker and thrust it downward with all his might. Piercing the bear's upper and lower jaw, it penetrated the Scorpion's tail and implanted into the wood, affixing the Scorpion to the wall.

Jason fell and witnessed the Scorpion desperately try to free itself from the wall. *GO! NOW!* Without hesitation, Jason rolled onto his belly and began crawling for the exit. The frantic screeches from the Scorpion reverberated throughout the smoke-filled cabin. The fires of hell caked every wall within Jason's den of isolation.

The heat burned his skin as he reached the door, smoke filling his lungs with each anguished breath. Attempting to stand, Jason collapsed, smacking his back into the corner of the wall and causing his old jacket to fall beside him. Jason grabbed the jacket he hardly used and placed it over his head, shielding himself from the thickening smoke.

Blinded by the ash sailing through the air, Jason continued to hear the painful screams of the Scorpion still trying to free itself from the wall. Try as it might, it couldn't escape. The Scorpion was another trophy mount affixed to the wall by Jason.

Feeling the corner of the wall, Jason grasped the ivory tomahawk he had placed near the door. *Get out! Now!* Desperately reaching for a door handle, Jason pushed as hard as possible, breaching the door and tumbling into the snow.

The coldness of the snow brought immediate relief from the fires of hell that burned within the cabin. Drums continued to beat through the night, echoing into the air as Jason crawled through the snow to get as far away from the fire as he could.

Each movement he made with his arms and legs grew weaker and slower the further he got. Soon, he couldn't crawl anymore. Jason remained on his hands and knees as he vomited a pile of blackness into the snow below him. The pain rose up in his esophagus and exploded out of him. An angelic relief flowed within him as he collapsed onto his back, facing the night sky above.

Jason used his arm to wipe the Scorpion's blood off his face, but it only spread the red liquid across the lower half of his face, just as Charging Bear had done with his war paint.

Above him danced rays of green and purple, an aurora borealis shimmering across the night sky, illuminating the white open field and majestic trees. Millions of stars shone throughout the black canvas, brighter than any he'd ever seen before. It was the most beautiful sight Jason had ever seen.

He sat on his knees and focused his attention on the burning cabin. *It's gone. It's all gone.* The building that had once been his final hope for survival was now burning in flames. Jason might have already been dead had it not been for this one place. Dead on his couch with a bullet in his head in Plattsmouth.

Jason came to Alaska to find peace in isolation; this cabin was his fortress of seclusion. It was the only thing that kept him alive; now, it was burning to the ground. He couldn't help but feel a great sadness in his heart as he watched the orange embers rise into the air.

The night was broken by an enormous screech from within the flames. The scream was more horrible than any he had heard before. It was as if thousands of souls were simultaneously undergoing the most terrible pain imaginable. Although terrifying, the sounds also made Jason's heart weigh heavy.

The cabin collapsed, turning into a burning pile of wood. The dark gray smoke rose from the flames, contorting its clouds into grotesque faces of pain and anger. Faces formed within the smoke and screamed in pain and agony at the sky above. Trapped in eternal flames, the darkness attempted to flee the cabin's burning confines. The spirits of rage, depression, and vengeance dissipated into the night sky as the smoky faces dissolved above the fire.

It's over.

Jason grasped his jacket and tomahawk as he watched the cabin disintegrate into the fire. Glancing up to the sky, Jason thanked everyone who had helped him recover from his pit of darkness. A mix of snow and ash fell from the sky, causing a beautiful veil of white that reflected the cabin's fire.

He viewed the surrounding trees around him, illuminated by the falling snow, and observed strange-looking deformations. Each branch appeared to have distorted bumps emerging on every tree surrounding the open snowy hill.

Ravens …

Jason realized that these were not just deformities or bumps of the tree but thousands upon thousands of ravens sitting on the branches, all staring down at Jason kneeling in the snow. *The raven who brought light to the world. The souls of our loved ones.*

"ORION!" The voice boomed throughout the night as logs and burned wood erupted from the smoldering remnants of the cabin. In unison, all the ravens looked toward the fire.

"COME TO ME!" Alone in the fire stood a contorted Jack, malformed and completely engulfed in flames, holding the iron bar that had trapped him in the cabin. The demon stood in the fire, a wolf's skull and hideous antlers bound to its head. Jack pointed the iron bar that had trapped him to the wall at Jason.

"COME TO ME, ORION!" Jack raised his arms in the air, holding the iron bar in rage. His skin was charred like a demon from hell. Blood covered the top half of his face, the opposite of how Jason now looked.

Jason grasped his tomahawk and stood, waiting for his demon to make the first move. Deafening drums pounded throughout the dark wilderness as the two stared each other down, breathing heavily in anticipation.

Suddenly the demon threw a massive burning log out of his way and began sprinting toward Jason, the iron bar gripped firmly in its hand.

"RRRAAAHHH!!!!" With a warrior's cry, Jason raced toward his demon with the ivory tomahawk in his right hand. He could hear and feel nothing except the pounding of his heart and the mysterious beating of drums as he sprinted through the snow.

His eyes fixated on the demon as it neared, its horrible, deformed antlers and wolf skull dashing toward Jason like a beast from the Underworld. The devil, now entirely free from the burning flames, ran through the snow, closing the gap between the two foes.

Jack unleashed a menacing, deep-throated roar as he raised the bar above his head, now feet away from Jason. With one hand on his tomahawk, Jason continued to move forward, undeterred by the evil in front of him.

I am in control.

As the two men clashed, Jason lowered himself and slid through the snow, avoiding Jack's swing of the iron bar that nearly took off his head. Jack spun with his iron bar raised. Having dodged the demon's swing, Jason rose to his feet as Jack turned to face him and thrust his tomahawk upward into the demon's lower chest cavity.

The ivory tomahawk embedded itself into the demon's torso with a fleshy thud. Jason gave the weapon one more forceful thrust upward as he shoved it deeper into Jack's gut.

Jason stared deep into his demon's eyes, only inches away from his face. The two men gazed at each other for a moment, surpassing space and time. Jason's blue eyes and Jack's dark, cynical pupils observed each other as the black liquid poured out of Jack's mouth, dripping down his chin in helpless pain. Jason leaned into the demon's face and whispered.

"You have no control over me."

Jack's face twisted with pure unhinged wrath as his eyes began to glow bright white. The carvings on Jason's tomahawk began shimmering in a golden glow. The weapon vibrated, and the ground began to quake as the light grew brighter from within the demon.

The howls of wolves, bears, cougars, and birds rang throughout the dark wilderness. An orchestra of tormented nature sang as the light burst from Jason's demon. Jack opened his mouth and let out a furious roar of madness as a blast of blinding light shot through his mouth, ears, and eyes. The darkened forest was illuminated under the explosion of a blinding white light as the demon exploded. Jason felt himself being propelled off the ground and thrown into the air.

All the trees surrounding the open hill were tilted away by the shockwave, causing thousands of ravens to fly up into the night sky and toward the northern lights.

Jason landed on the snow but felt only sand. His first thoughts were to search for his fellow soldiers—Brad, Diaz, and Sergeant Bass, the people he loved. He felt the left side of his face turn numb as the light faded away.

Struggling to lift himself from the ground, Jason collapsed, unconscious in the cold Alaskan snow. The northern lights danced above him as the cabin continued to smolder. Ravens flew through the sky, evading the blinding devastation.

The snow fell upon the earth. Jason lay alone in the coldness of the wintery Alaskan snow, destruction surrounding his unconscious body. There was no one near him. No animal, no friend.

No demon.

Chapter 28

Healing does not mean the damage never existed. It means the damage no longer controls our lives.
—Native American Proverb

Out of the Woods
Three Days Later

Gone. The negative inner voice was gone. Well, not gone, but quieted. Suppressed to the point of being inaudible. It had been three days since the intentional burning of the cabin. A decision Jason made out of pure survival. The will to live and the desire to progress forward in life had been more potent than the negativity that brooded inside him.

The cabin, a symbol of everything he worked for in his misguided escape from society, had gone up in flames. There was no turning back, no undoing the decision he had made. It was time to leave the wilderness.

Burn the boats.

In 1519 the legendary Spanish conquistador Hernán Cortés began his conquest of the Aztec empire. As they arrived on the shores of the foreign kingdom, he gave his men but one order. *Burn the boats.*

This immense symbol of finality was purposefully issued so his men would understand that there was no retreat, no way back, and no escape. The only path they could take, whether complicated or dangerous, was forward.

With the cabin in ashes, Jason had burned his boat—the boat he'd used to escape reality, society, and his own spirit. The only path for him now was forward, forward into the community that he had abandoned physically, mentally, and spiritually. His perseverance through the dark outdoors had toughened him into embarking on his hike out of the woods.

For the first time in years, Jason felt human. He felt normal. The sky was a bit more beautiful, the wintry air smelled more potent and fresh, and the sounds of nature rang an angelic melody in his ears that brought about peace and serenity. He didn't feel reborn. He felt recovered.

Rebirth would mean a new life. However, Jason was not walking into a new life; he was walking back to his old one.

He had entered the Alaskan wilderness with a broken soul. Like so many others, his spirit was harmed by the most terrible experiences humanity could expose him to: War. Death. Pain and loneliness.

Cracks and fissures spread throughout his spirit like the roots of a black tree growing more towering with each traumatic experience. In contrast to what Jason thought, isolation was no friend of his. The most dangerous time for him was being alone—alone with his thoughts, memories, and ideations. That was when his negative inner voice, his demon named Jack, took advantage of him. In those quiet moments, Jack saw the silence as a weakness. An opportunity to use this time of isolation to scream loudly within Jason's soul.

You're a failure! You're pathetic! You'll never be good enough! You're better off dead! Kill yourself ... You should feel guilt ... You should feel shame ... You deserve pain and misery.

You're hopeless and powerless, Orion. Give up ...

After the destruction of his cabin, Jason embarked on a three-day trek out of the Alaskan backwoods. He was exposed to many quiet moments during his journey. Quiet moments that, unusually, came without interference by his inner demon. Quiet moments that brought peace and internal reflection. It was a new but familiar experience, something he had not been exposed to since his father passed.

He spent the cold nights by an open fire hastily making shelters from sticks and pine branches. The weather, luckily, was not as overbearing as the seasonal Alaskan winter usually was. Jason was cold, tired, and sore ... but happy.

When Jason burned his cabin, he also burned everything inside it. All his survival gear, food, water, and clothing. Nothing was left except the clothes on his body, his old beaten-up jacket, and his tomahawk.

Most individuals would see themselves in these circumstances and panic. They would see the hopelessness of it all and wander aimlessly without direction or purpose into their demise. However, with years of outdoor experience, Jason was primed to persevere in the elements.

All the lessons he learned from his father, the military, and Charging Bear had prepared him for conditions where survival depended on living off the land and finding your way home. But, in a sense, Jason had been finding his way home since he left Plattsmouth.

When he chose to leave the small town he grew up in, he was not leaving home. He was leaving a city, an apartment. He was leaving empty beer cans and a society he could no longer tolerate. A home is more than a place you occupy. A home is a shelter from storms, all sorts of storms.

Jason, although not having a proper living space, was now at home. Every shelter felt peaceful. Sleeping under a pile of tree branches and sticks was home, napping against a tree was home, and walking through the woods purposefully to a destination was home.

Peace now began to flourish in Jason's heart. When you become trapped inside yourself, inside your negative voice, you miss the important things that lie outside your body by being too consumed with staring into the heart's abyss. Jason was now able to focus on more than the evil things. He was able to live again.

Like many soldiers throughout history, Jason had a wounded heart and an injured mind. And like many soldiers throughout history, his heart could not be mended alone. Doomed is the warrior who denies the help of others, convicted by his own pride.

Charging Bear, this mystical man who saved Jason from the brink of death, knew these obscure rules of life. His wisdom extended beyond the present. It drew from the oral histories and lessons of his ancestors. Lessons that many in society have forgotten.

We cannot fight our demons alone.

But that does not mean our support must be physical. It does not mean you need someone standing next to you. Because love transcends the physical world. A mother's love for her son, the son's love for his father, and the devotion between friends and partners all leave impressions within our souls.

We are never alone, even when we're lost in the woods.

Jason's soul was shrouded in the love of his father, mother, and friends who had left this world. Although he did not know it, they were beside him the entire time. Jason was so damaged, too focused inwards, poisoned by his negative inner voice that he could not feel that love because his pain was too overpowering.

The scars he had on his face, legs, and torso were nothing compared to the ones he had in his heart. Scars that never fully healed and continued to bleed with every emotional reaction to every trigger and memory.

They will never fully heal.

The acceptance of this fact was what began to equip Jason with the armor of perseverance. A complete acceptance and acknowledgment of the past and present.

To have a hopeful future, you must accept your past and acknowledge your present, for you cannot know where you are going until you truly understand where you have been and where it is leading you.

In a way, we are all lost in the woods. Some more than others. With a leap of faith, let the river of fate guide you downstream to your destiny, and you will find peace.

* * *

Jason reached the tree line. Tired, dirty, and hungry, his body was weakened, but his heart was strong. He found himself smiling during the cold hard times throughout his three-day journey. He was thankful his walk out of the woods was peaceful. No wolves, no Taliban, no demons. It reminded him of his long hikes with his father as a child, a core memory that stayed with him throughout his life.

I love you, Dad.

Jason took a knee as he finally saw the lone road he was dropped off at so long ago. The blacktop pavement popped through the trees, a unique man-made structure guiding a path to civilization. It was all Jason had been looking for.

* * *

The morning after the burning of the cabin, Jason had started his journey out of the woods. Cold and tired, he warmed his hands in his beaten-up jacket. It was then that Jason felt something foreign in his pocket, a crumpled-up scrap of paper that he first thought was a piece of garbage or a discarded receipt.

Uncrumpling the paper, Jason brought it up to his face and inspected it. It was a note in blue ink with a neat feminine touch of cursive writing. It read:

> *When the woods become dark and lonely, you can find a*
> *light in my home.*
> *Artemis 877-927-8387*
> *xoxo*

* * *

Jason's stomach rumbled as he looked past the edge of the tree line to the road. Surviving mainly off berries and small game meat, he was becoming adept at feeding himself from the earth. *There we go!*

Jason reached down and reaped a pile of mushrooms that grew near his feet. Pale white with tinges of black, he ate a few bitter fungi and placed the rest in his pocket for later. Jason stood peering beyond the tree line, then remembered something his father had told him long ago.

"Remember Jason, when a hunter returns holding only a handful of mushrooms ... don't ask him how his hunt went."

Jason smirked, took a deep breath, and stepped out of the forest.

Epilogue

Plattsmouth, Nebraska
Three Years Later

Back in Nebraska, Jason walked along the side of the road with cars speeding past him periodically, en route to whatever destination they had in their busy lives. His worn-out muddy boots were becoming a liability to his feet, creating blisters and sores from the long walks he embarked on throughout the years. *I need new boots—you guys have treated me well, but you've passed your prime.*

The snow-covered gravel crunched beneath his feet as he continued his pilgrimage to his old hometown of Plattsmouth. Jason had landed at the airport that morning. Ever the frugal type and still having the conditioning and marching habits the military bred into him, he chose to walk to Plattsmouth rather than rent a car or take a cab. After five hours, though, he was beginning to regret his choice.

Damn, no sense continuing like this or my feet will fall off. Time to ask for some help. There's no shame in that.

Jason turned to face the oncoming traffic and stuck his thumb out, hoping to hitch a ride with anyone kind enough to pick him up. He was clean-shaven and wore a beaten-up baseball cap covering his freshly cut hair. His skin was a bit more smooth than it had been three years ago, and his scars, while still visible, appeared to have faded a bit. As usual, Jason had his pack with all his necessities. He was always prepared and content with living off of what was on his back—yet another habit that was ingrained into him from the military and his father.

Many cars passed until he found success in an old gray short-bed truck that pulled off to the side of the road a few dozen yards in front of him. *Perfect, thank you!* Jason strolled to the passenger side window to see an older man in the driver's seat.

His hair was gray and long, tied back in a ponytail. His skin was leathery and gave the impression of a life of hard work and exposure to the outdoors. The man wore an old worn-out jacket with the distinct camouflage pattern of the desert battle dress uniform worn by the United States Army in the early nineties.

"Looking for a ride?" The man spoke with his hands still on his steering wheel. His back seats were filled with discarded clothing and other garbage, giving the impression that he lived out of this van.

"Sure am, if you don't mind. I'm only heading to Plattsmouth. My feet were starting to kill me."

"Hop in, son." The gray-haired man unlocked the door. "Throw your pack in the truck bed if you like."

Jason tossed his pack into the truck's bed and sat in the passenger seat. His feet began to throb as the blood flowed into his lower extremities, no longer obstructed by the pressure of his body weight.

"Man, that feels good. It's nice to get off my feet. These boots aren't as good as they used to be."

The gray-haired man leaned over to inspect Jason's footwear. "I have a similar style of boot. Once they hit a certain amount of time or use, they can be a pain in the ass. I hate breaking in new boots, so I try to get the most out of them."

"I know that feeling. That's one of the reasons I've been hanging on to these. Old habits die hard." Jason looked up from his boots and faced the stranger. "I'm Jason, by the way." He stretched his neck side to side and made himself comfortable as the truck pulled back onto the road.

"Nice to meet you. It should only be about a half-hour drive to Plattsmouth, so it shouldn't take long. Why are you out on the road anyways? Where are you coming from?"

"From Alaska, actually. I landed this morning. I do a lot of hiking up there, so I figured, why waste money when I can just get to my destination on foot? Of course, I didn't expect my boots would fail me." Jason rubbed the left side of his face, numbness still affecting him after all these years.

"Alaska? I've never been there. I heard it's beautiful. What brings you to Plattsmouth, of all places?" The gray-haired man spun the steering wheel as they made their way onto the freeway.

"It's my hometown. I grew up here. I haven't been here in three years, and I decided to come back for a week and visit a few places."

"Three years? Why now?"

"It's the tenth anniversary of an incident where I lost some friends. I wanted to come to pay respects to them and visit my father. They're buried in the same place."

"Oh. I'm sorry to hear that." The gray-haired man's shoulders seemed to slump as if he had just heard bad news about his loved ones.

"That's OK. Thanks for giving me a ride. You're really helping me out."

"Anytime. Not many people pick up hitchhikers anymore. Everyone is afraid of a human connection. They'd prefer to be on their phones."

Jason laughed. "I get that. My father used to say similar things about society." He stared out the window to view the snow-covered trees passing by the window in the distance, reminding him of Alaska.

"Do you have any family back in Alaska?"

"Yeah, my fiancée. We live just north of Anchorage. I wouldn't let her come with me, though. It's something I felt I needed to do alone." Jason stared down at the tattoo on his right hand and rubbed the soft part between his index finger and thumb.

After the proposal, Artemis and Jason got matching tattoos on their hands of two swans creating the shape of a heart with their necks—an ancient Greek symbol of love, a mythology that both of them were passionate about.

The man looked at Jason, inspecting him. "I get that. You can learn a lot when you're alone."

Jason raised his head a scrutinized the man in curiosity. "I never got your name."

"Jackson."

"Where'd you get that jacket, Jackson?" Jason eyed the desert camouflage jacket.

"It's an old jacket I wore back in the first Gulf War. Desert Storm in the early nineties."

"Oh." *Don't say it, don't say it, think of something else, Jason, don't say it!* "Thanks for your service, Jackson." *Dammit! I guess I understand why everyone says that. What else do you say?*

The gray-haired man laughed and looked at Jason. "I should be thanking you for yours."

Recognizing that he never told Jackson he had served in the military, Jason's curiosity perked up. "What do you mean by that?"

"Really? Black military boots, a pack with probably everything you need, deciding to hump it on the road to your destination? Along with the story of your dead friends and those scars on your face. I may be old, but I still know a warrior when I see one."

He's good.

Chuckling nervously, Jason smirked and looked at his boots. "That obvious, huh? Well, thanks. I appreciate that." As Jason directed his ride downtown, the men pulled off the highway toward Plattsmouth. After a ten-minute drive of twists and turns, they reached the outskirts of downtown Plattsmouth, and the sun began to set in the distance.

"You can just pull over here, Jackson. I'm basically at my destination."

"You sure?"

"Yeah, I'm going to stay in a hotel for the night."

"OK, well, here you go." The truck pulled off to the side of the road, and the doors unlocked, allowing Jason to grab his pack from the truck bed.

"Nice meeting you, Jackson. Thanks for the ride." Jason slung the pack over his shoulder and waved his hand at the gray-haired man as he began to walk away.

"Orion!"

Freezing in his tracks, chills shot up Jason's spine as he contemplated the name that was just called out to him. A name he hadn't been called in three years. His steely blue eyes widened with uncertainty and apprehension as he spun to face the gray-haired man sitting in his truck.

"What did you call me?" Jason dropped his bag to the ground and looked into the man's eyes suspiciously.

"That's my last name. O'Ryan." The gray-haired man leaned across the console to the passenger seat to get a better view of Jason. "Jackson O'Ryan. Just in case we ever meet again or run into mutual friends somehow." Jason felt a weight lift off his shoulders, feeling a bit ashamed of his immediate defensive reaction. *Guess I've still got some work to do.*

"Oh, sorry. I misheard you." He walked to the passenger side window as Jackson rolled up his sleeve and extended his arm for a handshake.

"Take care of yourself, Jason."

206

Jason reached in and shook Jackson's hand with a firm respectful handshake.

"You too, Jackson."

As the two men said their goodbyes, Jason caught a glimpse of a tattoo on Jackson's forearm that made him pause, stunned and perplexed at what he was looking at. Engraved on Jackson's forearm was an insidious black Scorpion with its stinger raised, ready to strike.

The stranger withdrew his hand and winked at Jason as he placed the truck into drive. The man drove off down the road and gave Jason one last wave out his window. The smell of exhaust lingered in the air with an odd tinge of sulfur. An odor Jason recalled smelling during his time in the backwoods of Alaska.

Jason watched as the man faded from view and looked up toward the darkening sky.

You will always be with me. But you'll never control me.

With an innate knowledge of what he had just experienced, Jason turned to make his way downtown. As the sun dipped below the horizon, Jason walked past the welcoming sign for the town of Plattsmouth. The sunset illuminated the large blue and white sign in an orange radiant glow. The falling sun gave the engraved lettering of the town's motto a divine ambiance.

Welcome to Plattsmouth. Honor the Past. Plan for the Future.

SHANE COWDEN
ISBN: 9798367651119

An author's longevity and success are determined by word of mouth and written reviews.

Please consider writing an honest review of **ORION** on Amazon!

Thank You

Thank you to everyone who inspired me to write this story. Every person in my life, and every situation I have been in, good and bad, made me into the person I am today. Your good and bad experiences mold you, and I would not be the man I am today without all the highs and lows that life brings.

Thank you to my wife, the strongest woman I know. I would still be lost in the woods if it were not for you. Your steadfast, dedicated, and loving commitment to your family is the only thing that allowed this book to happen.

When I started writing, I had no intention of writing a story about a veteran and his struggles. In fact, it was the complete opposite. I wanted to write something completely different. I used the method of "by the seat of your pants" writing that Stephen King is known for. That's where you sit down and write whatever comes to mind without a predetermined plot structure.

I tried hard to avoid the veteran influence but kept being drawn back to it. Eventually, I gave up fighting it and let the words flow onto the pages. ORION is not a story about myself, as many have asked. However, it involves experiences that I and others close to me have endured during their time at war and home.

You do not need to be a veteran or a first responder to understand the meaning and impact behind ORION. Every person deals with negative internal thoughts, whether that comes from traumatic experiences, childhood, or unfortunate events that have occurred in their life.

The lessons within this book that Jason learned from Charging Bear are lessons that I learned from many people in my life. My wife, friends, family, and doctors. I want to thank them all. They have all made a profound and lasting impact on my life that consciously or subconsciously made me who I am today.

Thank you to my three beautiful children. I hope you all grow stronger and wiser than your daddy ever was. You are my everything, and I love you to the moon and back. Thank you to my sister Shauna and brother Garrett. Your faith during my difficult times is something I will never forget. God bless your family. My uncle Rich. You know more about my story than most others, and I don't see how things would have turned out had I not had you by my side to support me. Enjoy your retirement from firefighting. It's well deserved. Remember the lessons from this book. Mom, Dad, thank you for your infinite love and support. I am grateful for everything you have done for me. I hope I made you proud.

To my brothers Mac, Ridge, Josh, Klunk, Fish, and Dusty, I love you. Our unwavering dedication to each other is a bond that cannot be broken. Thank you for looking out for my family and me. I think about each and every one of you every day.

The Orca Boys. You are the Orion of your own stories. Please stay on the straight and narrow, and thank you for walking side by side with me in the woods.

Warren and Sandra, Kyle and Lindsay, I'll never forget your support for my family. I'm blessed to have you as neighbors. Erica, Ana, Brie, Deb, and Veterans Affairs, your teamwork and dedication to others are beyond words. Thank you for your unwavering support.

Thank you to my editor, Amie Norris, for guiding me through the end process of my first novel and for the heartfelt attention you gave this manuscript.

And to everyone that has impacted my life in a multitude of ways. I could write a thousand pages about neighbors, coworkers, high school friends, Kadnar, Dawson, and others. Thank you.

Orion's ancient story is about an elite hunter that is prey to a creature of the gods, Scorpio. I endeavored to tell the tale of Orion in a modern way that relates to our current society. Many veterans are currently lost in the woods, some without a support network. If this book positively impacts one person in any way, then the year and a half I spent writing it was well worth it.

Many soldiers are currently fighting their war here and at home in silence. No one hears the thoughts that echo in their minds or the nefarious attempts to control their spirit. With love and discipline, they can beat it, but they can't do it alone. Their war is not over; and like all wars, it can't be fought alone. Conquer the negative inner voice within you and regain control of your spirit.

Thank you.

About the Author

Shane Cowden is a Canadian author debuting his first novel, ORION. Born in Hamilton, Ontario, his biggest fans are his wife and three children. Shane served in Kandahar, Afghanistan, in 2008 with the Argyll and Sutherland Highlanders of Canada, an experience that profoundly shaped his life. Having lost friends at war and at home, mental health is a subject close to his heart and the driving motivator for his first novel.

Having graduated from college with a diploma in journalism, storytelling is his natural passion. He currently resides in Bowmanville, Ontario, leading a nuclear security response team in defense of Ontario's energy sector. When he's not working, he spends his spare time coaching hockey, writing, or playing guitar for his children. If you want to contact Shane, please visit his website, www.SierraCharlieNovels.com.

If you enjoyed this book, please consider writing a review on Amazon!

VETERAN HELPLINES

Are you a Veteran in crisis or concerned about one?
You're not alone—Veterans Crisis Lines are here for you.

United States Veterans Crisis Line

The Veterans Crisis Line serves Veterans, service members, National Guard and Reserve members, and those who support them. How It Works Available 24/7: Dial 988 then Press 1, chat live, or text 838255. A caring, qualified responder will listen and help. Your call is free and confidential, and you decide how much information to share.

Veterans United Kingdom helpline

Freephone (UK only): 0808 1914 2 18
Telephone (overseas): +44 1253 866 043
Email: veterans-uk@mod.gov.uk
Normal service 8.00 am to 4.00 pm Monday to Friday

Veterans Affairs Canada Helpline

The VAC Assistance Service provides free and confidential psychological support that is available 24 hours a day, 365 days a year. The service is for all Veterans, former RCMP members, their families, and caregivers.
Toll-free: 1-800-268-7708 | TDD/TTY 1-800-567-5803

Australian Veterans Helpline

Open Arms - Veterans & Families Counselling on 1800 011 046
ADF Mental Health All-hours Support Line on 1800 628 036

Manufactured by Amazon.ca
Bolton, ON

34425949R00118